Retribu

by

Heaton Wilson

ISBN: 9798366321495

PUBLISHNATION

www.publishnation.co.uk

For mum and dad.

'Vengeance is Mine, and retribution. In due time their foot will slip;
For the day of their calamity is near, And the impending things are hastening upon them.' *Deuteronomy 32:35*

PROLOGUE

It had become a sacred routine: down several pints of the amber nectar at the Feathers; a quick march to Fatty Fry's for cod and chips; sit on a bench and eat out of paper; use said paper to wipe grease off hands and face; bin it at bus stop; stroll up new road; fall on sofa.

It happened every Friday, but that in no way diminished the pleasure. The beer gave him a glow, and the chips made him comfortably full, which was pretty close to the title of his favourite Pink Floyd track.

Time was, he would have got a warmer glow in the back of the car with the vigorous support of any woman who fancied it. But those days were long gone. And if he was honest, beer and chips were a pretty fair substitute. Plus, there were no complaints if it didn't last very long.

Jack wiped the grease off his lips on the front page of the Ashbridge Free Press motoring section, screwed the paper up, drop-kicked it into the bin - he'd only missed once in the last six attempts – then set off for home. After about half a mile, he turned left off the bright lights of the Manchester road onto the new, and as yet unlit, road they'd built as part of the new estate.

He heard laughter and turned to see a couple of blondes lighting fags as they waited at the bus stop.. They were surrounded by bags for life, no doubt after a spot of late night shopping at the new superstore.

Jack shook his head. What a way to spend a Friday night. He and his mates were unanimous. They wouldn't be seen dead in a superstore. Anyway, what was so super about them? He smiled. Like minds, they were. Funny how they agreed on most things, but maybe that's why they'd stayed friends for so long.

He thought about the old days. So many memories… happy, painful, good times, tough times - extremely tough times. But they'd always stuck together. Not so much mates, more like blood brothers.

He was so lost in thought he didn't hear it.

Seconds later, he was lying at the side of the road, arms and legs at odd angles, his eyes staring, blood pooling around his head.

The vehicle drove a short distance up the road, and did a three point turn. Its headlights came on as it rolled quietly back towards him. Jack was lying cruelly illuminated in the stark brightness, and his blood shone red as it began to flow into the gutter.

The driver got out and nudged him with his foot. Satisfied, he checked the front of the car, then eased slowly back to the main road, and joined the steady procession of late night traffic heading out of Manchester.

1

'Strike a pose, Jane. Think Meryl Streep.'

Allan knelt down to get a better angle for the shot as Jane put on her best pout and tried to look moody, which wasn't that difficult in this weather.

'Does it always rain in Lyme Regis?'

Allan laughed. 'Only when we're here. Anyway, come and look at this. You look gorgeous.'

Jane tiptoed across the dark wet stones that had been thrown together years ago to form the Cobb, the mini breakwater that made this place world famous when it featured in 'French Lieutenant's Woman', complete with Meryl Streep's cloak and stormy skies.

The stormy skies were still there, but Miss Streep had long gone. Jane had been fooled by the morning sun into wearing shorts, and now she was cold and wishing she was elsewhere too.

She gave the image on Allan's phone a cursory glance. 'God I look awful! Look at my legs!'

'What are you talking about? You've got lovely legs.'

'Yeah, for a donkey. Anyway, come on, I'm freezing, and I need coffee. You promised me good weather.'

Allan shrugged. 'It was all right yesterday.'

'Oh yeah? It stopped raining at three, just as the fossil walk ended.'

'Behave … Come on then, I'll buy you coffee and cake and we can plan our walk tomorrow. It's going to be sunny for our last day.'

Her eyes shone playfully. 'Promise?'

'Cross my heart and hope not to die if I'm wrong.'

Jane shivered and grabbed his hand. 'Come on, you idiot.'

As they hurried towards town, Jane remembered she'd had no expectation of being able to relax on this trip. It had come so soon after the Jamie Castleton case, and on the back of a strong hint from Chief Constable Hopkirk that she was in line for a step up. On top of that, she and Allan had been through a rough patch. He was twitchy about her getting even more responsibility, and him becoming even more of a house husband.

'You're already a DCI and Acting Chief Super at Ashbridge,' he'd told her. 'What more do you want?'

Jane was still wondering about that. What did she want? Promotion would mean even more time away from Allan, and less time for mum, just when both relationships were getting warmer. But could she turn it down?

She quickly cut that thought off. She had relaxed, by her standards. And things were looking up. The brisk walk had warmed her up, and she could see their favourite tea room a few yards up the main street. Suddenly, nothing mattered more than a hot drink in a warm room. Having seen herself in that photo, cake was out of the question…

******

DC Paul Rossiter stretched and yawned.

'Don't do that. You're sucking all the air out of the bloody room.'

'Sorry, Lorry.'

'Yeah, yeah, funny…never heard that rhyme before.'

'What's up? We always call you Lorry. Sorry.'

'Oh my aching sides … I know you do, and I know why. You haven't noticed how much weight I've lost, have you?'

'Course I have. And your point is?'

'I'm not built like a lorry.'

'Okay, what shall we call you instead? How about Pickup?'

'Pickup?'

'Yeah, as in pick up truck.'

DC Loretta Irons slowly pushed herself out of her chair and started walking over to Ross's desk. He quailed in mock fright, but the play acting stopped as the portly figure of DI George Creasey barged into the room.

'Just about to clock him one, Lorry?'

'Yes, sir. Do you mind?'

'Not at all. Just make sure it hurts.'

Ross laughed and moved smartly towards the kettle. 'Your usual coffee, guv?'

'Good idea, young man. Lorry, leave him alone. For now, that is.'

Ross blew a kiss at Lorry. She shook a fist at him.

George shuffled the papers he'd brought in, before leaning on his desk and reaching for a wine gum while he studied them. Without looking up, he said: 'Forget the coffee. You're going out, Ross.'

Ross grinned at Lorry and grabbed his jacket. 'What is it, guv?'

'Fatal RTA up at Summerlands.'

He sighed. 'What? Why us?'

'No sign of the car, and no sign of the driver either.'

Ross and Lorry exchanged looks of disbelief. George continued.

'Bastard's done a runner. It's probably one for Roads, but let's have a quick look, eh? On your way, son.'

Ross grabbed his phone and tablet, and marched angrily to the door. 'Ross! Calm yourself down. Get the full story and get back here. Then I'll decide if you can lose your temper or not, all right?'

Ross gave an apologetic smile and Lorry almost liked him, but only for an instant. 'Yeah, understood. Sorry, guv.'

George turned to Lorry as the door swung shut. 'You all right, Lorry? Is he giving you problems?'

'Nothing I can't handle, sir.'

'Good girl. Anyway, what are you doing here? You should be at home with Mark, not stuck in here doing homework.'

'Yeah, well, he's working, as usual. The exam's next week and I really want this, George.'

'I know you do. You don't want to end up like me, though, do you?'

'End up like you? You're a DI… sir! Who wouldn't want that?'

'Aye but it's taken me about 40 bloody years to get here. You're going to get there before you're 30, the way you're going.'

Lorry shook her head, but her cheeks flushed bright red. 'Awww, thanks George. But I'll never be as good as you, even if I've got the title.'

'Now you're taking the mick. Fancy a wine gum?'

*****

Allan and Jane held hands as they walked up through the gardens to their hotel. The rain had gone, the wind had dropped and the sky was dark velvet.

Looking back from the top, they watched the harbour lights shimmer off the water.

Allan put his arm round her waist and Jane smiled up at him. 'Where are you?' she said softly.

'I'm right here, with you, and feeling very mellow after that meal. You?'

'Same. It was great, Love seafood.'

'And white wine, I noticed.'

She gave him a sidelong look. 'Yeah, so?'

'So, nothing, You're worth it.'

'True.' Jane laughed. 'It's so nice to be away! That mad world we inhabit seems a long way away, doesn't it?'

Allan sighed his reply, but nodded all the same. 'Yeah. We need more moments like this.'

Jane stroked his hand. 'I know. We will.'

Allan pulled her closer. 'Promise?'

'Well I promise, but do you?'

He laughed. 'I do.' He looked as if he was about to say something else, but held it back.

'What?'

'Well … I do. It's like the marriage vow…'

'And?'

'And … well… do you think we should?'

'Get married?'

'Well, yeah.'

Jane pushed away so she could look him in the eye: something that was easier said than done, since he was at least eight inches taller. She hadn't seen this coming. They'd been partners, living together for over two years, with never a suggestion of making it permanent.

'Allan Gary Askew. Are you asking me to marry you?'

He took her hand and looked so serious, Jane wondered if he really was going to propose.

But he just seemed thoughtful and they carried on their slow walk to the hotel. Allan was clearly trying to find the right words, which was unusual for him: he'd been a journalist all his life.

Jane didn't mind the silence. It gave her some extra thinking time.

They'd been at each other's throats for ages over her late nights. Even on the way down here, Allan had made it obvious he feared the worst if she accepted the promotion that Hopkirk had hinted at. So what was this about? His attempt to tie her down? Or him accepting the situation for better or worse?

They reached the hotel entrance, its bright white paintwork uplit through palm fronds: more like Dubai than Dorset.

Allan paused at the white marble steps that led up to the sliding glass doors. 'I know I've been an arse lately, feeling sorry for myself. It just felt like I might as well be living on my own. But I don't want that. I love being with you -'

Jane smiled. 'Same here.'

'We're so close, so similar. Same sense of humour, don't find it easy to show our feelings…' he paused, a faint smile, 'and work too hard?'

'So what you're saying is we're as bad as each other.'

They laughed and hugged. Allan let out an exasperated sigh: 'I'm hopeless at this! It's probably coming out all wrong, but I just think, sometimes, well… why don't we get married? What stops us? Are we just scared of making it official?'

They moved to one side and nodded as an older couple walked up the steps and into the hotel, the sliding doors closing automatically behind them.

Jane frowned as she tried to organise her thoughts. 'I think we probably are a bit scared. I love being with you - I feel safe and you make me laugh, and more than anyone else I've ever met, you understand me. But I am a bit scared of going that next step - not because of you, but because of me. I know what I'm like.'

'So, where do we go from here?'

'We go to our room, have a nightcap and go to bed.'

'Hang on, it's only ten!'

'Good. That gives us plenty of time in bed before we feel sleepy.'

'Okay. I do like the sound of that. And Jane?'

'Yeah?'

'I'm a bit scared, too, you know.'

Jane stood on the step above him, wrapped her arms round his neck, and kissed him. 'I can't blame you, darling. I'm an animal in bed…'

*****

It was dark when he turned off into the woods.

The magic eye at the entrance did its job and the red and white striped barrier slowly swung upright.

There was never anyone about at this time of night; just lights behind curtains and squares of light from tv sets they'd probably fallen asleep watching. Even so, he let the car freewheel silently down the gravel track that led to the end of the row, and parked up against a hedge.

He locked the door on the key so the bleep of the alarm system didn't attract attention, then went in by the side door and knelt down to make a fuss of Bess.

She rolled on her back so he could rub her stomach, and he instantly felt the adrenaline seeping out of his system.

He drank a glass of water and filled up with a bowl of cereal at the kitchen table.

It was good to get the job done. Tonight had been a long time in the planning, but there was no time to relax: it would soon be time for the next one.

He kicked off his trainers and Bess lay on his feet under the table. He reached down to stroke her head, then opened his notepad and started reading through his notes.

2.

'So what's occurring?'

The paramedic snorted. 'Not another Gavin and Stacey fan.'

Ross winked. 'Yeah, sorry. I confess. Anyway, moving on... What's the situation, Lucy?'

Lucy shot him a fixed grin. It was always the same: no matter how grim the incident, there was always one smart arse who fancied himself. 'Well if I move out of the way, you'll be able to see for yourself. It's pretty bad. Are you sure you want to?'

'Not really, but… let's just get it over with.'

Lucy and her partner Nick were crouched over the body in their green uniforms, their bags and equipment piled up around them, forming a kind of barrier. The emergency lighting was already installed and as they moved to one side, Ross saw the mess that had once been a man.

Blood and brain matter were glistening on the road surface. The man's torso seemed to have been twisted out of alignment with his legs. His face looked remarkably intact, almost peaceful, but as Ross moved to one side, he winced and hid a gagging reflex as he saw the back of his head.

'You all right?'

Ross nodded, turning so the body was out of sight. 'Yeah, thanks. I will be… No other casualties? No-one else involved?'

'Nope. This is it.'

He cleared his throat. 'So, a hit and run.'

'Only explanation. I can't see him getting injuries like this any other way. This poor guy has been hit at some speed.'

'Was he alive when you got here?'

'No. We think he died straight away. His head must have hit the ground at a hell of a speed. It was quite an impact. Looks like he might have turned to face whatever hit him. Didn't stand a chance, but probably didn't feel anything. We got the call out from a girl who saw him from a distance. She didn't want to get any closer.'

'Can't blame her, can you? Is she still around?'

'No sign of her.'

'Have we got a name?'

'No, she didn't want to say, apparently.'

'Great. That sounds familiar. So, no witnesses.' Ross looked up and down the road. 'I suppose Control Room might have got her number?'

Lucy shrugged and Ross took the hint. 'I'll take a walk, see if I can find anything useful.'

Lucy glanced back at the body. 'I'm not trying to be clever, but don't you want to look for ID?'

'No. I'll leave that to our forensic guy.'

'All right. But we need to -'

'- Don't worry, I'm going to call him now. If you can leave him where he is for a bit longer, please. Road Traffic are here, are they?'

'Yeah. They're up at the estate end, taping it off.'

Ross moved out of the intense light, the beam of his torch exploring the road and pavement as he walked up the slope that led to the new estate. It was all very neat and new. There were rows of saplings sheathed in clear plastic tubes on either side, with fresh looking bark chippings covering the ground. At the top of the hill, mature trees stood guard in front of the dark silhouettes of new houses.

They called it Summerlands, which was a big leap of imagination. Lorry hadn't been impressed enough to put her and Mark's name down for one. As she rightly said: 'Who'd want a view of a superstore car park from the bedroom window?'

He'd occasionally asked himself if Mark had got the right idea. He'd handed in his notice straight away after they'd wound up the Jamie/Gonzales killings, and taken up a job at Greaves - one of the city's biggest companies - with his new best mate Adrian Fisher. They were both computer nerds, and they'd worked together on the investigation. Mark had been banging on about his salary, expenses, fancy bloody office ... Now he and Lorry were looking at new houses and other pointless things to spend money on.

Ross told himself it wasn't all about money. But even so...

He turned back towards the main road. His torch picked out the faint pattern of tyre tread in a lay-by. He tutted at himself -

'*it's a road, Ross, cars drive along it all the time.*' Even so, he took a few pictures with his phone camera.

It was puzzling that there was no sign of any of the fragments you'd expect to find after a car accident: like shattered glass. Did whoever smashed into this guy clear up before clearing off? But if there was no debris, was it definitely a vehicle? Could he have been beaten up?

It was time for reinforcements. He tapped speed dial and got a speed answer.

'Ross? What have we got?'

'Hello George. Looks a bad one. Poor guy is a hell of a mess. Would you be alright getting Phil out here? I don't want to touch anything, in case, you know.'

'All right matey. Stay where you are. Phil's working late anyway. Go home when he arrives, okay?'

*****

Forensic Phil was staring at his laptop when George walked in.

'Don't even think about going home, young man. Got a nasty mess for you to look at.'

Phil lsmiled happily. He'd come close to retiring only a week ago, but working on the Jamie Castleton murder had given him a new lease of life. The irony was not lost on him. He was the wrong side of 60 but still put in the hours. He turned away from the laptop and looked up at George. 'Nasty messes are my speciality. So … what's occurring?'

*****

By the time Phil arrived with his technicians, the road had been taped off, and the paramedics were sitting in the back of the ambulance looking at their phones.

Phil hopped into his protective overalls and pulled on disposable gloves and shoe covers, before kneeling beside the body. The other members of his team got on their hands and knees looking for evidence, and occasionally took pictures.

Phil checked over the body, then delicately searched Jack's pockets. He never hurried, and he treated every body with respect.

Ross stood a few yards away, reluctant to leave, reluctant to get any closer.

Phil called out over his shoulder. 'His name is Jack Cooper. No driving licence, just a couple of cards in his wallet … a debit card and a library card. And 15 quid and a bit of change.'

'Any address?'

'No, you'll have to check with his bank, or the library. But I suppose he lives near here.'

'Might not, though. Could have been visiting a mate, or something.'

'That's why you're the detective, Ross.'

'Maybe, and I'm not swapping.'

Phil shook his head, amused. 'No, I wouldn't either. I'll take a closer look at the poor lad, but it's pretty obvious this was the result of a vehicle collision.'

'Lad? Definitely not beaten up, then?'

'He's younger than me, which makes him a lad. And if he was beaten up, only the Incredible Hulk could have done it. No, the issue really is whether the head wound is a separate injury, before or after he was hit by whatever vehicle it was. The structural damage to his body is consistent with massive force - too much for any beating. High probability that it threw him backwards and smashed his head on the ground. We'll get fragments from the wound which should tell us what we need to know.'

Phil leaned in closer, and sniffed. 'He's had a beer or two tonight. And I'm getting a faint whiff of fish and chips off his clothes.'

'So he could have been a bit off his head and walked out in front of the car?'

'Yep, it's a possibility. I'll have a close look at him later. But for now, I'll just check with them.' He nodded towards the paramedics.

Phil felt his age when he had to crouch down for any length of time. The pain in his knees made him catch his breath. But, looking at Jack reminded him he was one of the lucky ones; that it was a privilege to be able to grow old. He slowly stood and arched his back, before walking stiffly over to the ambulance.

After a few minutes, he moved back to Ross.

'I think it's safe to say it's a hit and run, and a serious one at that. But beyond that…'

'What?'

'Well, was it deliberate or accidental?'

'We'll never be able to prove it either way, will we? Whoever did this knows what they've done and if it was me, I'd be bricking it enough to trash the car and leave the bloody country.'

'You could be right, Ross. But let's wait and see.' Phil nudged him with his elbow and smiled. 'Go on, bugger off home. Nothing more you can do here. Let us get on with it now.'

'You sure?'

'Yeah, I'm sure. See you tomorrow.'

Ross trudged back to his car and started the engine. He usually liked to hurry along when he was driving, but he'd be taking it slow tonight.

*****

Jane sipped her tea and flicked through the headlines on her phone as Allan mopped up the last of his egg yolk with a piece of toast.

He sat back with a satisfied grunt and patted his stomach.

Jane smiled. 'Enjoy that?'

'Just call me a full Englishman. Don't know how you manage on that parrot food though.'

'And what's wrong with muesli and soya milk, pray?'

'Nothing. But I bet you'll be gagging for a bacon butty by 11.'

'Whereas you'll be gagging for one by 10,' she shot back, flipping her hair over her shoulder.

'Now, now… You're not worrying about your weight are you? Look at you!'

'I'll take that as a compliment. And no, I'm not. I just want to eat more healthily, that's all.'

Allan reached out to put his hand on hers. 'After last night, I'd have thought you'd have more of an appetite.' He winked, and she rolled her eyes, her smile growing wider.

'Well you broke the calorie counter this morning, and no wonder. They'll be hiring more kitchen staff if we come here again.'

'Ha! Anyway, come on, it's our last day. Still fancy that long walk we sussed out?'

'Yeah, definitely.'

Allan poured out cups of tea. 'Anything in the news?'

'Climate change. Brexit. Scotland and England arguing over everything -'

'No change there, then. We should rebuild Hadrian's Wall - make it a few feet higher. If the Scots are that keen, leave 'em to it. What else?'

'That's it. Anyway, Mr Editor, you should be the one giving me the news.'

Allan laughed. 'Day off, remember? Anyway, come on, drink up. Let's go before that coughing couple get in here, spreading their germs.'

'Sure you can manage the stairs?'

'I'm not actually... But, while we've got the room to ourselves, thanks for last night, love. It meant a lot to me, It felt like we got close again.'

'I know. I felt the same. I've got that sad, last day of the holiday feeling now. Won't be long before we're thrown back into it at work. It's been so nice...' Her voice tailed off, and she frowned. These moments together didn't come round often enough.

'Yeah, we should hang onto this feeling. We're good together, aren't we?'

'Yes, we are. So, let's enjoy today, even if I do have to wait till 11 for a butty.'

Jane checked her messages while Allan brushed his teeth noisily in the tiny en suite bathroom.

One from George: '*All OK here, ma'am. Nothing to worry about. See you in a couple of days.*'

Jane tapped out a reply: '*Cheers George. I never worry. Thanks for looking after the place!*'

But as soon as she hit send, her brain began to whir. Why did he feel the need to say there was nothing to worry about? That must mean there was. She made a mental note to check out the local news website later, when Allan wasn't looking.

Relaxing and enjoying the last day of their break wasn't going to be so easy after all.

3.

Phil had been up most of the night, but, even on three hours sleep, he prided himself on looking and acting far brighter than the others. Ross looked like he'd slept in a hedge: hair all over the place, tie on crooked. Lorry was slumped back in her chair, white faced, and yawning.

Phil flicked through his notes, and the noise was enough to alert them to the fact that he was in the room.

'Oh, hi Phil.' Ross waved loosely and twirled a ballpoint pen around in the fingers of his other hand.

'Impressive.' Phil nodded at the pen.

Ross looked bemused. 'What?'

'The pen trick.'

'Right. Yeah.Thanks.'

Lorry decided to acknowledge his presence with a slurry good morning, and Phil bowed graciously.

'George not in yet?'

Ross looked at his watch. 'No, he's not. Slacker…'

Phil fought to hide his annoyance. Jane rated Ross as a detective but he was too cocky by half. 'What do you mean? He works harder than any of us.'

Lorry sensed Ross was about to come up with one of his throwaway lines that always caused offence. 'You're right, Phil, he does. Not like him to be late, is it? Anyway, can we help?'

'Got some results for you from last night, Ross.'

Suddenly, Ross was alert and businesslike. 'Great, Phil, thanks. What's the verdict?'

'No surprises. Frontal impact, not quite straight on but pretty close; got him around the thigh area. Thrown backwards, smacked his head on the ground - death would have been almost instantaneous -'

'- that means straight away, Lorry.'

'Shut up Ross!'

Phil carried on tersely. '- so he wouldn't have known much about it. Legs mangled as you'd expect, and major internal damage.'

‘Head wound showed impact with the road?’

‘Yes, it did. Curious thing, though…’ Phil pursed his lips in thought.

‘Yes?’

‘Well, let’s say the car or whatever it was, was going fast. Normally, the pedestrian would be carried over the top of the vehicle, and hit the road at the back.’

‘How do you know Jack didn’t?’

‘Markings on the road surface indicate hard braking at what I’d estimate to be the point of impact.’

Ross stared. Lorry chipped in, wide awake now: ‘Suggesting that the driver was anticipating the collision and braked straight away after the hit, rather than being caught by surprise and driving through him.’

Phil nodded his appreciation. ‘Top marks, Lorry. You should have no problems passing your exams.’

Lorry gave him the thumbs up. ‘Thanks Phil!’

Ross grumbled. ‘All right, get a room you two… So what are we saying exactly?’

‘Well nothing’s exact at this point. Those marks could have been made by a different car at a different time, but I’d lay money on the fact that this was no accident.’

Ross leaned back in his chair. ‘Any clues about the vehicle? Fragments on the road, or on Jack?’

‘A reasonable guess is that we’re looking for a bigger than average car. The lack of any fragments indicates that we’re talking about a very well built, solid vehicle. Or someone cool enough to stop the car, carefully sweep up, and take the debris away. And something else - the impact points on Jack’s body suggest this was no ordinary bumper - it perhaps had something extra fitted on the front…’

‘What are they called? Bull bars?’

‘Something like that. Whatever you call them, they certainly made their mark.’

Ross stood and walked over to the whiteboard, writing notes in green capitals.

Lorry looked thoughtful. ‘So, not just a hit and run accident: a deliberate act? Interesting.’

'Well, that's how it looks just now, Lorry. Early days, but I thought you should know. I know it doesn't give you much to work on, but I'll keep going.'

'Oh God. We've only just recovered from the last murder.'

Ross's tone was heavily sarcastic. 'Yeah, it's really inconvenient, so shall we just call it an accident?'

It was wasted on Phil. 'I'm not calling it anything yet. Just give me a bit longer. Oh, and can you tell George? I'm going back to the scene now, but I'll be back in an hour or so if he wants me.'

Lorry closed the door behind Phil and walked over to Ross. 'Let's see your notes, then, Sherlock.'

'Knock yourself out. I'll make us a brew, yeah?'

'Ross! Really? I love you! White without…'

She turned to face the whiteboard. Ross had only written a few words, messily: *HOME ADDRESS ... NEXT OF KIN... BOOKS ...REPAIR SHOPS ... CUSTOM CARS*

Lorry called out: 'What about next of kin? Any luck?'

'Don't even know where he lives yet. There are a few Jack Coopers round here, so I'll have to find him through his bank card.'

'Great. And what's this about books?'

'He had a library card. Random thought … it would be interesting to find out what sort of books he read. And the bit about custom cars might lead us to whoever round here fits those bull bars. If it was deliberate, the driver might have had them put on for the occasion.'

'Good thinking, my man. Seems a strange way to kill someone, though.'

'Yeah, that's what's getting to me. Why not just shoot him or spike his beer, or poison his chips?'

'That's why you're thinking about repairs and books… bit of lateral thinking going on under that lush hair of yours: the car itself is the clue.'

'Got it in one, Lorry. You know what, you should be a detective.'

Lorry grinned and held her hand out to accept the mug of tea Ross was offering. 'Cheers, Ross. I don't know why I put up with you.'

'Cos you love my hair and I make superb tea?'

Lorry grimaced. 'Not quite. You've put sugar in this you numpty!'

*****

Allan was already regretting promising Jane fine weather.

It wasn't just that the dark clouds seemed to be deliberately targeting the route of their walk to Uplyme, leaving Lyme Regis basking in sunshine. It wasn't just that the further north they went, the windier it seemed to get.

Jane's impending tantrum was based on the fact that when the sun eventually did come out, it was accompanied by a downpour.

Allan's mad-eyed positivity as he pointed to the faint outline of a rainbow didn't seem to help either.

They took shelter under a tree. Below them a spectacular brick aqueduct stretched across the valley, seemingly only there now to provide shelter for a flock of sheep. Allan took pictures, which gave her enough time to wrestle her rain jacket out of her rucksack.

Allan helped her into it with more upbeat words of cheer: 'It's clearing up now.'

Jane resisted the urge to push him back down the hill. She opted for a more mature response: 'Hoo - bloody - ray.'

Allan persisted: 'Come on, it's only a mile to the pub. We just have to get to that stile, then we're on a gravel track that brings us back to the main road. We can get the bus after, if you don't fancy walking.'

Jane yielded to his relentless good humour. She stuffed her jacket back where it came from. 'Right, come on. Let's do this!'

They were the only ones in the pub, and the landlord was almost as endearingly enthusiastic as Allan.

The menu ran to five pages, but the food was surprisingly good - steak pie for Allan, mushroom omelette for her - and Allan raved about the beer, as always.

They sat by the window, looking out over the river valley. The sky was pale blue and the sun looked like it might decide to stay. Jane drank the last of her white wine spritzer and patted Allan's knee. 'Come on then, let's walk back, shall we?'

‘Really? Great, just give me a minute. The gents is calling - if I could only find it…’

‘I’m sure the landlord would love to tell you. He must be desperate to talk to someone.’ Jane laughed.

Allan headed off to the bar and she watched amused as he got into deep conversation. She took her phone out of the rucksack. No more messages or emails. Nothing on the local news site either, apart from a fatal RTA up at Summerlands. She put the phone away as Allan returned.

‘He says we’re better off going back a different way. Reckons a lot of the river path will be too muddy after the rain.’

‘Good advice. We should give him a bonus for that.’

Allan smirked. ‘Don’t worry, I’ve already added a 10 per cent tip. I told him he’d probably saved my life.’

‘Cheeky bugger!’

‘Ready?’

‘Yeah. You?’

‘Yeah. Starting to feel sad. Packing the bags tonight...’

‘I know. Let’s make a deal to come back here again.’

‘Fine by me. What, after the next murder, you mean?’

‘Do not say things like that! I still haven’t got over the last one.’

‘Sorry, that was stupid. It brought back bad memories for you, didn’t it? You ok?’

‘Think so. It was good to finally tell someone what happened, and I’m glad you were there to listen.’

‘I still can’t believe that teacher got away with it. You were so young.’

‘Let’s not go there again, eh? Come on. The landlord wants to lock up, and we’ve got hours of holiday ahead of us.’

‘You’re right. How did we get on to talking about work anyway?’

‘It was your fault.’

‘Mine…?’

‘Of course…’

They were still talking as they shut the door behind them. The landlord moved slowly over to wipe down their table. A woman with bright pink hair and tattoos on her considerable biceps came out to join him.

'Any more orders, boss?'

He managed to sigh and smile at the same time. 'Nope. The lunchtime rush is over, my lovely.'

*****

He loved to see Bess loping along, nose to the ground, not a care in the world.

She'd been a racing greyhound but she was no use to the owners when she got arthritic.

Bess loved the open spaces out here, and no wonder, after spending most of her life in the back of trucks or in cages.

She'd looked so pathetic, lying quietly in the RSPCA kennels while the other dogs went berserk. He'd looked into her eyes and saw the pain, and knew she was the one.

When he eventually got the go ahead to take her home, he told her he wasn't doing her any favours; they were kindred spirits.

It took her a while to trust him, but she was fine now, and she loved it when he came home during the day to give her a run out. It was like Crufts first thing in the morning out here. Too crowded by half.

He'd checked the vehicle this morning to confirm what he'd seen by torchlight last night. No front end damage. Not that he'd expected any. All those hours in the garage had paid off.

He wouldn't be needing it again for a few days, so he'd driven it into the trees and put the cover on.

He whistled and Bess jogged back to his side, nuzzling his coat pocket for the treats he kept in there.

Back home, he dished up her canned food and mixer, topped up her water, then settled her onto her floor cushion while he went to the workshop.

*****

Jane and Allan rounded things off with a nightcap in the hotel bar.

Allan sipped a double cognac. Jane was enjoying an Irish coffee, and decided to take advantage of the mellow mood.

Her opening move was meant to be disarming. 'I've loved being away with you, you know.'

Allan swirled the golden liquid in his glass and sniffed appreciatively. 'Me too. It's been good. Home tomorrow, though.'

That was the link she'd been hoping for. 'Back to work.'

'Yep.'

Jane braced herself. 'I'll probably find out if Hopkirk is going to make me an offer.'

'Oh. Yeah.'

'Had any more thoughts about it?'

Allan yawned and stretched an arm across the back of the sofa. Jane took that as an invitation to move in closer. This was going better than she'd hoped. 'Not really. I know it's been on your mind, but I've tried to keep it to one side.'

She frowned. 'Because you're worried?'

'Not worried, no. I just feel that what will be, will be, and we should be strong enough to deal with it.'

Jane felt the creamy warmth of the whisky sinking deeper inside. She kicked off her shoes and hitched her legs up onto the sofa. 'That's how I feel. So we're all good then.'

'Yes, we are. If it's meant to be, you'll get a promotion -'

'- and we'll still love each other and the extra money will come in handy.'

'That's true.' He sipped his drink and let his head fall so far back against the seat cushion he was almost horizontal. 'I could consider retirement, in that case.'

She hadn't seen that one coming. 'You what?'

'I quite like the idea of living off your earnings.'

Jane laughed rather too loudly for the only other couple in the lounge, who were in the opposite corner, nearest the open fire, sipping delicately from their tea cups. She offered them a sheepish grin by way of apology. 'Oh really? And what would you do all day?'

'Watch Pointless and Bargain Hunt, take up Sudoku, have pub lunches… you know, that sort of thing.'

'Right, that settles it. If I get offered it, I'll refuse. Then you'll be sorry.'

Allan winked at her, annoyingly. 'Actually, who's to say I won't get an offer I can't refuse?'

Jane leaned in, stroked the back of his neck, and whispered. 'Well, perhaps you will, if you come upstairs with me now.'

He snorted. 'That's so cheesy.'

'I know. But are you complaining?'

'Come off it. I love cheese.'

4.

Jack Cooper had lived alone at 14 Meadow Lane, Summerlands: a newly-built three storey town house in a row of similar properties. According to the developers, they'd all sold within a month at around £200,000 apiece. There were 35 properties of various sizes on the estate. Ross and Lorry got side-tracked into doing their sums, and agreed they were in the wrong line of business.

His bank account showed two sources of income, netting £2,500 a month. One was a building company, and Lorry was planning a visit rather than relying on her powers of persuasion over the phone: anything to get out of the office. The other was a finance company based in Durham, and Ross was trading emails - at least, he was for the time being.

Jack hadn't been a big spender. He'd paid out for TV entertainment and sports channels, mobile phone - though, curiously, he didn't have it on him at the time, car, and insurances. He was paying £600 a month on his mortgage, which suggested he'd not had to borrow too much to buy the house.

There was no next of kin because he'd never been married, his mother and father were both deceased, and he was an only child.

Neighbours knew him by sight, and had never seen him receive visitors, though one of the local curtain-twitchers said he was always out on a Friday night, and always back around closing time.

As Ross said to George while he was typing this into the log: 'Where do people find the time to spy on their neighbours?'

George chewed a wine gum thoughtfully. 'Well, there's nothing much on the telly, is there? Anyway, is that all you've got?'

Ross ignored the implied criticism. 'Up to now, yes, boss.'

'So we need to find out what that finance company payment was for. Who were his mates? If he was out every Friday, where did he go? If Phil is convinced he was killed, that's good enough for me. Jane's back tomorrow, so I'd like to be able to give her the full story, and show her we've covered all the main angles, even if we haven't cracked the case yet.'

'Crack the case? Have we even got enough to prove it was deliberate? Give me a break, boss!'

'Ross, my boy, you can have a break,' George smirked slightly, 'when you give me something we can work with. Come on, get on your bike; you can fill out the log when you've got something useful to say.'

Ross swivelled his desk chair, flashing a petulant frown in Lorry's direction, but it was wasted because she was busy keeping her head down to avoid being George's next victim.

Ross sighed dramatically as he turned back to George. 'Right then. I'm off to the bank. Want me to get you anything while I'm out?'

George smiled. 'You're a good lad, really. A bag of wine gums would be nice.'

Ross saluted as he closed the door. 'All righty. As long as you save me the green ones. See you later.'

George chuckled, turning to Lorry. 'I suppose you think I'm too hard on him.'

She thought for a minute. 'You're not, but I think we all underestimate him because he's such a joker.'

'I know. He reminds me of me - a long time ago.'

'Well, he should turn out all right then.'

'I shall reward you for that. Get round to Summerlands and start asking questions, will you?'

'Anything specific?'

'I want to know about anyone and everyone on that estate who owns a big car - what do they call them these days? - an SUV, whatever that means. Or a pickup. May as well start close to home. And if they have those bull bars on the front, make a note of that, too. I've got a couple of uniforms standing by, so you can go up there together. I want people on the estate to know we're on the case. If they're innocent, they'll feel safer. If they're not, we're more likely to flush 'em out. All right?' George nodded emphatically, clearly pleased with his plan.

'On my way, boss.'

'And Lorry?'

'Yes boss?'

‘Meticulous is the word. Every house, on every street. And if there’s no answer, make a note so we can go back.’

She smiled. ‘Meticulous it is.’

‘It sounds good, doesn’t it? Any idea what it means?’

‘I don’t want to push my luck, George, but that is just the sort of thing Ross would say. And it doesn’t fool anyone. He’s a clever devil, and so are you.’

‘You’ll go far, young woman. Now get on your bike.’

George was on his own when Lorry left. He looked at the empty desks and it set him thinking about his decision to retire.

Phil had told him he’d change his mind when it came to it and George had scoffed at the idea. But now, he wasn’t so sure. Phil had been set to leave until he realised the job was still giving him a buzz, still challenging him. ‘The biggest surprise, George,’ he’d told him over a pint, ‘was that I’m still learning. I really thought I’d seen everything.’

George had a feeling the same thing was happening to him. While Jane was away, he was running what could be a murder investigation.

But was it? Ross was right. The forensic evidence suggested it was deliberate, but there was no proof, despite Phil’s confidence. The driver could have been blind drunk, not concentrating, and smacked into Jack. The road wasn’t lit by street lamps and Jack was in dark coloured clothes. And Phil’s idea about the car braking at the point of impact could simply mean the driver had realised what had happened, got out and seen the damage, then no doubt sobered up instantly and decided to get away quick.

George tried to imagine what Jane’s reaction would be. She could easily go ape at the resources he’d put into it.

He sat at his desk and looked through the notes he’d made last night while Dorothy was watching Downton Abbey on catch up…

…we don’t know it was murder; no evidence to help track the killer down; no eye witnesses; the killer could be out of the country; why use a car to kill someone? to make it look like an accident?

He grunted. Jane would take one look at it and tell them to treat it like a hit and run, until the evidence showed otherwise.

George fished the last wine gum out of the packet and leaned back in his chair, his mind churning over the prospect of retirement. Could he? Should he? Jane had talked him out of it once, and she would no doubt have another go. Dorothy said all Jane had to do was flutter her eyelashes and he'd cave in. George had told her that was utter bollocks, but she was half right. He'd do anything for her. Jane was the first superior officer he had total respect for. She was direct, honest, led from the front, and stood by her team; allowed people to make mistakes as long as they learned from them.

What mistakes were they making now? Probably over-thinking that car crash, for one.

His brain was working overtime and he needed coffee. He automatically looked over to Jag's desk. Jag had always brewed up for him - until the bastards that killed Jamie and Gonzales found him searching that empty storage depot and gave him a beating. Jag had lost sight in one eye, and his wife Moraji said he had impaired vision in the other, but he was hoping to be back home in a couple of days, and back at work in a couple of weeks.

It was part of the price they paid for helping to maintain the thin blue line. They all knew the risk, and many had paid the ultimate price.

George said a silent thank you for being spared, to a God he didn't believe in, and tried not to grumble at having to brew up for himself.

*****

After just three days away, Manchester seemed bigger, brasher, and busier.

They took turns driving from Lyme Regis, and it was Allan's turn to navigate through the madness of the local traffic on Princess Parkway.

By the time they got home, they were ready for another holiday.

Playing housewife didn't come naturally to Jane, but she fought off the urge to phone George for a catch up, and put on the chef's apron Allan bought her last Christmas. Allan spread a stash of mail out on the kitchen table and began sorting them into neat piles. Jane scrambled their eggs energetically while peering to see if there was anything on her stack bearing the Greater Manchester Police crest.

'Anything for me?' she asked innocently.

'No, apart from the usual junk. I've got one, though…'

'Anything exciting?'

Allan gave her a curious glance and she realised she'd overdone the excitement. 'Remember I told you about that company that's been sniffing around looking for acquisitions?'

'Yeah, the one you mentioned rather smugly last night? I thought you were kidding me at first.'

'Well, they've sent me a letter.'

'Well… come on, open it.'

Jane arranged the eggs to hide the slightly charred sections of the toast, and carried the plates over as Allan opened the envelope. He read annoyingly slowly, then folded the letter neatly and put it back without a word.

Jane waited, not very patiently. Her culinary skills had been completely ignored. Back to the ready meals tomorrow, then. 'Well?'

He sighed. 'I can't take it in.'

'What is it? Bad news?'

'No, the complete bloody opposite.' He grinned, pausing for dramatic effect. 'They only want to buy me out and put me on their board of directors.'

'My God, Allan! Really? That's amazing!'

Allan looked as though he'd suffered shell shock and his voice seemed at least an octave higher. 'They've offered me a quarter of a million. What do you think?'

Jane slammed her knife and fork down and pulled Allan to his feet so she could hug him. 'You're a bloody star, that's what I think. That's just - wow! Quarter of a million?'

'Yeah, and I get £35k as well. I can't believe it.... £35k! I'll have money for the first time in my life. I don't know what to do.'

'You're wondering if it's a fair offer?'

'No, it's a bloody good offer, considering how tough things are. Circulation is holding up, but advertising revenue has dropped through the floor. It's just...well, I've built the Free Press up, and the worry is they could turn it into a run of the mill local rag - full of recycled press releases and pictures of Rotary Club dinners. It would mean me stopping doing what I love; what I'm good at; and poncing around in a suit, having meetings and stuff like that… It's scary. But £35k a year…?'

'If they want you that much, you can dictate how you want it to be. Just tell them, you want to be hands-on.' Jane stopped, the news starting to really sink in. 'And just think of the money. My God!'

Allan obviously was, because he'd already reached for his jacket. 'You're right. Come on. Those eggs look good, but I reckon we should be eating out tonight. Let's get a cab to Chinatown, yeah?'

Jane wasn't in need of further encouragement. She scraped the food into the pedal bin without a word.

They collapsed into bed just before midnight and Allan was asleep in seconds. Jane stared at the ceiling. The excitement of a small fortune in the bank had kept them buoyed up for most of the night, but when they began thinking about what they'd spend it on, they realised it wasn't actually a life changing amount.

Allan was all for buying a nicer house, which would probably account for most of it. And he was already dropping hints that his new salary would take the pressure off her being the breadwinner.

That set alarm bells ringing. She was determined to be positive on his behalf, but she'd sensed the way the discussion could go once the euphoria had faded. Allan would instinctively and subconsciously try to pigeonhole her. She could imagine the conversation…

'There's no need for you to work all the hours you do any more. We could settle down, think about a family, move to a nicer area, have more holidays…'

Allan was still a working class lad at heart, with all the traditional attitudes that came with it. A woman's place, and all that… He'd just see it as a natural progression for them.

But settling down was the last thing she wanted. She'd always believed that people *settle down* when they're too old to do anything else. And anyway, should money be the deciding factor in how her life changed and their relationship developed?

She was still waiting for Hopkirk to make her an offer, and she'd made up her mind she'd accept a promotion if it was presented to her. There might even be a letter on her desk tomorrow - or was that today? If that came off, it would mean more responsibility, more commitment, longer hours. How would Allan react to that?

If he became a director, would he be out more, travelling to other company sites?

Could she end up being the one kicking her heels at home?

The clock LED silently flicked through the minutes and the hours, casting its blue glow over the room.

5.

As predicted, George got an instant answer.

'Treat it as a hit and run for now. There's nothing to show it's anything else.'

'Phil's convinced it's deliberate, ma'am.'

'What he *thinks* isn't enough. We both know that. I need much more than that if we're to move straight into a murder investigation, especially while we're still mopping up after the last one. Keep an eye on it, but let Roads do their stuff first; see if they can find the driver.'

'Understood. Welcome back, ma'am.'

'Have you missed me?'

He wasn't prepared for that question. 'Well…'

Jane smiled. 'That's ok, George… you don't have to answer. Now, go on; clear off. I've got about three tons of paper to read, and Lord knows how many emails.'

Jane shuffled through the envelopes and files in her in-tray. There were plenty of them, but there was no sign of the one she really wanted - one marked PERSONAL from the Chief Constable's office.

She'd talked to mum on the car phone on the way in and told her how excited she was about the prospect of promotion. Mum's response was that Jane needed to make more time for holidays and spend more time at home with Allan.

Jane tapped her fingers on her desk as she thought it through. Allan clearly felt his offer was the perfect opportunity to make some changes. But the only change she wanted was another promotion. She was already the first woman in the North West to make it to DCI; and the first to become an Acting Chief Superintendent. Hopkirk had told her she'd been 'noticed', so she told herself to be patient: it was just a matter of time before that recognition turned into something tangible.

Her mind was made up. To hell with other people's expectations. If she was going to *settle down*, she'd be doing it in a bigger office with a desk chair that didn't make her bum ache.

*****

Ross had finally worked his way through the digital maze that was the finance company's online service.

Jack Cooper had been receiving a monthly pension from the Army. He'd retired a year ago at the age of 55 after reaching the rank of Staff Sergeant. He'd served in Ireland, the Middle East and Afghanistan, and been awarded the Military Cross five years before.

Ross felt his anger about the incident rising again as he told Lorry. 'He was a bloody war hero for Christ's sake!'

Lorry had been busy too. A visit to the wonderfully named Rob the Builder yielded the information that Jack was a handyman on a zero hours contract, helping out on a few smaller scale domestic projects, and liked a pint at the Feathers. The eponymous Rob said Jack was reliable and good at his job, and had never been involved in any of what he called 'the usual argy-bargy you get on building sites'.

The more they found out, the more Ross and Lorry felt driven to get justice for Jack, and they couldn't hide their disappointment when George told them Jane's decision.

'Thanks for your work, you two. I'll pass on the info to Roads and Transport Policing at HQ. It's up to them for now.'

Ross shook his head. 'But, George… Phil is certain it was deliberate…'

George didn't mince his words. 'You've heard the decision, Ross. Get on with the case work that's on your desk. If Phil comes up with anything more, I'll be the first to say we should dig deeper, but until then …' George shrugged. 'We've got a backlog to clear, so let's get on with it.'

Ross and Lorry exchanged glances, and Lorry shrugged her shoulders in reluctant acceptance. She'd never seen Ross so affected by a case before.

*****

Allan reckoned the opening of Aunt Betty's tea room on the ground floor of his rented office space in Ashbridge was as much cause for celebration as his windfall.

He'd already qualified for their VIP card, and he munched away on a chunk of their fruit cake as he skimmed through emails.

There were a few unsavoury messages about Jamie's murder, claiming there was nothing wrong with watching porn videos, and those children wouldn't have been in them if they didn't want to.

Allan couldn't believe anyone could feel like that. Not only was it disgusting and offensive, it was an insult to those abused children; and to Jamie, who'd died because he'd exposed the whole sordid business.

He was about to press delete, but saved them instead, so he could forward them to the police. Jane would know who to send them to.

It was another example of the good and the bad of being at the sharp end of the newspaper business. He'd reported on tragedies like house fires, road accidents, and plane crashes; seen at first hand the seedy side of life that the emergency services experienced every day; interviewed rich and poor, and found the poor ten times more generous of spirit.

He'd been proud and a little surprised that he hadn't grown a thick skin. He also found that he still cared. The good people and the good things they did could still move him to tears, and the bad stuff, while it made him seethe, didn't destroy his optimism.

So what would it be like to climb a few steps, and leave all this behind? Would the comparative wealth be worth it?

He had to respond to the offer soon, and, although he was celebrating like a cup final goal scorer last night, he was hesitating now.

There was so much to weigh up. It gave him a sudden hankering to go out for a blast on a bike. But that wasn't going to happen. He'd sold his beloved Triumph soon after shacking up with Jane… a knee-jerk decision he now regretted: the bike, not Jane, of course.

That settled it. He wouldn't be rushed into making a decision about the NW Media offer, however much money they were offering. Though a new bike was very tempting.

Whatever the ultimate decision, he resolved to look forward to a few more days of being an editor. An update on the Jamie murder was a must. If the next edition of the Ashbridge Free Press really was going to be his last, he'd make sure it was a belter.

*****

Jane lasted a week before giving up hope that Chief Constable Simon Hopkirk would make her an offer she couldn't refuse.

In that time, she'd seen Allan enthused, chattering away about the stories he'd lined up, and still debating whether or not to accept his offer. She tried to be supportive, but almost lost it when Allan butted in when she was, with Jag's return in mind, reading a long complex procedural note about making the workplace accessible for people with disabilities.

It was tough enough getting used to the idea that Jag's life and career prospects had been so damaged, but Allan made it impossible to concentrate. He'd been humming to himself while clattering away on his keyboard. Then, just as the noise subsided, he slammed down the screen and thumped down on the sofa with her.

'I still don't know what to do, Jane.'

Jane rearranged the papers he'd dislodged, and kept her eyes fixed on the folder. 'About what?'

'You know what! The offer!'

She fiddled with the folder in her hands. 'Why not toss a coin then?'

'Oh that's nice. Thanks. Yeah, that's a great way to plan the future... Come on, tell me, seriously, what do you think?'

Jane sighed and put the folder down. She could tell he'd already decided. 'I've told you what I think. You should take the money.'

'You really mean it?'

'Yes I do. I need a new coat.'

Allan laughed. 'Okay then.'

'So you've made your mind up? I can go back to my very important procedural note?'

'Yeah, go on. I promise not to say another word.' He zipped his lips with his finger, and won a smile in return.

'Good. Kiss my cheek, get us a drink, and take a vow of silence.'

'Yes ma'am. Your usual vat of prosecco coming up.'

'Thank you. Hurry along.'

Then, just as she was getting back into it, he was back with her drink. 'What about you, though? Still nothing?'

'Nope.' She said it without emotion, but he could easily see through her.

'Do you think Hopkirk was having you on, or what?'

'No, I just think he's busy with other stuff and it's gone out of his mind.'

'You okay about it?'

'Not really, but there's nothing I can do.'

'Oh, come on...That's not the Jane I know. What would you say to me? *If you really want something, there's no point waiting; you have to take the initiative.* So, remind him.'

Jane thought for a minute, slammed the folder on the coffee table and walked off to the kitchen.

'What's the matter? What have I said now?'

'Nothing. That was such good advice, I'm getting you a drink.'

'So you'll do it?'

'Yes, I bloody well will.'

*****

The Jack Cooper investigation had yielded precisely nothing.

There was no trace of the vehicle that hit him; no evidence at the scene that would confirm or undermine Phil's suspicions; and the regional Serious Collision Investigation Unit had drawn a blank, but at least promised they'd keep the file open.

The investigating officer called George to pass on the news. 'Between you and me, the paper pushers want us to drop it - write it off - but no way. That is not going to happen. He's ex-Army. So, if you come up with anything, let me know, all right?'

Jane read through the report. 'So, nothing doing.'

'Can't be helped, ma'am. We tried.'

'Ross still think we didn't try hard enough?'

'He does, but he's ok. It shook him up a bit. Not seen him get so involved before.'

'What's that about?'

'No idea, ma'am.'

'Find out, will you? I don't want anything festering under the surface. It's a small team. We can't afford any atmospheres.'

George scraped a hand over his stubble and nodded. 'It's the inquest later. I was thinking of taking Ross with me.'

Jane simply nodded, preoccupied by something on her screen, and George closed the door quietly behind him.

She stared at the email. She was still seething when she read it out to Allan that night.

'Jane. Quick note to say thanks for your work covering for Charles Aston, and especially for the diligence with which you pursued the murder investigation. As you know, we are continuing to mop up the porn video operation now, and the CPS is confident of success in the various court cases that will soon follow.

'I am pleased to inform you that I have now appointed Roy Cooke to the permanent position of Chief Superintendent, Ashbridge Division. Roy has done sterling work at various divisions, and I am confident he will be a great asset and provide the leadership and support you and your team at Ashbridge deserve.

'Chief Supt Cooke will be taking up the appointment on Friday, and I am sure you will make the necessary arrangements, and give him a warm welcome.'

'He's having a laugh.'

'I still can't believe he's done that to me. *You've done a great job, Jane; you've been noticed, Jane; oh and by the way, I've appointed someone else to do that job you were covering...* What happened to the promise of better things to come? I'm bloody furious.'

'I suppose he might be planning something else for you.'

'He already has - more of the same. Bastard. Roy Cooke is the biggest slimeball in Greater Manchester. He doesn't walk through doors; he slides under them. I can't stand the guy, and now he's going to be my boss! And he's younger than me. Jesus!'

Allan slammed the microwave door and set the timer. 'What are you going to do now?'

'I'm going to tell Hopkirk what I think of his idea, and how offended I am that he's completely overlooked me.'

'Don't be too hasty. Like I said, this might just be step one of a cunning plan. For all you know, he might have something else in mind.'

'Well if he hasn't, I certainly have. Wonder if there's any vacancies in Lyme Regis?'

Allan opened a bottle of Malbec and found two clean glasses in the dishwasher. 'Come on. Have a glass of this. You've got a few days before he starts, so don't rush into anything. Calm down first. Then plan your revenge, if that's the way you want to go.'

Jane sighed as she sat down. The wine tasted good, and had an immediate anaesthetic effect. 'You're right. Sorry. Anyway, what's your news?'

'I've written the letter accepting the offer, but I haven't posted it yet.'

She frowned, confused. 'Why not?'

'Fear, I suppose. I keep thinking ... I've spent a lifetime at the sharp end, and I wonder how I'll cope being a man in a suit.'

'But you won't be. It's not in your nature. You'll get stuck in, and I'll be cross if you don't. Just send the letter. You'll adapt. We'll both adapt.'

'Yeah, I suppose. Blimey...It's all happening, isn't it? Oh, yes, and I went to the inquest today - you know, the Army guy who died in the crash?'

'Jack Cooper, yeah.'

'Open verdict. Really odd that, for a road accident. I'm going to be following that up tomorrow. Could very well be the last piece I write for my own paper.'

'Well don't interview me, whatever you do.'

'I can't promise that. I might have to phone you up about the new Chief Super.'

Jane laughed. 'It could be the best quote I've ever given you. And the last.'

*****

The road was clear, as it had been at this time every day for over a week.

People thought they were free, but they were just slaves to routine; doing the same things, at the same time, day in, day out.

Like the old guy who drove out here to walk his dog, parked in the same place, facing the same way; spent 30 minutes, more or less, walking up the track into the woods and back. Every. Single. Day.

It was all so predictable, and it was just the same with the guy he was waiting for now.

He'd be walking back from the pub in about five minutes, because he always did. Probably got a programme he wanted to watch, so he'd give himself enough time for a couple of pints, and a quick walk to clear the head before he sat down on his own.

He was just like Jack Cooper. Another creature of habit. Good phrase that. Summed it up pretty well. They were certainly creatures - vermin ...and they were being eradicated.

He smiled as another phrase came into his head... roadkill. Yeah. If he was writing the headlines, that would be the one.

The smile faded when his target appeared.

He did his usual 360 degree observation, then turned the key. Three litres of power sprang into life with a deep growl.

*****

Sergeant Alex Gledhill was smiling politely at a portly gentleman annoyed about the fact that the spray from a neighbour's garden hose was leaving spots on his car. 'And it has happened more than once, you know'.

Alex patiently suggested to him that it wasn't really a matter for the police. The gentleman was indignant and growing redder in the face while threatening to write to the local paper, but Alex was a big man, and he decided to stalk out with as much dignity as he could muster, while threatening to write to the local paper.

He had dealt with some idiots during his 20 years, and he'd often wondered how he managed to keep a straight face. But he invariably did, at least until the coast was clear, anyway.

Alex turned to PC Sykes and laughed: 'Well, Eric, we sorted that major incident out, didn't we?'

Eric allowed himself a half smile, and turned back to the procedural manual he was studying. He was wary of getting too relaxed around his boss. And anyway, he knew he was hopeless at making conversation.

He was desperate to advance, especially after fouling up so badly during the last murder inquiry.. He'd spent too much time looking at his phone when he was guarding a hospital room, and didn't get a look at the intruder who'd knocked the guy off. He got a severe bollocking off the Acting Chief Super for that, but she'd given him a second chance. The guy had been dressed like a doctor, so he probably wouldn't have given him a second glance anyway; and they'd caught him eventually,. But there was no way he was going to switch off again.

Eric wasn't one for chit chat; he was much happier reading, or playing Fortnite. So he was relieved when the phone rang. He grabbed it gratefully. *'Ashbridge Police. PC Sykes. How can I help?'*

He listened, then began taking notes. Alex gave him a questioning look and Eric wrote three words in capitals, then turned the sheet towards him: *HIT AND RUN.*

6

The driving licence in his wallet provided identification, which was just as well since his face had been smashed to pulp.

He was pronounced dead at the scene: a quiet road on the outskirts of Ashbridge, just before it began the gentle climb that marked the transition from municipal to moorland.

The incident had been called in by an 82-year-old who was under sedation and on the way to hospital for treatment for shock. He'd been driving home after walking his dog in the woods half a mile further on, but he hadn't seen anything.

The weather was overcast, visibility was average at best, and the road surface was wet from the mist which the locals said seemed to hang here permanently. When Eric got there, traffic had closed the road, organised a fingertip search, and were taking pictures of tread markings.

The victim's name was Andy Fry. He lived in a terraced house nearby, one of a row built of grey/brown stone. The traffic guy said there was a pub about a mile up the hill, and they thought he might have been walking back from there when he was hit.

'It's a narrow road, and visibility isn't great, as you can see,' he said. 'He only needed to be a bit unsteady on his feet after a few pints, and this is the result.'

Eric's Casio G Shock showed 1852. He was tempted to say it was a bit early to get paralytic, but what did he know. He never touched the stuff.

He moved closer to get a better view of the body, but it was still surrounded by paramedics, and from what he'd been told, he'd be better off not looking too closely.

The light was fading rapidly now, and Eric shaded his eyes against the flashing blues and yellows of police cars, ambulances and fire engines.

He turned his back and radioed in. 'Nothing much I can do here, sir.'

'All right. Get yourself back here and do your report. I might even let you go home after that.'

Eric didn't need reminding about doing his report, but he'd be in no hurry to get home. Apart from his natural instinct to take his time and do things properly, he didn't really fancy another night with mum, staring at classic episodes of Coronation Street.

He drove back to the station against the flow of traffic heading out of town.

He wondered about the hit and run driver, trying to imagine how he or she was feeling now. Would guilt win in the end? It often did; people frequently turned up at the station a few hours later, owning up to minor collisions. But to smash into someone and leave them... Eric shook his head. Surely no one could live with that kind of guilt, and it would take guts to own up to it now.

Eric couldn't escape the feeling that, if it was him, he'd be too traumatised to even think of escaping. The shock would make most people freeze, wouldn't it?

Questions kept forming. Was there a passenger in the car? Was the car in a garage now, being repaired? Looking at all the cars on the road now, on just one route out of Manchester, how on earth were they going to track down one car, one driver?

As he turned into the station car park, he saw Ross getting into his car. Ross had told him there'd been a hit and run not too long ago. Another fatality, too..

Jane Birchfield told him once that you should never ignore a connection. He made a mental note to look up the details while he was writing his report.

*****

'So what are you saying, George?'

'PC Sykes made the point; we're now looking at two hit and runs, two middle aged men dead, both on quiet roads with no CCTV, no passers by, and light was poor. And no debris found at the scene, just tyre marks that look similar.'

'...But no evidence to suggest they were anything other than bad accidents about ten days apart. The drivers panicked and left the scene. It happens.'

George paused; wondering how far he could push it. 'You know yourself, ma'am, sometimes, you get a feeling, a hunch.' He stopped, considering his next words. 'It's got to be more than coincidence. I just think it's worth looking into: see if anything turns up.'

'Okay George. I've been known to go out on a limb before. And I do owe you one for covering for me while I was away.' Jane sat back and folded her arms. 'Go on. I'll give you a couple of days to come up with something, then we move on, all right?'

George scraped his chair back as he stood. 'Right you are, ma'am. Thanks.'

Jane gestured at him to sit down again. 'Did you get anywhere with Ross?'

George wriggled his considerable bulk back into the chair. 'Oh, yes, sorry. Turns out his grandfather was in the Army. Awarded the Military Cross, same as Jack Cooper. They were very close, apparently. Almost a second father....'

'Were very close?'

'Yeah, he died last year.'

'Okay. I'm glad you talked it through. I bet Ross appreciated it.'

'He did. That's down to you, ma'am. I avoid stuff like that.'

'Try it again sometime... Anyway... You've heard about the new Chief Super?'

George's face fell so much it almost hit the desk. 'Yes ma'am.'

'Thoughts?'

George cleared his throat. 'Honest opinion?'

Jane scoffed. 'Of course.'

'Well, you know I'd been thinking about retirement? Let's just say this has made my mind up. I'm leaving, ma'am.'

Jane shook her head sadly. 'I know how you feel. I'm not exactly jumping for joy, but we have to make the best of it.'

'I know. But...' He hesitated for a second, disappointment written all over his face. 'We all think you should have got the job, ma'am.'

'Thanks George. I'd have loved to take it on, but let's be honest, no-one could ever replace Charles Aston. Maybe it's better this way. A completely fresh start...'

He didn't look convinced. 'If you say so, ma'am.'

Jane smiled. 'I don't know what I'd do without you. You've been a rock, especially these last few months.'

'It's a pleasure to work with you, ma'am.'

She nodded. 'Likewise. We understand each other, I think.'

'I think we do.'

'So, promise you'll talk to me again before you make up your mind about leaving. We can't afford to lose our best people.'

George nodded and left quickly, closing the door behind him.

From the look on his face, Jane was pretty sure he'd retire, and soon. She leaned against the door and stretched her back, which was playing up after too long in the chair, then snatched up the phone and put a call through to the Chief Constable's office.

*****

The police press office wasn't going out of its way to help, and Allan decided a bit of bluster might do the trick.

'Come on, Cheryl. All I want is a comment about how unusual it is to have an open verdict about a road traffic accident. It's not that difficult is it?'

Her voice was annoyingly polite, like a hotel receptionist dealing with an unreasonable customer. 'Yes, but Allan, it's not for us to comment on a coroner's verdict. You should be talking to their office, not me.'

'You know very well they won't talk to me. if you can't comment officially, just give me something to work with. I won't quote you. I won't attribute it. It's just one angle in the story, and all I want is to be able to say that it's unusual.'

'Allan, that RTA is still an open file. I can't say a word, you know that…'

He cut her off. 'Final answer?'

'Sorry. Yes.'

'Okay. Which famous film star said *I'll be back*?'

He could practically hear her smirk. 'Can I phone a friend?'

'No you can not.'

'All right … Arnold Schwarzenegger.'

'Yes, the terminator. And that's me right now. You have been warned.' He tried to sound threatening, but Cheryl just laughed.

'Don't be like that. When was the last time we let you down?'

‘Last week, probably. Thanks anyway. See you around, Cheryl…’

Allan replaced the receiver and leaned back, swivelling round in his chair, as if that would help him think. He’d set his heart on getting a different angle on the hit and run. The police had appealed for witnesses, but they always did that.

His interest in the coroner’s verdict was just a not very original ploy to unlock information. Open verdicts weren’t unusual at all; they were often given when there was an element of doubt. But it had given him an excuse to pester the lovely Cheryl, so that was good… And she’d confirmed that the file was still open. So this was more than a hit and run. And Jane’s team had been looking into it as well. Why all this special attention? Because it was murder? Now that would be a story...

What’s more, his daily call to Ashbridge nick had revealed there’d been another. Coincidence, or a front page headline? … *Killer at the wheel.*

He had two days to deadline. He needed to get off his backside and get down to the station for a bit of face to face. It was always the best way. What was that desk sergeant’s name… Alex?

Allan reached for his notebook, then stopped. The hunt for a story always made him come alive. He was really feeling the buzz, and time was flying today. How would he survive without it?

As he jogged down the stairs, he wondered again whether accepting the offer would turn out to be the biggest mistake he’d ever made.

*****

He used the last of the daylight to get underneath, spray oil on the subframe, and check the bolts with a torque wrench.

Then he parked under the trees, stowed his overalls neatly in the back, and put the cover on, before weighing it down with a couple of branches.

He nodded politely as the couple from a few doors down walked past with their yappy terrier. That was a surprise. They weren’t usually out at this time. He gave them his best smile, but it made him uneasy.

‘Lovely evening. Enjoy your walk?’

‘Oh yes, thank you. How’s Bess?’

‘She’s cross with me for not taking her out. But I’ll make up for it in a minute. It’s her dinner time.’

They laughed and waved before walking on.

He frowned as he closed his door. They couldn’t have seen him with the vehicle or they would have said something. Normally, they couldn’t resist commenting on anything, so he’d probably got away with it, this time.

Even so, he couldn’t afford any more errors. The job wasn’t over yet.

7.

Jane stopped on her way out to thank PC Sykes for his report on the hit and run.

He blushed straight away and the acne on his forehead glowed bright red. He was too shy, or embarrassed, to look her in the eye, but she was rewarded with a smile when she told him they were looking at potential links between the two accidents.

His commitment to the job reminded her of the time she first met Jag. He'd offered to be her runner on the Fiona Worsley case. It was her first murder investigation and his diligence was a godsend. It had given him the encouragement he needed to work towards a move out of uniform and into CID; and she'd been able to give the impression of remembering every detail, thanks to his copious note taking.

He'd always been first to hold his hand up to the unglamorous jobs, like viewing CCTV footage, or working through files to find the fact that could close a case.

Now, even though he'd lost most of his vision after the attack, he hadn't lost his spark. He was still eager to carry on, and refusing to indulge in self pity. Jane had vowed the day it happened that she'd do whatever it took to keep him in the team.

She walked to her car and reflected on the fact that if Eric was half as good as Jag, he'd go far.

Jane was on her way to meet Hopkirk to talk about her future, and no doubt listen to him extolling the virtues of Cooper. Only two more days till that prat moved into Charles Aston's office.

But she'd become intrigued by the hit and runs. Now was a good chance to see where they happened, and a bit of fresh air wouldn't do any harm before she met the boss.

She walked slowly up the as yet unnamed road where Jack Cooper died. There'd been a few showers since it happened, but you could still see the stains where he'd lain bleeding. It was only about 50 yards from the main road.

Jane turned to look back. There was a lot of passing traffic even at this time of the afternoon, and that made it a high risk location, if it was deliberate. But, hang on… that could be the point. She'd been here for 15 minutes and no cars had come down here. And why would they? There were only a few houses on the estate at the top, and there were easier and less busy ways to get there than via the main road. Plus, it was a new road that most people didn't know about yet.

Jane leaned against her car and closed her eyes. This was the way she worked; feeling the atmosphere of a place, allowing herself time to absorb what happened. Her uncle Bill was a DCI in Yorkshire, and he was full of advice for her when she followed in his footsteps. She still missed him. One thing he said had stuck with her over the years… 'Try looking with your eyes closed.'

So she did…

She could hear the rushing noise of traffic on the main road. It was a 50 mph limit on that stretch, so not much chance of a passing car looking up here and seeing anything.

Jack Cooper walked here every Friday night after his trip to the pub. If you were planning to mow him down, you'd have to be sure of his route, and the timing. The killer would probably drive here and park up to observe.

Or maybe they'd follow him on foot a few times. In which case they'd have to walk, or drive, on the main road.

Jane opened her eyes and pulled out her phone. All her love of detective work had come flooding back, and she wondered for a moment why she was so keen to grab promotion. It would definitely mean more meetings, more time behind a desk... Uncle Bill wouldn't have been impressed, that much was for certain.

She jabbed the speed dial number for CID.

'George? We need CCTV footage from the cameras on Manchester Road, 200 yards either side of the road where Jack Cooper died. No… just the hour from 9.30, every Friday night for the last six weeks. Oh, and get someone out here to check for any track marks off the road. If he was mown down, someone must have been watching him for a while. Maybe they parked in the trees up at the top.'

She put the phone back in her pocket, checked her watch, and cursed.

There was no time to check the other location: it wouldn't pay to keep Chief Constable Simon Hopkirk waiting.

*****

DC Jahangir Desai, better known as Jag, sipped tea and checked his watch. 3pm. The CID room would be buzzing now, and yet here he was, sitting in his armchair watching a repeat of *Law and Order.*

The hospital had told him that he needed to rest and avoid sudden movement, to safeguard his one good eye. He'd laughed. Good eye? He could only just see well enough to read, the TV was still blurry, and it'd be another week before they'd even consider letting him go back to work.

It didn't help that Moraji was being so brave. She was determined to support him, even though she was juggling work, and looking after him and baby Aarav. His name meant peaceful, but he was anything but.

Nights seemed endless. If Jag wasn't squirming to try to find a comfortable position, Aarav was disturbing the peace. Moraji was still working part time at the school, too, despite the cost of child care. But they'd agreed that if it kept her sane, it was a price worth paying.

Jag had resigned himself to the fact that the beating he'd been given had not only wrecked his sight, it had also wrecked his career prospects.

Jane had been great: she'd visited him every day in hospital, and promised that his desk was waiting for him and that he'd be welcome back. She'd told him that he would always have a place on her team. But even she couldn't hide the fact that his hopes of continuing his progression through the CID ranks had been knocked back.

Moraji had told him he had to man up. 'Obstacles are there to be overcome,' she'd said, as she bathed his eye earlier.

Jag smiled. He loved his wife, but she was like a walking Facebook meme, at times.

He turned his attention back to the television. The police had found all the evidence they needed in the first half hour, and the suspect was already in court.

His smile faded. There would soon come a point where he would have to appear in court and face the man who beat him up that day. The memory was still so vivid… *The dingy warehouse;*

the surprise discovery of the new film set where they'd shot the porn videos; the sound of footsteps coming nearer; the explosion in his head.

Jag flinched as he remembered, before repeating his daily mantra that he would not be defeated. He would get back to work and he would fight back against his disability, and he would make Moraji and Aarav - and Jane Birchfield - proud.

*****

Ross was back to his annoying best, and Lorry didn't know whether to clout him or kiss him.

He'd shown another side to his personality over the last couple of weeks, and she was moved that he'd been so close to his grandad. But the other Ross was in the room now - the cocky, smart alec Ross that had grated on her from the first day she joined the team to help out during the Fiona Worsley murder case.

Still, she felt a residue of warmth towards him, even when he conned her into thinking it was her turn to brew up.

Now she planted his mug of coffee on his desk with exaggerated firmness.

'Your coffee, sir.'

'Thanks minion.'

'You're looking pleased with yourself.'

'Why not? I'm good looking, I've got a decent job, and I won £50 at poker last night,' Ross said with a shrug.

'Not sure your first point would stand up in a court of law, but I'll let you off. How's the hit and run thing going?'

Ross switched to serious, and became instantly more endearing. Lorry sat down at her desk and swivelled round to face him.

'I haven't told George yet, so don't say anything, but there's a clear link between the two victims. They were both ex-Army, and not only that, but they also served in the Royal Lancashires together.'

'Wow, that has got to be more than coincidence.'

'Exactly what I thought. But there's more.... Turns out they are both on Army pensions, and they left at roughly the same time

- within a couple of months of each other. Jack got the Military Cross, but there's no record of decoration for Andy Fry. However -'

Lorry flapped her hand impatiently. 'Go on. This is getting good.'

'- they served together, on the same tours… Ireland, Middle East, Afghanistan. So they must have been pretty close.'

*****

Jane had arrived on time, but Chief Constable Hopkirk was running late, so she found a desk and read Ross's info as soon as he'd keyed it into the log.

She messaged George: *Ross has done well, but be careful. We want to keep this under the radar. If this gets out, we could have a very public panic on our hands. The Army connection is too strong to ignore, so let's find out more about that - any history, enemies within. That sort of stuff.*

George replied. *That'll be a challenge, getting the Army to open up!*

If anyone can, George, it's you.

We don't know too much about what they did when they left the Army. We need to catch up on that, as well.

Okay. If we're right, then there's a killer driving around on our patch right now.

There's plenty of catching up to do. That's my fault for telling you to back off.

Made sense at the time, ma'am.

That'll count for nothing if the trail's gone cold. Got to go. Keep me posted.

*****

Allan couldn't have timed his visit better.

By the time he climbed the station steps off the High Street and pushed through the heavy oak doors, everyone was already talking about the hit and run investigation.

Allan put his Aunt Betty's paper bag on the counter and bashed the bell.

Alex Gledhill grinned, but he was looking at the bag, not Allan.

'Little gift for you, Sergeant.'

'Don't tell me… jam doughnuts.'

'The very same.'

'You're a star, mate. Now, I suppose you want something in return?'

'Cynic… But yes, I do, now that you mention it. What's happening with the hit and runs?'

Alex had only just found out himself, and it was so fresh in his mind it seemed natural to talk.

Allan only wrote a few key words in his notebook. He'd learned that shorthand notes could easily terminate what was supposed to be a matey conversation.

Alex tapped the notebook. 'I didn't tell you any of this, did I?'

Allan smiled reassuringly. 'Of course not. It'll just be me weaving a few things together that are already public. And I'll be careful. We don't want people getting frightened of going out, do we?'

Alex smiled, clearly relieved, and looked inside the bag. 'I'm slipping. I should have checked the contents first.'

'You do that, while I go and check out the Feathers.'

'Why the Feathers? That's not your local.'

'No, but it was Jack Cooper's.'

'So, off to the pub on business, then. Some people have all the luck.'

Allan thought about that as he walked to the pub. He'd thought he was lucky, getting offered a small fortune for the paper, and a tidy salary on top. Now that he was on the trail of what could be a cracking news story, he wasn't so sure. Again.

*****

George saluted sarcastically as he slammed the phone down.

'Bollocks!'

He'd been in a bad mood all day, and, despite the entertainment value, Lorry and Ross had decided to keep their heads down.

Unfortunately for them, their lack of response was now irritating him even more than that phone call.

'Are you two going to just sit there in silence all bloody day?!'

Ross reluctantly peered over the top of his monitor. 'Sorry, George. What's up?'

'I'll tell you what's up… the Army, that's what's up. It's like getting blood out of a stone.'

They'd been listening intently anyway, not that they had much choice, but Lorry feigned innocence.

'No luck then, George?'

'No!' he snapped back, the veins on head popping up. 'I've been on the phone three times to their so called Staff and Personnel Support unit, and every time they've told me they're waiting for the Adjutant General's office to give permission to release information. It's just -'

'Bollocks?' Lorry suggested.

'Exactly the word.'

'Makes you wonder what they're so worried about. It's not as if either of them died in service, is it?'

George heaved a sigh, and levered himself out of his chair with a grunt. 'I'm going to see Phil. He's got a mate in the Army and he might be able to pull a few strings for me. Behave while I'm gone, alright?''

Ross winked as the door closed behind him. 'I've never seen him so grumpy. Wonder what's up?'

Lorry shrugged. 'He's just having a bad day.'

Ross didn't sound convinced. 'Yeah… but he was really peed off about that guy Cooke taking over, wasn't he? Maybe that's what's really bugging him. Don't know why, though; I heard he was a cool dude, full of new ideas…'

'That's it then.'

'What is?'

'George is pushing 60 now. He probably doesn't want new ideas.'

Ross scoffed. 'That's ageism, that is.'

'Bollocks!'

'Don't you start…'

They were still laughing when George walked back in, but he surprised them with a smile. 'Good news,' he said as he reached for a wine gum. 'Phil's going to phone his mate. He reckons he'll give us everything we need to know about our two victims.'

'Fancy a brew to celebrate, George?'

'Don't mind if I do, thanks Lorry. And Ross?'

'Yes boss?'

George walked over and dropped a £2 coin on his desk. 'Nip over the road will you, there's a good lad. I've run out of wine gums.'

*****

Simon Hopkirk's white shirt was almost as bright as his teeth. He stepped out from behind his desk to greet Jane and shook her hand with just the right degree of firmness, considering he was over six feet and built like a fast bowler.

He was the youngest Chief Constable in the force's history, and probably the best respected too. He had a reputation for standing up for his people, and providing opportunities for under-represented groups.

Jane realised she was probably here for that reason. He couldn't afford to blot his copybook by closing doors in her face.

She accepted the cup of tea he offered, but turned down the chocolate digestives. The small talk was over.

'So, Jane, you wanted to see me, I believe?'

'Yes sir. I wanted to ask what your intentions were for me, if I may. You remember we spoke not long ago ...'

He smiled and leaned back in his chair, but his eyes never left hers. It was yet another of his skills... eye contact, also known as observing your prey. 'Is this prompted by my decision to appoint Roy Cooke, by any chance?'

That threw her, and she almost took the bait. But, instead, she chose to buy time by sipping from her empty tea cup and decided on diplomacy rather than diatribe. 'It is, sir. To be honest, I was surprised. I'd hoped that after your encouraging comments recently about how well I'd done covering for Charles, that it was a clue about your intentions for me.'

He leaned forward, his elbows now on the desk. 'Sorry I gave you the wrong impression there, Jane. Look, let me be upfront with you. I rate you very highly, and it's no secret I want to provide more opportunities for women at the highest level.' He paused for effect. 'And I mean, the highest level... Look, I want you here at headquarters, but I can't fix it straight away. It would be unfair on one or two people if I told you my intentions now, so I'm going to have to ask you to trust me.'

He held a hand up to stop Jane butting in. 'I need you to work with Cooke for a little while. I know you don't see eye to eye, but I know you can rise above any personal feelings. I'll have something for you very soon. Believe me, I wish I could make it happen now...'

Jane's good humour lasted well into the night. She amazed Allan by getting home before him, prepping his favourite shepherd's pie, and buying a bottle of red from the top shelf of the supermarket.

She was even singing Adele while she was serving... '*Hello from the other side...*'

It was enough to get Allan up off the sofa and into the kitchen. 'Have you won the lottery, or what?'

She stifled a laugh. 'In a way.'

'It must be a bloody good way. I've not heard you sing for months.'

'Yeah and I bet Adele's worried.'

He raised an eyebrow. 'The next door neighbours will be.'

'Cheeky sod. I'm dishing up. I'll tell you my news when we're sat down.'

'Yes ma'am!'

He made the right noises, but Jane could tell it had given him pause for thought. He tried to hide it, but his first reaction was to think about the impact of her good news on his, rather than the instinctive loving support she'd been expecting.

It confirmed her original fear - that he'd been hoping his new money would change their status. He'd want to move house, have holidays, take her out for meals... he'd become the dominant male. And he couldn't understand why she resented it, or even rejected it.

She sat, brooding while he loaded the dishwasher.

On the surface, they'd had a good meal and they'd talked about the good things that were happening. But maybe they were both wondering if they were *good things.*

Jane drained her glass and poured another. Was she just being a brat because her good news was being overshadowed by his? Or did she understand only too well that Allan was using his good fortune to manoeuvre her into submission?

She thought back… He'd been sulking about her late nights for weeks: he'd even buggered off to Lyme Regis on his own a couple of weeks ago, saying he needed time to think. Their trip to Lyme Regis was supposed to bring them back together. But right now she felt like they were anything but.

She slumped back on the sofa, feeling drained. Her head was beginning to spin, and it wasn't just the wine. Was this the beginning of the end, or was she over-reacting? Either way, she couldn't go on like this.

Jane took another gulp of wine and decided she wasn't going to stew overnight. She'd have it out with him. Even if that meant ending it right now.

8.

Allan took his time stacking the dishwasher to his exacting standards, and finally reached a decision.

He drank a glass of water to clear his head, then sat next to Jane. She didn't even look at him.

'Can I say something?'

She just nodded.

'I'm not going to accept the offer.'

Her voice was flat. 'You've already accepted it.'

'Well, I'm going to withdraw my acceptance.'

Two minutes ago, she'd been ready to throw wine in his face and walk out. Now she didn't know what to say. Allan took her silence as a cue to carry on.

'Hearing your news made me think again. I was already wondering why I was being such an idiot. We don't need the money; we're ok as we are. I love what I do. I can't see me lasting five minutes being a director. Just imagine all the bloody stuffed shirts I'd be mixing with! I'm just a journalist. I don't belong anywhere else. So…' He shrugged.

Allan reached for the hand that wasn't holding onto the wine glass, and Jane saw the sincerity in his eyes. '...I'm really pleased for you, and I wish I could have come across a bit happier about it, but it's just - well, it's been on my mind, and you set me off thinking again. I just want us to be happy, and I think this is the best way. So grab your promotion. You deserve it. I'm happy as I am. So, yeah, that's it, really.'

Jane put the glass down, leaned back against him and closed her eyes. She'd been steeling herself for a shouting match, and now it was all she could do to not to cry. She couldn't even trust herself to speak without her voice shaking.

She'd misjudged him, and though she loved him even more, she loved herself less.

Her head was resting on his chest and her voice was almost a whisper. 'So we carry on, and you promise you won't mind me putting in the hours?'

'Yes, I promise, and yes, we carry on - well, I hope you want to. I want to carry on building up the paper, and I want to carry on being with you. I still hope that one day…'

'...We'll get married. Yes, I hope so too.'

'You mean it? God, I never thought I'd marry a chief constable.'

'I never thought I'd marry an editor.'

Allan gently pushed her away and then held her hand. 'If I'm honest, I can't actually remember how we got to this point, so can I just rewind?' He took a deep breath… 'I love you, Jane Birchfield. Will you marry me?'

Jane held his hand and pressed it over her heart. 'Yes, Allan. I will.'

*****

Phil was smirking rather obviously. 'You look like you had a good night, Jane.'

'And you look like you need a good night.'

He laughed. 'Charmed, I'm sure.'

'Come on, Phil, what've you got for me?'

'George asked me to call in a favour with a mate of mine in the Army, and it was interesting. Turns out both our hit and run victims were in the same platoon, and did the same tours of duty, most recently in Afghanistan. That's where Jack Cooper got awarded the Military Cross.'

Jane leaned forward. 'For what?'

'Saving his mates when they were ambushed on patrol, apparently.'

'Was Andy Fry one of the mates?'

'My contact didn't know. He just said there were a lot of casualties on both sides, but that Jack was a hero.'

'So, ok; if we assume that he and Andy Fry were mown down by a vehicle deliberately, what motive could there be? It may be nothing to do with the Army, tempting as it is to make that link. Allan's looking into the story, and he went to the Feathers, where both of them used to meet up there on a Friday, with a couple of others. The landlord reckons they were all ex-Army, but who knows what they were up to after they retired. The motive could be closer to home than Afghanistan, or wherever else they went.'

'Sex or money?'

Her deadpan delivery was perfect. 'Not today, thanks.'

Phil spluttered as he sipped his water, but recovered quickly as Jane smiled at him, innocently. 'So, there's plenty to think about.'

'Yes. We both trust our instincts don't we? Mine is telling me to concentrate on the Army.'

'And you are rarely wrong... Anything else I can do, ma'am?'

'Not for now, thanks. Oh - there is one thing. Convince George not to retire, will you? I need him. The new Chief Super starts tomorrow.'

Phil stopped as he was about to close the door behind him. 'May God have mercy on our souls.'

*****

It was a clear night, with a half moon casting a misty grey wash over the street.

The usual morons were lurching around, colliding with lamp posts but somehow never dropping their cider bottles.

He stood in the shadow of incongruous gothic arches that formed the entrance to a shopping precinct; waiting, as he'd done so many times. He was good at it, too. Had lots of practice over the years, and much more recently. He'd learned to switch off so he wasn't counting the minutes. In fact, the only moment he became aware of time was when the target appeared.

Target 3 was looking fairly straightforward. This was the fourth night of observation, and he'd appeared at roughly the same time so far, walking at a brisk pace at the end of his shift, as though he was keen to get home, even though there was no-one there.

The route never varied, but this section was a no-go. There were too many people around, even if most of them were out of their skulls.

And there he was... right on cue.

He started the stopwatch and stamped the cigarette out, before easing into the street, keeping well back, baseball cap pulled down tight, collar up. It was about a 20 minute walk, and the route would make this slightly more difficult. The only safe time to strike would be when he reached the quieter streets near his home, which didn't leave much of a window.

There was an element of risk, and he knew that; but he'd lived with risk for a long time. The priority now was to keep well away from CCTV cameras. He knew where they were, but it was impossible to go completely invisible. If a camera didn't catch you, a random passer-by might.

But if you really want something, you'll work for it, and accept that you have to take a chance now and again. And he'd never wanted anything more than this. It would all be over in a couple of weeks and then he'd be going off-grid, never to be seen again.

The target turned left, and he followed, crossing the street with his head down. He checked his watch. Half way. The next victim would be home in 10 minutes, and he had no idea what tomorrow would bring.

*****

Ross sat at a corner table, nursing a Guinness and making the crisps last.

He looked round. He wasn't the only saddo in the Feathers. There was one on every evenly spaced bar stool, and quite a few hogging tables for four. The only people talking were a creepy looking man in a suit, who was obviously piling on the charm for his date for the night, who was on her second G and T and still didn't appear impressed.

Ross crunched another salt and vinegar crisp and checked his phone for messages. Nothing. So this was what a Friday night out looked like when you were middle aged. There wasn't even any music, just a big telly on silent, showing Bundesliga football.

George had said Jane's partner Allan had been sniffing around the story, and came in here a couple of nights ago, so he asked would Ross mind checking it out: seeing who came in, any signs of ex-soldiers meeting up, and chatting up the staff to get some names.

Ross sighed, drained his glass and slowly walked up to the bar.

At least the barmaid looked lively. 'All right, love? What can I get you? Same again?' She smiled brightly, and Ross smiled back.

'Just a half, please.'

'Not seen you in here before.'

'My first time. Actually, since you're so observant, who are the regulars? Any in tonight?'

She looked up and down the bar and pursed her lips. 'All of them. Why? Oh, don't tell me, you're the police… right?'

Ross grinned and flashed his ID. 'Blimey, you're good. Yeah, we're trying to find out more about Jack Cooper and his mate, Andy. Anyway, what's your name?'

She put the glass on the bar and waited for it to settle. 'Amy. They were in here every Friday. Lovely blokes.'

'Just them?'

'No they were always there with two others.' She walked to the other end of the bar and peered round, before coming back, shaking her head. 'No, they're not in.'

'Know their names? That'd be useful. We just want to know more about them.'

'Why? It was a road accident, wasn't it?' Ross simply shrugged. 'Alright. Their mates were Colin and Chris.'

'Surnames?' Ross lifted his glass to take a sip.

'Colin Flynn. Don't know the other one. He was the quiet one. They played cards, bought a round each… that was the routine.' Amy now seemed upset. 'And Jack would always put a pound on the counter for me on his way out.'

She topped up his glass, and Ross handed over the money. 'You've been great. Look, it's not that busy… can you spare me five minutes for a proper chat?'

Amy frowned. 'You're not going to chat me up, are you?'

Ross held his hands out in a gesture of innocence. 'Me? You have nothing to fear from me, Amy.' He could see she immediately understood. 'No, I just want to tap your brain about Jack and his mates.' He leaned closer . 'I won't keep you long, I promise. And you'll be doing me, and maybe Jack, a big favour.'

Ross told her about Jack's Military Cross and that he wanted to find out more about him because of his own grandad.

Amy knew Colin Flynn fairly well. They used to work behind the bar together at the King's Arms near Ashbridge bus station.

She'd started at the Feathers because they offered her more hours and a better hourly rate, but she thought he still worked there part time. She even remembered his address - well, the name of the street ... Box Avenue.

She couldn't enlighten Ross about the enigmatic Chris, however. 'He laughed at all the jokes but you never heard him tell one. Always so serious; on his guard, like. Bit weird, if you ask me.'

'There's a lot of weird in the world.'

'You sound like my dad!'

Ross chose not to take offence. 'Oh that's nice.'

'How old are you?'

'29... Hey, I'm supposed to be interviewing you.'

'Are you really gay, or was that just a trick to get me on my own?'

'You don't hold back, do you? Actually, yes, I am. But I don't often admit it.'

'No, I could tell. You had that sort of look. Like you were already wishing you hadn't let on.'

Ross realised that he was talking to this girl more than he'd talked to anyone since grandad Frank died. 'You're a good observer, you are. You should join the police.'

She simply laughed, so he carried on. 'You're the first person I've told since my grandad died. He brought me up after my mum and dad split up, and I was terrified of telling him. He was a war hero, for Christ's sake! I told him one night. He'd had his usual glass of whisky before bed, and I just went for it - blurted it out.'

'That was brave. How did he take it?'

Ross turned away so Amy couldn't see his face. He fought hard, but it was too late. He felt tears stinging his eyes and the wet track as one rolled down his cheek.

Amy put her hand on his arm and whispered. 'It's ok. No-one's looking.'

Ross wiped his face on the sleeve of his jacket. 'He just put his arm round my shoulder and said: *Doesn't make any difference. And did you think I didn't know?*'

'That's lovely. But no-one else knows, even at work? Really?'

'It's the police, Amy. I just don't know how it would go for me if it came out - if I came out...'

'Have you got a partner?'

'No, you?'

'Nah. Look around, not much to choose from is there?' She laughed. 'Actually, I thought my luck was in when you bought me a drink.'

Ross smiled. He could stay here all night, but he decided to see if he could track down Colin Flynn. 'Sorry Amy. Not your night, is it?'

'I'll get over it. Come back soon, yeah?'

Ross felt like he'd made a new friend. 'I will. Be seeing you.'

*****

Chief Superintendent Roy Cooke checked himself in the mirror and called out in answer to the knock on the door. 'Enter!'

'I just thought I'd check everything's ok and say welcome to Ashbridge, sir.'

He sat down and pulled a shirt cuff out an inch or so from his jacket sleeve. 'Thanks muchly, Jane. Yes, all good, so far. Though the office is too cramped. And this chair needs replacing. I don't know how you put up with it. Or Charles Aston for that matter. Might have to think about finding a bit more space... Anyway, sit down while you're here. Probably a good time for a quick catch up, yes?'

Jane ran through current casework, but the only time he showed any interest was when Jane mentioned the hit and runs. He'd clearly been briefed already, because he was quick to come back on it when she finished.

'So, the two hit and runs... accidents, yes?'

'Well, we don't think so. They were so close -'

'You don't think so? I see... Tell me, Jane, how much resource is going into your investigation, on the shaky ground that you *don't think so*?'

Jane stared him out and kept her voice low. She was damned if she was going to let this bully intimidate her. She'd heard about his love of trying the male domination routine on female officers.

'Actually, sir, very little. We've done some basic checks on the victims and their backgrounds -'

'- And?'

'Sir, if I could finish...' Jane said through her fake smile. He waved a hand dismissively but she was pleased to see that at least she'd rattled him. 'And we know they were both in the same regiment, if not the same platoon; on the same tours of duty; and they met once a week at a local pub. So you might think it's more than coincidence they should be the victims of apparently random road accidents.'

He smiled. '*More than coincidence*....Oh dear. Jane... I know this must be difficult for you, having sat in this chair for a while, to have me come in and start calling the shots. But, as you know, that's my job here. And I will be calling the shots. We need more than coincidences to launch expensive and time consuming murder investigations. And you need to keep me briefed on a daily basis from now on.'

He stood in an obvious attempt to terminate the discussion. Jane stayed seated, until he reached the door and opened it.

'Thanks muchly, Jane. I'll read the log, and I'll let you know about the hit and runs.'

'Thank you, sir. Welcome to Ashbridge.'

*****

Allan got the full force of her wrath that night.

'That man! Complete tosser! *Thanks muchly*... for crying out loud!'

'So, looks like being a bumpy ride, then?'

'For him, yeah. He thinks I'll just roll over. Well he can dream on. I don't need lectures on policing from a squirt like him.'

Allan put on his most innocent and supportive face. 'You just can't make your mind up about him, can you?'

It took a second to sink in, but she laughed despite herself, and it was enough to snap her out of it. She thought, not for the first time, how much she relied on him to keep her sane. 'Sorry, Allan. How was your day?'

'I got a stroppy email from that company about the takeover. Sounds like they've never been turned down before. They obviously think it's a negotiating ploy and they want to talk.'

'Blimey. Sounds like you could name your price then.'

'Yeah, but I'm not going to. My mind's made up.'

Jane chuckled. 'You're as stubborn as me.'

'Huh… and that's saying something. Hey! Still want to marry me?'

'Well… I'm wondering what would happen if I turned you down. Would you think it was a negotiating ploy?'

'No. I'd think you'd lost your marbles.' He gave her a pointed look, earning a grin in return. 'Anyway, you can't turn me down. Come here and give me a kiss, Mrs Askew.'

Jane wanted to keep the banter rolling, but that stopped her in her tracks. 'Mrs Askew... Mr and Mrs Askew … I like the sound of it.' She smiled and put her hand on the back of his neck. 'If you want a kiss, Mr Askew, you'll have to come here. And that's non-negotiable.'

*****

Lorry was on her fourth set of CCTV files, and was beginning to lose the will.

As she'd said to Mark last night, it would help if she knew what she was looking for. 'It's just a load of cars going past. How am I supposed to pick one out of that lot?'

'If you were working with me, we'd develop a computer program to do the search for you.'

'Yeah, well I'm not, am I? Anyway, how's it going at Greaves these days?'

Mark didn't dare get too enthusiastic because he knew it was irritating. But he was loving life at one of the North West's biggest companies. He'd been offered a job by Adrian Fisher, who had been a massive help on the Jamie Castleton case. Jamie had hacked into the Greaves online betting system - affectionately known as GOB - from one of the company's internet cafes.

The boss of Greaves - Graeme Hargreaves - had shut down the cafes and the servers, and tasked Adrian with finding out who was behind it. He'd worked closely with Mark, and they'd got on well. So well,in fact, that he was offered the chance to leave the forensic unit at Ashbridge and jump into the private sector with a hefty pay rise, his own office, and a fancy title - Head of Cyber Security. Adrian's PA even brought his coffee and biscuits in. On a tray...

Lorry had been happy to start with. The new money got them a new flat with views over Manchester, and they got engaged. But she missed seeing him in the canteen, and the contrast in working environments and job satisfaction was making her jealous, so Mark played it cool.

'It's going alright, but it's tough keeping up with the hackers. You wouldn't believe the tricks they get up to.'

'That's why they took you on, though. You're the best.'

Mark smiled. 'Too kind. If I am, it's because I had the best grounding, working with all of you at Ashbridge nick.... And that reminds me what I was going to say.' He cleared his throat. 'I know the work can be boring at times -'

'- Bloody right it can!'

' - but that place has got a great reputation. So stick with it a bit longer, and you never know…'

'Yeah, you're right. I'm learning all the time. Might even make it to sergeant soon. I shouldn't complain.' Lorry sighed.

'No, it's fine. I used to, all the time.'

Mark closed his laptop but showed no sign of switching himself off. 'I've got some time off tomorrow. Want me to see if I can come up with a bit of software to help with the CCTV thing? Do you think George would mind?'

Lorry yawned. 'Nah, he's a big softy. Just bring him a bag of wine gums and you'll be fine.' Mark opened his laptop again. 'What are you doing?'

'I just had an idea about those hit and runs… You were saying there's no sign of debris on the road each time, right?'

‘Yeah, so?’

‘So I’m thinking where would you find vehicles that could stand up to that sort of impact.’

Lorry groaned petulantly. ‘Oh come on Mark. It’s bedtime.’

‘You go up. I’ll be there in a minute…’ He walked over and kissed the top of her head. ‘Trust me, you’ll thank me for this tomorrow.’

9.

There was something not right about Jack Cooper's house.

George frowned as soon as he saw it. He'd never met the guy, but it just felt wrong. It was basically a garage with a house on top, and George couldn't imagine why a middle aged Army man would choose something so modern.

He rubbed his chin. Ah well, each to his own.

The ground floor was a garage with nothing in it - no car, no shelves full of tins of paint, no random pieces of wood; not even an oil stain on the white concrete floor.

A side door opened onto a narrow hall leading into a small utility room and a toilet. The stairs led up to an open plan living room and kitchen. More stairs took you up to the top floor, with one bedroom and a box room, a bathroom and a separate toilet.

It wasn't just the layout that troubled George; it was the complete lack of any personal touches. It was neat and tidy, as you'd expect from an ex-soldier, but there were no pictures on the wall, no photos, no photo albums or address books … no books of any kind.

The only items of any interest were his laptop and mobile phone.

George bagged them, then phoned forensics when he found a few items of clothing in the built in wardrobe, including a couple of Army uniforms. There might be some traces on the clothes, but everything looked so clean, and he wasn't holding his breath.

George sat in his car, buying himself time to think, as Jane was always telling him to do.

Why was the house unnaturally clean? Did Jack have something to hide? It almost looked like he'd set things up so he could make a quick getaway...

Maybe that was the way he'd lived: carry the minimum, always ready for action.

George watched as a woman in tight jeans, high heels and a short black puffa jacket came out of the house next door, locking the door behind her.

Later, over a cup of tea with Jane, he shared the result of his meditation: 'Maybe his house was spotless because he was always next door.'

Jane clearly wasn't impressed. 'I thought you said she looked about 20? Anyway, if that's your theory, why didn't you ask her?'

George winked. 'Well, I was tempted, ma'am, but I didn't want to go wading in on just a theory. Thought I'd sound you out first.'

Jane rolled her eyes. 'OK George, point taken. You're right to think the unthinkable. Let's mark that one as noted, and see what else turns up. Not that the boss wants us sniffing around, of course.'

He held out his hands in supplication. 'Of course, ma'am, wouldn't dream of it.'

Jane smiled. 'Thanks George. Can you give me a few minutes? I need a bit of thinking time, too - you've set me off.'

Jane took a few gulps of water as George closed the door, then leaned back in her chair and closed her eyes. In one way, it was good to be back in her old office, *doing a bit of detectiving,* as she told her mum. But she couldn't help resenting the fact that Roy Cooke was sitting next door - in Charles Aston's chair.

Charles had been a friend and a mentor, supporting her through the chauvinism that made her life difficult without it ever appearing deliberate. She'd watched Charles decline rapidly after his diagnosis, and the hospice visits usually left her in tears. Now he'd been replaced by someone she had no respect for, and it made the loss even harder to take.

Simon Hopkirk was offering hope that she'd get the step up she craved, but how long could she wait?

She moved to the window and wiped a square of condensation so she could see out. The dark clouds were piling up like grey wool, leaving just enough room for a spotlight of sunshine that lifted the colour on the hills beyond.

Jane took a deep breath and turned back to the paperwork. She could almost hear her mum exhorting her, like she always used to: 'Get your work done first, then you can start fretting about yourself.'

She flicked through the papers, just as an email from George pinged up on the screen.

'Mark Manning's here. He thinks he knows what kind of vehicle was used in the hit and runs.'

*****

It seemed that the good people of Box Avenue were taking their street name seriously. Just about every one of the tiny front gardens had a neat box hedge.

Ross couldn't see the point of gardens, let alone hedges, reasoning there were better ways to spend time than mowing, trimming and weeding.

It was a short street of tightly squeezed houses that managed to look identical, without being. Different coloured front doors; a small tree in a garden to break the line of hedges all the same height; some with net curtains, some with roller blinds, some with venetian; but all unified by their red brick walls and grey slate roofs.

Amy at the Feathers hadn't been able to remember which house Colin Flynn lived in, so Ross was trying to work it out. He worked nights at a pub, so chances were he'd be sleeping it off. There were four or five upstairs windows with the curtains still drawn, but only one where the garden wasn't up to the Box Avenue standard. Number 18 had moss growing between the stones on the path to the green front door.

This was the one. But should he wake him up, or leave him dreaming?

Ross caught a faint scent of coffee, and remembered there was a greasy spoon round the corner that one of his poker mates swore served up the best fried egg balms anywhere in the known universe.

Colin Flynn could have his extra half hour in dreamland after all.

*****

Bess had that sulky look he knew well. It said: 'Please can we stay out a bit longer?'

But she knew better than to resist too long. The minute he started walking purposefully across the soggy field towards her, she put her head down and trotted up to him.

He ruffled the back of her neck and she looked up at him with her big soft eyes. 'Good girl, come on. I've got to go to work.'

He'd surprised himself, talking to a dog.

He'd always been the quiet one; simply because he never felt the need to foist his opinions on someone else, and pouring out your troubles to other people with troubles of their own seemed pointless.

But dogs were different: their actions did the talking for them. That was the way he'd been raised. His dad was a sergeant major and his mantra was '*speak less, say more.*'

He got to the end of the gravel path, and was just about to turn left for home when those bloody neighbours appeared again, kitted out in full hiking gear for a walk down the lane and back. It was too late to ignore them so he put on his friendly smile: 'Morning!'

They returned the greeting in stereo. He could tell the man wanted to make conversation, but he wasn't expecting his opener: 'That's an impressive vehicle you've got round the back there. What make is it?'

It took an effort to keep his cool. 'Oh it's just something I'm working on for a customer. Pretty basic stuff really. Nothing special.'

But he wasn't letting it drop. 'Oh right. I must say it looks special, though. Never seen one like that before. Very distinctive. No wonder you covered it up. Protection, I suppose?'

'Not really. It's just special to him, so I thought it best, you know.' He paused, thinking quickly. 'It's meant to be a surprise for someone, so I promised I'd keep it well hidden.'

His wife smiled politely, but she obviously wanted to get on with the walk. And so did their terrier, which was pulling on the lead, drawn by an invisible but obviously important scent. Finally, he took the hint. 'Ah well, must be going. Can't keep the dog waiting. Wish it was as well behaved as yours… Be seeing you.'

'Enjoy your walk. Bye now.'

He shouted in frustration as soon as he was in the kitchen, but got himself under control before settling Bess down, then went out to check the truck as the first spots of rain began to fall.. It must have been windy overnight, or he hadn't weighted the cover down properly, because the front end was visible.

He cursed under his breath: '*stupid bastard*'. It was a bad mistake. It may only have been his first, but he'd told himself when this began that it would only take one to blow the whole thing.

At least it would soon be over. The third target was scheduled for tonight. He told himself he just had to keep cool and stay focussed, because there was no turning back now.

He checked his watch. The rush hour was over. He walked to the end of the track to check there was no-one around, then eased the truck out from under the tree. He quickly attached the number plates with their Velcro backing tape, folded the cover, and drove off to the workshop.

*****

Colin Flynn came to the door wearing pyjama trousers, and nothing else.

The shaved head and broad chest told the world he could look after himself. He was wearing a hostile expression, but if Ross was intimidated he wasn't going to show it.

'Morning Mr Flynn. DC Rossiter, Ashbridge Police.'

Flynn's tone of voice confirmed the original impression. 'What do you want?'

'We're looking into the deaths of Jack Cooper and Andy Fry.'

'What's that got to do with me?'

'You were friends. Met every Friday at the Feathers by all accounts.'

'So?'

Ross kept the smile on his face. He enjoyed challenges like this. He was famous at the station for being able to cope with the most obnoxious customers, and Mr Flynn was rapidly falling into that category. 'So, Mr Flynn, you knew them well, and we're trying to work out what happened. We'd appreciate your help. Can I come in?'

'Work out what happened? They were knocked down by a nutter in a car. Anyway, why do you need to come in? I can't tell you anything.'

Ross sighed theatrically and glanced up and down the street. 'OK, Mr Flynn. Let me put it another way. Can I come in and have a quick chat with you, or would you like to come to the station and be interviewed for the rest of the day?'

After a moment's consideration, he opened the door and impatiently waved Ross in.

The living room pushed the concept of minimalism to its limits. It was a white painted box containing a new-looking two seater leather sofa, a dining chair, and a tv on a cabinet. And nothing else - unless you count white roller blinds over the bay window. Flynn scraped the chair across the wooden floor nearer the window and motioned Ross to sit on the sofa.

'Right. Get on with it then.'

'Wouldn't say no to a cup of tea.'

'I'm right out of tea. Sorry.'

'Right you are. How long had you known them?'

'Twenty or thirty years.'

Ross scribbled a note. This was going to be like getting answers on Mastermind. 'How did you know them?'

'We were in the Army.'

'Which -'

'- Royal Lancashires. Various tours.'

'And you stayed in touch when you retired.'

'Don't know why you're asking. You already know, don't you?'

'Let's try again, shall we? You stayed in touch when you retired?'

'Jesus! ... Yes!'

'OK, good. Doesn't it strike you as odd that two close friends should be killed in hit and run accidents within two weeks of each other?'

'When you've been in the Army, nothing surprises you.'

'So it doesn't worry you?'

'That's right. It doesn't. Anything else?'

'Can you think of any reason why anyone would want to kill them?'

'No.'

'Did they have any enemies?'

Flynn smiled for the first time. Or was it a sneer. 'Plenty. That's one of the perks of being in the Army. Trouble is, most of them are on your side.' He looked pointedly at his watch. 'Have you finished? I can't tell you anything. They were good mates, but that's all.' He paused and sighed, looking out of the window behind Ross. 'Look… Ok, I'm sorry they're gone, but -'

Was that a trace of human emotion? 'But what, Mr Flynn?'

'...Nothing. I've got some jobs to do, so …'

'Go away?' Ross stood and looked round slowly. 'Looks like you're all packed up and ready to leave. Moving house, Mr Flynn?'

He stood and stepped in so close Ross could smell his aftershave. 'None of your bloody business.'

Ross turned towards the door, then stopped. 'OK. Thanks for your time. But don't go anywhere without letting us know, will you Mr Flynn? We'll need to talk to you again. And just one more question, where do you work?'

Flynn sneered. 'You already know.'

'You're right, I do. I've just thought of another question. Can you tell me where Chris lives?'

'Chris who?'

Ross laid it on thick to make the point. 'Oh you know Chris! The chap you meet at the Feathers every Friday. Quiet bloke but always gets a round in…'

He was unmoved. 'You're a real smart arse, aren't you?'

'Yep. So?'

'No, I don't know. His second name is Seymour, and I think he said he's got a flat out towards the Peaks.'

'Well, thanks, Mr Flynn. Be good, and stay safe. I'll see you again. I'll let myself out.'

Ross sat in the car and tapped notes into his tablet. Flynn kept accusing him of already knowing, but Flynn knew more than he was telling, too. He's a tough guy, but why wasn't he just a tiny bit scared? Most people would be, after losing two mates in exactly the same way. You'd be thinking, *is it me next?*

He started up the engine to get the heater going, closed his eyes and leaned back against the headrest, letting the thoughts filter through.

He opened his eyes and gazed out through the windscreen. Flynn's not scared because he knows why it's happening.

10.

George took Ross's call and gave him the OK to keep an eye on Flynn for the rest of the morning.

He was starting to feel the team was on the lower slopes of a murder investigation, especially with Mark Manning back in the office.. He only left just over a week ago, and yet here he was, face buried behind a laptop screen on Jag's desk, looking up occasionally to exchange soppy looks with Lorry, when she broke off from scanning CCTV footage.

George groaned: 'Come on you two. Save the lovey stuff till you get home will you? You're putting me off my wine gums.'

Mark grinned. 'I've missed you, George.'

'Bloody liar. Anyway, where's this key evidence you promised me?'

'Just coming. Boss…' Mark winked at Lorry, and she stifled a laugh.

Two minutes later he slapped the desk forcefully. 'Gotcha! Come and see this, George… Lorry.'

He pressed a few keys and the screen went blank, then touched the return key. They watched as a programme began to draw a sketch.

Mark loved working at Greaves, but it felt good to be back. 'I've taken the results of Phil's analysis of the first victim's impact marks and the damage he sustained. I've used that to estimate the size and weight of the vehicle, factoring in clues from the tyre treadmarks as well, and its likely speed. And I've added in the fact that there's an Army connection.'

George looked puzzled as a drawing began to take shape. 'Keep it simple, will you? What am I looking at?'

Lorry leaned in, her chin almost resting on Mark's shoulder. 'It looks like the front end of a vehicle.' She touched the screen. 'See how it's shaped? And how high off the ground it is?'

Mark discreetly patted her arm. 'Correct. Think of this as an artist's impression. And using that as a starting point, I fed the parameters into a web search and found... this…'

He pressed another button and the sketch faded to be replaced by a colour photograph of a sand coloured Army vehicle that looked more like a tank.

George looked doubtful. 'What the hell's that?'

'That, George, is a Foxhound patrol vehicle, as used by the British Army in Afghanistan. It's got a V shaped profile to make it less vulnerable to explosive attack, and look at that front end… its height and configuration is a dead ringer for the vehicle that killed Jack Cooper. You see? The angle of the front end is such that the impact would be more likely to throw a body back, not lift it up and over the bonnet; which was Phil's point. And, one more thing... if it's strong enough to survive a Taliban explosive device, it won't be shedding debris when it hits a pedestrian, even at forty or fifty miles an hour.'

George arched his back and sighed. 'Come off it, Mark. Who's driving one of these around Manchester? It's an Army vehicle! You're not going to get one on ebay and stick it on the drive, are you?'

Lorry chipped in, laughing as Mark looked in danger of succumbing to George's deliberate provocation. 'No George, but what if you were a mechanic? If you'd got the gear, what's to stop anyone building one of these? Mark found it on the internet, so anyone could look it up.'

George walked slowly back to his desk as Mark pushed himself out of the chair with a grunt. 'That's right. I'd bet it's based on a Land Rover chassis. There are plenty of them around on the second hand market. A bodywork specialist could make a fist of it. Anyway, George, I'll leave it with you. I'd best get going - it's my day off, you know, and I haven't had any breakfast yet.'

He grabbed his coat and car keys and stopped at the door, reaching into a pocket. 'Oh, nearly forgot! I got you a present.'

George smiled. 'Wine gums… good lad.'

'Nice to see you again, George. I really think it would be worth another look at CCTV.'

'And maybe we could start checking out some back street garages, George?'

'Yes, Lorry, thank you. I had already thought of that. Are you volunteering?'

Mark laughed, waved farewell, and closed the door.

'Yes, George, I'll volunteer.'

George winked and offered her a wine gum. 'Good answer. But you'd better go back over the CCTV first, like your fiance said. And you can tell Mark I think he's got the right idea. I'm impressed.'

Lorry smiled proudly. 'Really?'

'Yeah. I'm off to get some breakfast too. I could murder a bacon buttie.'

*****

Jane skimmed through her case files, determined not to be caught out by Smart Alec Cooke.

Five minutes to go - just time for a dash to the loo and a quick mirror check... God! She wondered why she was acting like a nervous schoolgirl. Probably because there's so much at stake; not least the Chief Constable's approval of the mature way she's dealing with Cooke being parachuted in...

Yeah, right.

Just then, a tentative knock at the door, closely followed by George's face, looking apologetic. 'Sorry, ma'am, but this is interesting.'

'Tell me as quickly as you can, George.'

'We've identified the vehicle that may have done the hitting and running.'

'Great work! Tell me more.'

George ran through Mark's analysis, and Lorry's discovery of a similar vehicle on CCTV close to both locations before the incidents. 'What seems to clinch it, ma'am, is that the reg plates on the vehicle are invented - fake.'

'Which makes it even harder to trace.'

'Well, nothing's impossible, ma'am. I've got Lorry looking at back street garages, workshops etc. Oh, and Ross has spoken to a close friend of both victims - a Colin Flynn, who was aggressive and unhelpful. Ross is puzzled by how little he seems affected by it, so he's keeping an eye on him.'

‘Brilliant, thanks George. I’ll pass that on to sir…’ She glanced in the direction of his office. ‘Let’s hope it’s enough to convince him to pursue the investigation.’

‘I’ll keep my fingers crossed, ma’am.’

‘You should. Oh, and you can stop calling me, ma’am, ok? I’m the DCI not the Chief Super, remember?’

George smiled as he turned away, then turned back. ‘Right you are. And good luck with Cooke… Jane.’

‘Thanks. I wonder what’s on the menu?’

‘Bloody smoothies, I shouldn’t wonder.’

Jane’s laughter echoed down the corridor as George headed back to CID with a broad grin on his face.

*****

Jane decided to go through the routine stuff before the hit and runs.

She noted that Cooke had got his priorities sorted. He already had a new desk and a new black leather chair. Apparently, the decorators had been in to give him a quote, too; if Doreen on the switchboard was to be believed.

He kept his gelled head down, writing notes in a black spiral bound notebook, as she highlighted progress on a spate of burglaries in a block of flats; surveillance of a suspected paedophile lurking near a school; shoplifters targeting corner shops; and an outbreak of graffiti and other vandalism on the Dukeborough estate.

She sipped from her water bottle and cleared her throat. ‘Re the hit and runs, sir…’

He looked up for the first time, holding the pen ready, and she noticed it didn’t have a nib. He caught her glance and gave her what her mum would have called a matinee idol smile. His teeth were, of course, perfectly whie. ‘It’s a special pen and notebook, Jane. I write as normal and my notes are automatically transferred to my computer as Word documents.’

‘Good lord.’

‘Awesome yeah? So, you were saying…?’

Jane updated him, and, by the end, she felt she'd done more than enough to convince anyone that these were no ordinary hit and run accidents.

But Cooke needed more persuasion. 'So we're basing this on the fairly random and totally unofficial thoughts of an ex-employee, and the probable coincidence that a similar kind of vehicle appeared on CCTV at some stage an hour or so before each incident.'

Jane steeled herself. 'Sir.'

'Let's think it through, Jane. Ashbridge is - what - about five or six miles square. So, not a massive area. Population?'

'Around 80,000.'

'So, fairly small. Tight knit... And therefore, it's not so improbable that a distinctive looking vehicle should turn up at two locations. I mean, the incidents were only about a mile apart, weren't they?'

'Yes, sir.'

'And at roughly similar times?'

'Light fading, yes sir. Probably chosen for that reason.'

'Probably...Hmmm.' He sat back and adjusted his cufflinks, the gold catching the light from his desk lamp. Jane sat back too, resigned to the inevitable.

He studied her for a moment, caught her mood, and then caught her out.

He leaned forward, elbows on the desk, smiling. 'Tell you what, Jane... I'm not convinced by this theory, but you clearly are. I respect your strength of conviction on this. So let's make a deal. I'll give you the next three days to come up with something more ... persuasive. If this vehicle is as distinctive as your ex-colleague says, you and your team should be able to find it and bring the culprit to justice - or not - in less time than that. OK? Deal?'

Jane wanted to tell him what a spineless, slimy little worm he was for passing the responsibility onto her. If Charles Aston was sitting there, he'd be saying yes or no, and taking the flak himself. But she'd save all that for this evening's rant with Allan.

Instead, she simply nodded. 'Deal. Sir.'

He grinned, and opened the door for her. The space was tight, no doubt deliberately. She caught the scent of cologne and coffee as she brushed past him with inches to spare, and flinched as he patted her on the back.

'Thanks muchly, Jane,' he said.

*****

Ross's vigil had yielded nothing new. Flynn only left the house once to go down to the corner shop, and came back carrying bread, milk and a magazine.

Lorry was chatting on the phone with Mark when he got back. She covered the receiver and called out as Ross walked in. 'We found it! That vehicle, looking just like Mark's picture!'

Ross threw a questioning glance at George, who popped another wine gum in and raised his eyebrows in response. Lorry blew a kiss down the phone then hung up.

'So what's next George?'

'Don't get too comfortable, Ross. Lorry's narrowed down some possibles on CCTV. Remember, Jane asked us to check for repeat pedestrians?'

Ross laughed. 'Sounds like an illness.'

'Whatever. I want you to have a look at the images, too, then you and Lorry need to start searching for workshops and garages that could have built the vehicle Lorry's talking about, and see if any of them have an employee resembling any of the images.'

'So, we're treating it as murder?'

'We are, but Cooke isn't. We've got three days to convince him, apparently.'

Ross smiled. 'Loads of time. I don't know why you're all against him. He seems a switched-on sort of guy to me.'

George snorted. 'Don't tell me, you fancy him?'

Ross didn't even stop to think. 'No George, he's not my type.' George looked distinctly uncomfortable, but Ross knew there was no turning back now. 'I know this'll come as a bit of a shock to you both, but I've wanted to say this for such a long time...'

Lorry moved over to him and put her arm through his. 'So, say it, Ross.'

Ross breathed in deeply, his eyes fixed on George, who seemed very interested in the pen on his desk. 'OK... I'm gay.'

Lorry squeezed his arm and leaned in to whisper. 'Tell me something I don't know.'

'What?! You knew all along?'

'Course we did. Didn't we George?'

'What? Oh… yes.' He stood up and looked awkwardly formal as he shook Ross's hand. 'Makes no bloody difference, son. You're a good lad and a damn good detective.' He turned to look at the blank whiteboard. 'Speaking of which, there's work to do, you know.'

Ross was tempted to plant a smacker on George's cheek, but he kissed Lorry instead. 'Right then, glad that's out of the way… Ok Lorry. Show me the car, and then shall we divide up the garages and find the bastard?'

*****

Jane sat on the bed in her bra and knickers, watching mountainous dark clouds sliding across the twilight sky towards her, devouring the last feeble light of the day.

Downstairs, she could hear Allan clattering about in the kitchen, as he laid the table for tonight's ready meal. Pizza. Again.

She was thinking how unjust it was that Roy Cooke had replaced Charles Aston. Everyone says *life goes on,* but it doesn't always. Sometimes, life comes to an end. Charles had gone, and it still hurt her; made her feel empty.

She pulled on a pair of sweatpants, and felt guilty that she hadn't made more of the fact that she and Allan had decided to get married. She hadn't even told mum, maybe because she couldn't face her fuss and over-excitement, particularly after all the years of estrangement. But was that just an excuse?

Why wasn't she full of the joys? Simon Hopkirk had pretty much promised her a big new job at regional HQ; the man she loved had asked her to marry him; and she was back leading a team of great people, doing what she did best, tackling crime.

She'd never suffered depression, but she knew people who had. Phil, for one. He was broken after his mum died, withdrawn into himself. He'd smile and joke on demand, but the happy face was like a short-lived firework.

Was her inability to see the positives right now a sign of depression, or was that just her way of pre-empting the disappointment of dreams not coming true? A case of feeling let down before she actually was?

She pulled on a t shirt, so lost in thought that it almost came as a surprise when she looked up to see that the clouds had turned a deeper shade of charcoal and stolen all the light.

Allan called out: 'Grub up!'

'Coming!'

Jane splashed cold water on her face and gave herself a pep talk as she patted dry. A mindless night in front of the telly was what she needed now.

Then her mobile phone rang out like a musical alarm clock. It was the station ringtone.

*****

The man's body was lying in the gutter like road kill.

He was a complete wreck: so broken and bent the paramedics winced as they knelt beside him in their green and yellow.

Jane looked on, screwing her eyes against the flashing lights that reflected off the rain soaked pavement. Fifty yards beyond, a small group of people huddled under umbrellas up against the police tape, white faces flash lit like ghouls.

After a couple of minutes, a paramedic twisted round on his knees, caught her eye, and slowly shook his head.

A traffic officer moved next to her. 'So, another one, ma'am.'

'Afraid so. Any clues this time?'

''Fraid not. The rain hasn't helped, and this is an old road surface with dozens of tread markings. It's often used by speed merchants - kids mainly. No traces of metal or glass. We'll keep looking, and see if anyone saw anything. We're on that now. Sorry, ma'am.'

'And it's definitely Colin Flynn?'

'Yes, ma'am. ID is confirmed. The boss said he'd send a copy of everything through to your forensics team.'

Jane sighed gently. Another life lost. How many more could she take? She began to walk towards where the body lay, the rain already beginning to soak through her mac. 'Thanks, Graham.'

He had to strain to hear her. 'Yes, ma'am.'

She knew there was nothing she could do here, but it would feel like betrayal to walk away. Three middle aged men - at least one of them a decorated war hero - their bodies smashed into the ground by a coward. What kind of sick mind could do this to someone once, let alone three times?

And then, the guilt, again. Could it have been stopped? Could at least one of those lives have been saved if they hadn't been arguing among themselves about resources?

Jane lifted her face up to the rain, as if it might wash everything away, put the fire out inside.

She thanked each member of the NHS team who were now making room for a senior doctor, then walked up to the sightseers.

No-one saw anything. They seemed more interested in complaining about shoplifting at the corner shop. Jane promised the police took every offence seriously and wondered aloud why no reports of shoplifting had been recorded in this area. No answer.

She walked away, seething at their indifference. The Jamie Castleton murder inquiry, and the discovery of child exploitation, had been traumatic, and she knew she hadn't got it out of her system yet. But she felt a different kind of rage about what now looked like three horrific and methodically planned murders.

It didn't help that it felt like she'd been smashed up by uncertainty; her on/off relationship with Allan, the tantalising prospect of promotion, Charles's death and Cooke's arrival, George's retirement. It was quite a list.

She felt a hand on her shoulder. The doctor, looking composed, professional; everything she should be. He spoke with a soft Irish accent that on another night would make her drool. 'The poor man died instantly. He wouldn't have known at all what was happening. Will you be wanting a forensic examination?'

Jane thanked him and said she would, please.

'All right, good. I'll let the hospital know. Tomorrow, will it be?'

'It will… thank you again for all you do.'

'We just do our jobs, don't we, all of us? God bless.'

Jane watched as he walked quickly back to his car, talking into his mobile phone. No doubt on his way to the next life or death situation, and taking it all in his stride.

By the time she'd reached the other end of the street, the cold and damp had cleared her mind a little, and the anger was cross-fading into more familiar determination. She told herself the only thing that mattered now was finding the low-life that had killed three people.

As she drove slowly away, she wondered how she'd react now if Hopkirk offered her the step up she wanted, in the middle of the investigation. But she knew the answer: she would never forgive herself if she didn't see this one through.

The flashing blue lights were still blinking faintly in the rear view mirror as Jane joined the slip road onto the dual carriageway for the 15 minute drive to the station.

It only took a minute for the realisation to set in that the killing might not be over.

An hour later, she'd called the team in and Lorry was handing out the coffees.

Jane took a sip. 'This is now officially a murder investigation. Three victims. All male, ex-Army, same regiment, and drinking pals, too. First priority - find the fourth drinking buddy. Ross. What do we know?'

'First name, Chris. According to Flynn he lives out towards the Peaks - so maybe Mottram, Glossop way? The barmaid at the Feathers said he was the quiet one, never seemed to join in the banter.'

Jane dunked a custard cream in her coffee. 'He could either be the killer, or the next victim. Either way, we've got to track him down. A surname would help. Can you try your mate in the Army, Phil?'

George grunted. 'It'll be a damn sight quicker than phoning personnel.'

Phil nodded and headed for the door. 'I'll call him now.'

Jane walked to the whiteboard and picked up a marker. She flicked a glance towards Jag's empty desk. 'Lorry, can you keep notes for us tonight? Thanks. Now, thanks to Mark, we have an idea about the vehicle that's being used. It's distinctive and apparently based on an Army patrol vehicle called the Foxhound.

It looks a match from the CCTV, so we need to push on with the search. Any luck with that, Lorry?'

'No, ma'am. We got round to about a dozen places between us, but no joy. We were thinking, it's just as likely to be a rented garage, and there must be thousands of them.'

'Fair point. OK, tomorrow, we circulate a description. We need to hear from anyone who may have seen this, or anything resembling it, over the last six weeks.'

'We should circulate that to the car parts businesses too, ma'am - sorry - Jane.'

Jane nodded. 'Good idea, George. Yeah, add that, would you, Lorry? OK, plenty to get going on. Anyone got a theory about why?'

Ross pushed his chair away from the desk and frowned.

'Ross?'

'Well, we're assuming the Army is the big connection. But it might be something else.'

Lorry nodded. 'Like what, though?'

'Something personal. They met up every Friday, with this other guy Phil. Why? Were they up to something? Who knows, they might have had a racket going and it all started going wrong…'

'... and they fell out over sharing out the spoils…'

Jane wrote on the whiteboard. 'Good, thanks. You're right, we can't afford to pre-judge this. For now, the Army is the best link we've got, so we have to follow it up, but we stay open to all other possibilities, and - ' She swivelled round as Phil walked in. 'That was quick. Any luck?'

Phil stood next to Jane, looking pleased with himself. 'I can't tell you where he lives but his name is Chris Seymour. He's about six foot tall, brown eyes, and…wait for it ...'

George laughed. 'Bloody hell, Phil, you're not announcing this week's star baker! Get on with it!'

Jane hid a smile as Phil flushed slightly. 'All right, George, keep your thinning hair on ... Corporal Chris Seymour was an Army mechanic.'

It was a massive lead, but Ross had something else on his mind: 'Good God! Don't tell me you watch Bake Off, George…'

*****

Jane allowed herself a smile as she walked back to her office.

It was good to see their team spirit, and confidence, growing. She'd always known that Ross had the potential, but he was showing signs of maturity and judgement that surprised her. George had told her about Ross coming out, and, though it came as no surprise, it was fantastic news that he felt confident enough in his colleagues and in himself to say it. Lorry was blossoming, too, her desire to learn undimmed. And George was playing it to perfection, combining stern discipline with a warm heart, and his dedication set a great example.

It only needed poor Jag to return … but there was no time to fret about that now.

She sipped cold coffee and read through the case log on the first two victims. Could Ross be right? Were the Friday night pub sessions the key to this? Or did the motive for murder lie in the past?

She sat back with her eyes closed and tried to relax; let the facts float around. One thought kept coming back - the brutality of it. It was shocking - like terrorism. A murder weapon modelled on an Army vehicle - one that was so tough it could withstand explosions. The victims - all ex-Army. The killer would be lynched by the public for that, and God help him in prison.

He was making a statement, and taking a hell of a risk driving it around on public roads, so it must be significant. No, the Army connection was the key to the whole thing. Had to be.

But why was he doing it?

Only one explanation seemed to fit. Jane wrote it in big letters on her whiteboard: *RETRIBUTION.*

11.

The tiredness overtook him as soon as he lay back on the sofa.

Bess climbed up and rested her head on his stomach, and sleep came quickly.

Next thing he knew, the sun was shining and Bess was whining at the back door.

He was still wearing his camouflage gear. 'Just hang on a minute, girl. I need to change.' But Bess started scratching to let him know it was urgent, and she ran into the garden as soon as he opened the door.

Then he heard voices, and frantic barking. Peering carefully out of the window, he saw the old couple hanging on to their terrier, which was having a go at Bess.

Not them again… There was nothing for it. He'd have to go out and get Bess back inside.

He tried calling from the door. 'Bess! Come on girl! Here!'

'I think you'll need to grab her if you don't mind.'

They stared as he walked down the side of the house and grabbed Bess by the collar.

The old boy looked pleased with himself. 'Dressed for action then…Joined the Army?'

'Well, I prefer to hide at this time in the morning. Not a pretty sight.'

They laughed and he turned, stooping as he held onto the dog.

'Still got that car? I'd love to have a proper look at it.'

He turned, fixing a smile. 'No, it's at the garage, sorry. And sorry about Bess, she's just being sociable.'

'Only I hope you didn't move it because of me? Sorry, my wife thought it was rude of me. I wasn't being nosey. Just interested, you know.'

'No, that's fine. Well, I'd better give this one her breakfast. Bye now.'

He watched as they walked away, the terrier trailing behind them, its eyes fixed on where Bess had been.

He scraped food out of the can and topped up Bess's water bowl, then sat down with a glass of water.

The job was done, and now it was time to start mopping up. He'd been seen by hundreds of motorists over the last couple of weeks, but he'd been well away from home, with false plates, so that was all part of the calculation, the balance of risk. If the police were smart they might even have caught it on CCTV, but it wasn't going to help them. Foxy would soon be scrap metal.

But he'd made two big mistakes on his own doorstep, and that old guy - and his missus - could match him with the vehicle. He was a nosey sod with nothing else to think about, and he'd be gossiping about it for days, which would be no surprise. He'd spent his life switching between park homes and barracks, and they were all small communities full of people watching one another.

He watched from the window as they walked back to their place; the dog trailing behind them, reluctant to go home.

They were a normal harmless couple. But these weren't normal times, and they no longer qualified as just your average nosey neighbour; they were loose ends.

And loose ends had to be dealt with before they unravelled everything.

*****

Allan heard the news on the radio on his way in to work. It was billed as a fatal RTA and the police were 'appealing for the driver to come forward'. So that confirmed it: yet another hit and run.

There was no suggestion they were linked, but Allan knew different, and that put him ahead of the opposition. Now, though, careful timing was needed.

The rival Ashbridge Times came out on a Thursday - a day before his paper, the Free Press; which meant their deadline was a day before, too. Jane was instinctively cautious about press statements, so if she held off for a day or so, there was a good chance the Times wouldn't make the connection in time.

But how was he going to get his exclusive without embarrassing Jane? Going behind the police's back now and again to get a story was fine, but only if you weren't planning to marry the DCI.

He needed info from someone who wasn't directly connected. But who?

He pressed the button and took the ticket that raised the barrier at the entrance to the multi-storey car park, and inched back into his reserved space.

He was still mulling it over as he queued up for takeaway coffee and his favourite bread and butter pudding at Aunt Betty's. Then he remembered Amy at the Feathers. She'd told him about the Army lads who met there every Friday, and she obviously liked a natter. Two of the gang were dead, but what if the latest victim was one of the Feathers friends, too? It would be a hell of a story if Amy was to confirm that.

He hummed as he shuffled forward in the queue, tapping a reminder into his phone calendar… 'lunch at Feathers'.

He saw that Betty herself was serving this morning. She looked gorgeous, as always, in her bright red branded apron and baseball cap. Allan had no idea why someone who looked like a film star and baked the best cakes in the universe would still be single. But he'd never dared to share that opinion with Jane. He could imagine her outrage: '*So you're saying that getting married is the only measure of a woman's worth - apart from looking fit and making cakes?*'

Allan shuddered at the thought, then took a step forward. Betty called out 'Who's next, please?' She saw it was Allan and gave him a smile: 'Good morning, love. Your usual?'

He smiled shyly, like a lovesick teenager. But it consolidated his feeling that today really was going to be a good one.

*****

Lorry and Ross had arranged to meet at the Green Cafe around 11, to give themselves a break and a reviving brew after two hours of touring garages.

Ross got there first and took a table by the window, looking out over the High Street. He sipped a large and very hot cappuccino with a dusting of cinnamon as he went through his list. A couple of nice looking girls gave him a look as he sat down. He smiled. If they only knew ...

He counted up. Eight premises ticked off, but no sign of anything resembling a rebuilt Land Rover. In fact, no sign of any bodywork at all, which made you wonder how they were surviving.

The grainy CCTV images of pedestrians who Jane suggested may have been following Jack Cooper hadn't been much help, either. It was impossible to identify anyone, especially from shots taken in semi--darkness in drizzly weather, of folk wearing caps of some description.

As one irritable garage mechanic pointed out: 'That could be Marcus bloody Rashford, for all I know.'

He was half way through his drink, and there was still no sign of Lorry. So he called George, and got the news that they'd put together a list of more than 20 Seymours that needed checking out.

'So give the garages a rest, for today, will you?'

Ross leaned back in his chair with a smile. 'All right, George, if you insist.'

Lorry arrived in her usual rush and dumped her bag on the chair before heading off to the food counter, returning with a Cornish pasty the size of her head. She was attacking it almost before she'd sat down.

'A bit peckish, Lorry? I thought you said you were dieting.'

'Keep your nose out, Rossiter. These are to die for.'

'You're probably right. Anyway, are you ready for some good news?'

She nodded, chewing enthusiastically. Ross was trying not to look too closely, but she seemed to be putting on weight before his eyes.

'No more garages today. But we've got about a dozen Seymours to see.'

Lorry picked up crumbs from the table and smiled. 'Well at least I won't have to be chatted up by grease monkeys with page 3 girls on the wall for the rest of the day.'

'No luck then?'

'Nah, you?'

Ross shook his head and looked gloomy. 'No. Not been chatted up once.' He had a sudden thought, and frowned as he leaned forward. 'Do you think we need more people in there with us? We've only just sorted the last murders, and we're straight into another. I like Jane but I wonder if she fights our corner enough.'

Lorry almost choked in her eagerness to speak. 'Shut up! Course she does. She's an amazing boss… '

'Don't get them in a twist; I'm just thinking that maybe if we laid it on a bit thick, we might get some extra help. We're still a man down, you know.'

'Yeah, Jag won't be back anytime soon, will he? And then what will he be able to do?'

'Exactly. Admin I suppose, poor sod. He might recover, but how long do we wait? I think it's time we put a bit of pressure on. We don't want to be taken advantage of, do we?'

Lorry shook her head and washed the last mouthful of pasty down with a swig of coffee. She looked at Ross's cup and saucer and reached across. 'Are you not eating that biscuit?'

*****

Phil was viewing three sets of hit and run SOC photos on his computer; elbows on the desk, reading glasses on, staring at close ups of road surfaces.

George had been in once and asked him if there wasn't anything better on daytime tv these days. Phil had smiled patiently and explained his theory.

'It's safe to assume that if you were going to kill someone this way, you'd want to make sure the job was done. It's not like a shooting or poisoning where you could pretty much guarantee the outcome. But this way, there's a chance the target could hang on to life long enough to give the police a clue. The killings would need to be well planned, and anyone that careful would want to be certain of the outcome, wouldn't they?'

George was nodding, so Phil ploughed on. 'So you'd get out of the car and double check. In which case, however careful you were, you'd leave some trace: something that didn't belong there - a fragment from the sole of the shoe, a footprint, a strand of fabric from the carmat, even a few flakes of skin; just … something.'

George had looked convinced, if a little bored, and that was enough for Phil to tell Doreen he didn't want to be disturbed for a few hours because he was peering at Tarmac.

'It's your life, dear…' she said.

He often gave talks to students at the police college in Hendon: it was one of them that had given him the Forensic Phil tag. And he always told them he treated every dead person with total respect, and he never gave up on them.

He'd become a fan of photography, and he'd surprised them by revealing that its use in crime investigation could be traced back to 1851 when a photo of a forged document was produced in court.

He was also fond of telling them that while it may be true that there's nothing new under the sun, '*this old man has never stopped learning*'.

Technology changed as frequently as people, and cameras could now capture images in incredible detail, particularly with macro lenses… and that's what he was pinning his hopes on now.

Phil remembered the excitement when he produced a Polaroid camera at his mum's 70th birthday party. Everyone was amazed at the technology that could print the image direct from the camera, within a couple of minutes.

It was fun, but he was more excited about the close ups he was looking at now.

Every one of them could be useful if and when it came to court, but was it too much to hope that just one of these images would be enough to help Jane nail the swine who'd done this?

Phil poured a cup of tea from his flask and studied the screen. Seven down; about 200 to go…

*****

Chief Supt Roy Cooke slowly placed his tea cup back in the saucer and savoured the last mouthful of the only hot drink he allowed to pass his lips - Darjeeling black tea.

It was buying him the time he needed to judge his response to Jane's confirmation that the latest hit and run victim was the third in the series. She was sitting on the other side of his desk, looking at a paint colour chart Doreen had brought in while she waited for him to sign off on a full blown murder hunt.

He didn't have a choice, he knew that. The only question was how much of a role he wanted. Jane Birchfield was a golden girl, as the Chief Constable kept reminding him, but he didn't want to be completely outshone.

The issue he was pondering was that he'd actually got very little experience of murder inquiries, other than assisting a couple of years ago; and if he took control and messed up… On the other hand, if she took control and messed up…

He cleared his throat; decision made.

'Right Jane, let's get on with it. It's your case, and I'll support you, of course. Keep me briefed, all right?'

'Thanks for that, sir. One problem - we're a person down in CID...Jag's still on sick leave and will be unable to carry out normal duties on his return… can we -?'

'- Yes, is the answer. Of course. Get someone in. Anyone in mind?'

'It's back up and admin support and organisation we need, mainly. There's always a lot of hard boring slog to do ...as you know. I've had an eye on PC Sykes for a while, and I think he'd be ideal. He's unassuming, hard working, totally dedicated to the job, and I'm sure Alex could spare him.'

He nodded. 'Go for it, then. I'll sign it off for you. Anything else?'

'No sir, thank you.'

'No, thank *you*, Jane… muchly.'

'Oh, one thought, sir.'

'Oh yes?'

She pointed at the paint brochure. 'I quite like the duck egg blue.'

'Right … thanks.'

They exchanged smiles as she left, and for the first time since he moved in, he wondered if they might actually get along.

Maybe he needed to relax; learn to let go. The light touch...wasn't that what leadership was all about? if she really was the golden girl, giving her free rein now would reflect well on him.

He frowned slightly. It would pay him to be careful. There were rumours that Jane could be in line for a step up in the near future. And if that happened, she could end up managing him. So it was in his interest to keep her on side.

He opened up the calendar on his tablet; maybe lunch sometime?

*****

Allan's day was getting better by the minute.

The Feathers had Robinson's on draught; the pie of the day was to die for - if that was the right expression in the circumstances; and Amy was full of info.

Yes, Colin Flynn was one of the group. He wasn't exactly a bundle of laughs but she'd got on with him when they worked behind a bar at the King's Head a few months ago. He lived at Box Avenue. Bit of a tough guy - shaved head, muscles. One look from him would be enough, and he'd saved Amy from a few creeps who were trying it on.

'So a real gent?' Allan suggested.

'Definitely. Heart of gold, too.'

'Why do you say that?'

'He was the one who got us to collect money for this...' She rattled a charity box with *Ashbridge Children with Disabilities* picked out in red letters.

'Why, do you know?'

'No, he just said it broke his heart to see a child suffering. That's all he said, and you never pushed Colin. The others were all for it, too.' She blew her nose and turned away, and Allan took that as his cue to leave.

He was running through storylines as he walked back to his car.

'Ashbridge mourns the loss of its third hero. Tough soldier with a heart of gold. Raised funds for disabled children. Viciously mown down by a maniac...'

This one would hit the national headlines, and he'd be the one to break it.

He slid into his car and started the engine, just as the traffic warden came round the corner. He nodded and smiled as he drove slowly away, thinking '*Today, I can do no wrong*'.

Next stop, Box Avenue.

*****

Jane tapped her coffee mug on the table. She loved the atmosphere and the banter, but she did feel a bit like teacher controlling a rowdy class.

'Right, you lot. We've made a solid start. The more groundwork we can do now, the better. So, who's going first? Yes, Lorry...'

'No joy with the garages as yet, and we're getting through the list of Seymours, but ...'

Ross saw her hesitation and jumped in straight away. 'We've been wondering, ma'am, about whether we could get an extra pair of hands to help. It's a bit tough without Jag, to be honest.'

Jane kept her expression neutral. 'You're quite right, Ross, and thanks for being upfront. I've got some news for you, but I'm saving that till the end, ok?' She saw the relief on their faces, and smiled. 'So how many more Seymours and garages to go?'

'We reckon we'll get through them tomorrow.'

'Grand. Phil?'

'Still going through SOC evidence, especially photographs, looking for any trace evidence. I'm sure whoever did this got out of the car, so I'm hoping we'll pick something up.'

'Definitely, keep up with that. No more clues on the bodies?'

'Just the consistency of the impact areas. It really confirms Mark's conclusion about the vehicle.'

'Indeed. We've got to track it down. I also want you to map out the movements of each victim leading up to the time they were hit. Yes, and one of you talked about back street premises, and private garages. Any progress?'

George said he'd been going through newspaper ads to find the hobby and sole proprietor car repairers and dealers, and had come up with a list of names. 'Our problem now is, like Ross and Lorry said, finding the manpower to get out there and work through them all.'

'Thanks for the cue, George. Ok, I'll put you out of your misery. I've had a word with the Chief Super and he's ok'd an extra recruit. PC Eric Sykes will be transferring from uniform as from tomorrow. He's mad keen, totally dedicated, and he'll be a great asset.'

She took the silent nodding of heads as approval, and carried on to explain that Jag was still recuperating, getting stronger, but wasn't ready yet, and she was working with HR to agree a phased return to a work, ensuring a monitored environment that would allow him to continue his employment, at whatever level suited him.

'He's keen as hell to get back here, and I know you'll give him a fantastic welcome when the time comes. But we'll need to be sensitive to the new Jag, and be careful about the jobs we allocate to him. That will be for George and myself to manage, with HR support.'

She took a pause and looked each of them in the eye.

'You all need to take care. Make sure someone else knows where you are and how long you'll be. There's a brutal killer out there, and do not underestimate how dangerous he is… or she is.

'Everything stays in this room, as usual. There'll be plenty of public reaction when this gets out, so let me handle that. Understood…? Now I suggest you clear off home, get an early night. The hard slog starts tomorrow, and I want you all at the height of your superpowers, all right?'

'We should give ourselves a new identity!'

Jane rolled her eyes. 'Any suggestions, Ross?'

But for once, Ross was too slow. George butted in with a big smile on his face: 'Superdicks?'

She could still hear the playground laughter when she reached her office. Phil was close behind.

'Everything all right, Phil?'

'Yes, fine thanks. How's it going with the new boss?'

'Good thanks. Don't tell anyone in case they get jealous,, but he's invited me out to lunch next week.'

'Good God! Don't tell me romance is in the air?'

'Say that again and I'll hit you in the eye.'

Phil took a step back. 'You'll have to catch me first.'

‘Actually, I withdraw that threat. I might need you to come and rescue me if it gets out of hand. Now come in here and talk to me about those photographs…’

12.

He was desperate to catch up on sleep. But it wouldn't come.

It was meant to be a healing process; but he hadn't yet found the peace he hoped it would bring.

They'd finally paid the price for what they'd done, it was true; but it actually felt as if he'd done them a favour. It was over for them now, unless there really was a Hell, in which case they'd be meeting up again before long.

But he was still here, living with the memories, and even though justice had been done at last, he realised he'd been naive to think that it would take away the pain.

It had happened eight years ago, but the disgust and the horror still burned inside. It had been replayed in his head day after day, eating away, until he knew there was only one way to stop it...

Kabul 2013. The attack on the patrol; wide-eyed panic; the wild return fire; finally, dead silence. The stealthy recon through the wrecked house. Me waiting, engine running, clock watching... Then the crouching run, sun blazing. Looking through the hole in the bullet scarred wall. Bodies on the floor at crazy angles. Men and women. Civilians. Blood on the ground, the walls. A bundle of rags, like a doll, moaning and thrashing. Cooper shooting it in the head. Looking round, fist bumps, making the pact. Me running back through the dust like a coward, shaking, sweating. Flynn, in my ear - we saw you: one word and you're dead. Me nodding, driving us back to base...

He leaned over the sink, splashing cold water on his face, and sat looking out as the first hint of daylight began to suffuse the darkness. Bess tiptoed back to curl up in her bed. She'd endured stress and ill treatment, until he rescued her. But no-one had rescued him. No-one had listened. He'd lived in fear ever since: kept quiet until they left. But no-one listened even then... they didn't want to believe him.

Why did you wait so long? You're making it up. Hacked off because you didn't get a medal?

To them, he'd betrayed his comrades and his uniform with his false accusations. He was a marked man. They gave him a choice: leave now and lose your pension, or stay and lose your looks. He was more worried about losing his mind. It was time to get out.

But he could never forget the gut wrenching cries of the child before Cooper silenced it forever. He'd survived on anti-depressants, and the only motivation to get out of bed in the morning was to make them pay. Finally, after months of indecision, he'd come up with the perfect way to do it.

The last thing they would have seen was the front end of a Foxhound. He hoped that image would bring the shame of that day back. What better way to remind them in the instant before they died?

He put the kettle on and pulled on his overalls. No point wallowing in it, there was work to be done. The first job was to dismantle Foxy. The second was to decide what to do about the loose ends...

*****

Jane woke up in a bad mood.

After what felt like a lifetime lying awake, she'd just dropped off when Allan turned over noisily and almost bounced her off the bed. Then he had the nerve to start grumbling at her for getting up for a glass of water just as he was starting to nod.

Still, at least they were still talking to each other this morning, although the chat over her muesli and his fry-up was all about the hit and runs.

He'd been cagey about the story he was working on last night, but his guard was down now, so it wasn't difficult to get him to reveal all. She waited till he was attacking a fried egg with a piece of crispy bacon.

'So who've you been interviewing for your story?'

'The barmaid at the Feathers.'

'Helpful?'

'No comment.' He laughed as he saw her narrow-eyed look of menace. 'Yeah, she's good. Knew the latest victim, so I'm hoping to find out more about him today.'

Jane looked suspicious. 'Today? I thought you said you were out hunting last night...'

'All right, yes - I did go round to see if I could find the fourth gang member. I got to know Mottram extremely well, but no sign of Mr Seymour.'

'Hmmm. You're slipping'

'Apparently, yes.'

'So the barmaid reckons he lives in Mottram, then?'

Allan chewed thoughtfully, taking far more time over it than he normally would, and carefully avoiding Jane's steady and increasingly annoyed expression. He prolonged the agony by sipping tea before deigning to reply. 'Why? Don't you know?'

Jane jokingly threatened him with a teaspoon and he held his hands up in

surrender. 'OK! Yeah, she remembered him saying he loved it there because it was near enough to Manchester, and close enough to the hills.'

'Will you write down where you looked, just for me? It would save a lot of doubling up, and I know how much you love working with us...'

'Well all right, as it's you, but what's in it for me? Got anything to share with your husband to be?'

Jane remembered Allan's paper came out a day later than the Times, and that fitted much better with her plan for a controlled approach to releasing the news, which the newly supportive Chief Supt Cooke had agreed. The Times editor would give her some earache for it, but she could handle that, and the main thing was that she could rely on Allan to co-operate on the wording.

'Actually, there is something...'

'In that case, I'll make us another brew.'

*****

Phil had been through every photograph and whittled them down to a dozen possibles.

He'd assessed each of them as worthy of further investigation. Now he needed a witness so he could verify that the process did not lead to manipulation of the images, otherwise none of it would stand up in court.

He phoned through to George's office: 'Come on down, Eric Sykes…'

It was only when Eric asked why he said it like that, that he realised he was showing his age. 'It was a TV game show.... Oh don't worry about it.' He decided that telling Eric he had the same name as an old British comedian would be a waste of breath, too.

Eric had cottoned on quickly; noting the evidence number of each frame as it came up on screen, writing down the level of magnification it was getting, and the result.

They struck gold, or near equivalent, on the fourth image.

Phil pointed at the screen. 'Look, see that?' But Eric looked blank. 'That my friend is a bull's eye. It's a fraction of a footprint.'

Eric gazed into space. 'Was that the name of the game show?'

'What?'

'Bull's Eye. I'm sure my dad used to watch it.'

'Good Lord, yes, yes - I think it was!' Phil grinned and turned back to the screen. 'We can print that off now, and then all we need to do is match it to a suspect's footwear…'

Eric resisted making the obvious comment that they didn't actually have any suspects.

Phil cropped the image and pressed print, then moved on to the next.

Eric wrote down the reference number and leaned forward to check something. He jabbed a finger on the screen. 'That looks like it might be something.'

'Well spotted, young man. It is indeed something. What do you think it is?'

Eric frowned. 'I'm not sure...a feather?'

Phil grinned. 'Excellent! Yes, I think it is, part of one. And why would there be a fragment of feather on a wet road in Ashbridge, right next to a hit and run?'

'Could it be from a farm?' Eric was enjoying this, and Phil gave him time to think. 'Or, could it be from one of those puffa jackets? They've got feathers in them…'

'Genius. That was my first thought, too. Let's have a closer look… I think it looks too pure white to be from a farm, so best guess is a down jacket. Maybe it caught on the door when he got out of the vehicle, do you think?'

'Or he'd been with someone else and the feather landed on him.'

Phil smiled his appreciation, and Eric's face flushed a deeper shade of pink.

'True, or our man has a tear in his jacket. So far, I think the footprint looks our best hope. Let's get these uploaded onto the case log so Jane and the others can have a look.'

Eric watched carefully, taking notes of every move Phil made. He hadn't slept much last night - too excited; but when he did, he had a vivid dream about the murder. It was like a video game: a man in camo gear with a machine gun strapped to his back; a monster truck with devil's horns on the front, smashing through the gates into the station car park, where Eric was waiting with a pair of handcuffs.

He'd heard George didn't mince his words, so he decided he'd keep that to himself.

*****

Lorry gave thanks to Allan. She'd only seen him once, but his foot march round Mottram had nicely narrowed down her search for Chris Seymour.

Walking the streets where the woollybacks live didn't feature at all on her list of favourite pastimes. But there weren't so many of them, and a newsagent had saved the day by not only having a stock of Mars bars, but pointing her in the right direction; though why he was wearing a flat hat behind the counter was anyone's guess.

'He lives down there, I'm sure of it - neart' junction of Hyde and Stalybridge roads. Comes in for a paper now and again. Nice lad...'

Mottram in Longdendale is about a dozen miles from Manchester, close to the border with Derbyshire and slowly being pushed towards the Peak District by urban sprawl. It is home to about 10,000 people, and contrary to unkind rumour from city dwellers, none of them have an extra finger, bay at the moon, or get intimate with sheep.

Lorry chewed on a chocolate bar and looked curiously at a statue of one former resident, wondering who on earth L S Lowry was, and why he was sitting on a bench rather than stood up looking heroic in bronze, like a proper statue. Google soon made it all clear: he was an artist. That explains it...

Lorry shrugged and steeled herself for another door knocking session. The sooner she was out of the rain, the better.

Her mood improved when a lady with bright white permed hair and a gleam in her eye opened the door and announced in a voice that could have been heard in Ashbridge that Mr Seymour lives two doors down. She thought he was a nice lad, too.

Lorry held onto her umbrella as a stiff breeze propelled her in the right direction, and stood in front of an impressive green painted front door with bright brass fittings. She remembered Colin Flynn had told Ross that Seymour lived in a flat… this obviously wasn't, which may or may not be important. But there was a warm red glow coming from the front window, so she had high hopes of finding her man, and warming up at the same time.

She rapped the knocker, and a tall man, whose thinning hair and pronounced limp clearly disqualified him as a lad, came to the door so quickly it made her jump.

'Oh! Mr Seymour?'

'That's me. Come in, you're soaking wet.'

Lorry didn't need a second invitation. She smiled and stepped into the vestibule. The stained glass on the inner door gave the place an ecclesiastical feel.

'Thanks,' she said, as he helped her off with her coat. 'Sorry to be cheeky, but is there any chance of a cup of tea?'

*****

Ross phoned in to confirm he was outside a repair shop behind Market Street, and was about to go in. It was his fourth of the morning, and it was only 10am.

'I don't want to sound negative, George, but can you put these words in their correct order for me … goose, chase, wild.'

George was typically direct. 'Shut up and get on with it. Call me when you've done. I've got a few more for you.'

Ross disconnected first, told George what he thought of him, then turned his attention to the workshop.

It looked a bit like images he'd seen of shanty towns, with its corrugated iron roof, concrete panel walls complete with green mould and graffiti, and a hand painted sign - Crayford's.

But it looked like business was booming, relatively speaking. There were two bent and battered cars waiting for some love and attention on the pavement outside, and Ross could see sparks flying inside.

A man hiding behind a visor was lost in his work. Ross looked round discreetly as he waited.

No sign of a Land Rover, or the Foxhound lookalike. Just a back wall full of shelves with mystery objects on them, and equally unfathomable machines dotted around, looking more like instruments of torture.

Then, a voice: 'Can I help?'

He was a couple of inches shorter than Ross's six feet, but his arms were as thick as Ross's thighs, and his chest was even broader than his Lancashire accent.

'Hello. DC Rossiter, Ashbridge Police.' Ross showed his ID and handed over a calling card.

'Oh aye? What's up?'

'Do you ever work on Land Rovers, Mister…?'

'Name's on the door. No, I don't.... Why?'

'Just an investigation. We're checking workshops in the area, that's all.'

'There's a shop down Albert Road specialises.'

'Yeah, been there, thanks.'

'Well, anything else?'

Ross was suddenly struck by how tidy the place was, by comparison, and by the fact that much of the equipment looked new-ish. 'How long have you been here?'

''Bout three years.'

'You seem to be doing well.'

'What?' He followed Ross's gaze. 'Oh, well, yeah. I make a few quid, it all goes back into this place. That's a 20 ton push ram. Got it for £75. You got to have the right gear, but I get most of it on discount - it's the only way to survive.'

'Mind if I look round?'

His tone of voice suggested he didn't care. 'Go ahead. Mind if I carry on?'

Ross smiled back. This guy was a bit too smooth.

Crayford pulled his visor down and crouched down as the sparks began to fly, filling the place with light. Ross made the most of it to check the darkest corner by the back wall, then waved on his way out.

Mr Crayford stopped and called out. 'All ok?'

'Yes, thanks. If anyone comes in looking for a Land Rover repair or rebuild, let us know.'

'Will do.'

Ross stopped. 'If I wanted to scrap a car, where would I go? Where would you take it?'

'You'd get the best price from Lovatt's, I reckon. Not that I'd know. It's my job to keep cars on the road.'

'Yeah, of course. All right. Cheers.'

He waited till the detective had gone, then counted to ten, and turned the MIG welder off.

It was only a matter of time before the police cottoned on, but he hadn't expected it to happen so quickly. He checked no-one was hanging around outside, then put the closed sign up and locked the door. Moving quickly to the far corner, he unlatched a series of black painted catches and stepped back as the back wall swung towards him.

He'd worked on his hidden room for a couple of weeks, then spent a bit longer building Foxy, buying parts and panels in small quantities from a range of suppliers all over the country. Now it looked more like a skeleton. He'd already taken off the doors, roof and front panels, but there was still plenty to do.

It would all need to disappear as scrap the same way, in small amounts to different dealers, so it wouldn't arouse suspicion. He'd got a list of the back street guys, one man bands. No way would he be using Lovatt's. Everyone went to them, and that DC was probably on his way there now, with a bit of luck.

It was all in the planning, and confusing the enemy was the best tactic of all.

He reached for a ring spanner and squirmed under the chassis. It was going to be a long day. Bess would be getting her tea late tonight.

1

13

Chris Seymour was friendly enough to qualify for the *nice lad* label, but Lorry sensed he was holding something back.

It wasn't helped by his disconcerting habit of keeping eye contact when she was asking a question, then looking away when he answered.

And he took his time, too, stroking his chin elaborately as he considered his response. He spoke slowly, and was painfully keen to balance everything he said. Lorry felt it was like watching a politician on Question Time.

He'd even been evasive about the limp. 'Oh, just a little injury, way back… Erm, how's your tea?'

She put her mug on the coaster he'd placed on the coffee table, wondering idly why it was never called a tea table. 'How well did you know your Friday drinking mates?'

He stared over her shoulder. 'Now then, I'm not sure I'd call them mates… I wouldn't say I knew them that well.' He shrugged. 'We enjoyed a drink together once a week, for old times' sake, you know… But we all kept ourselves to ourselves.'

'But you were in the Army together? Same regiment?'

'Yes and yes… but I wasn't in the same gang as them. I was on the mechanical side of things, you see. No great rank. Just a corporal. Servicing and repairs…'

At least he'd confirmed that bit of Flynn's story. 'So, you repaired vehicles?'

'As I said, yes, general servicing. Some repairs...a few... Occasionally a vehicle. Keep them fit for purpose, that sort of thing.'

'So you'd be very familiar with the Foxhound…'

He looked beyond her, as if he was admiring the view. 'Well, yes, but only in as much as it was one of the vehicles used at the bases over there… one of many, you understand. Oh we had all sorts, different shapes and sizes… Forgive me, but why is the Foxhound of interest?'

He'd gone defensive suddenly. Lorry smiled innocently and ignored the question. 'Were there any… incidents over there, involving the three of them - or the four of you?'

He looked down at the coffee table. Was he trying to remember or trying to concoct a story? 'Incidents… well there were always incidents. Do you mean engagement with the enemy, or internal bits and pieces?'

'Either, please, Mr Seymour.'

'Call me Chris please. Let me see … well, I remember Jack getting his medal. That was a good day. Proper ceremony, you know, and drinks after… He was never boastful about it; quite reticent really. But he told me the story one night at the pub. Oh, he was the talk of the regiment at the time. Fought off an attack while out on patrol, apparently - vehicle surrounded, fought back, led his men out to engage the Taliban.' He shook his head sadly. 'A few civilians in the crossfire, I'm afraid. But that's the price of conflict isn't it? Innocent people often get hurt. Jack wasn't one to make a meal of it, though the other lads said he was a hero, leading from the front.'

'Was the vehicle they were in a Foxhound?'

He stroked his chin. 'I suppose it would have been. But I can't say for sure.'

Lorry sat upright, ready to ask the one question that was really troubling her. 'Mr Seymour, you know your three friends are all dead, don't you?'

He looked genuinely upset. 'Yes. Amy at the pub… she told me.'

'I'm just wondering why you haven't come forward at any stage. They were your friends, after all. And doesn't it bother you that whoever is doing this seems to be targeting your Friday night group, and … you are the only one left?'

His shoulders slumped and he rested his elbows on his knees, gazing into his Manchester United mug.

'I did wonder, but I wasn't with them in Afghanistan, so I didn't see how I could be a target -'

He stopped, and Lorry wrote a note: *...Afghanistan, he's just told me the motive.*

'So you think they were killed because of something that happened in Afghanistan, do you?'

He seemed to gather himself. 'Well, I really don't know, of course. I just can't think of any other reason, can you? It's either that or someone objects to us because we hogged the same table at the pub every Friday. And like I said, I don't see how I could be next. I was on the outside of their group. Just enjoyed the company once a week, got a round in.'

He smiled. 'Can I get you any more tea?'

Lorry sharpened her tone, just to see if it would produce any response. 'Not for me, thank you. Before I go, can I check … was meeting for a drink the only reason you were all in the Feathers every Friday? It's a long way to go for a pint for you, isn't it?'

This time, his answer came quickly. 'Well I lived round there for a year or so when I left the Army. Got quite attached to the place. Nice people … you know … So I just kept going. Then they started coming in and that sort of clinched it.' He put his mug down and centred it on the coaster. 'It's a fair drive but it got me out of the house, and it's only once a week.'

'What about Mrs Seymour?'

'Oh, there's no Mrs Seymour.' He smiled and winked. 'Not for lack of effort on my part, oh no… No, it's just me… Now, are you sure I can't get you another?'

But Lorry had heard enough to convince her to stay a while longer. She leaned forward, pen poised over her notebook. 'Do you still repair vehicles, Chris?'

*****

'I took your advice. What do you think?'

Chief Supt Roy Cooke lined his stylus neatly against his smart notebook as Jane dutifully admired the new paintwork in his office.

'Very nice. Good choice…'

'Your good choice, Jane, thanks muchly. Want me to get your room done out?'

'No you're alright, thanks sir. I'm quite partial to grubby magnolia.'

He laughed, and Jane wondered - not for the first time - how long it took him to get ready in the morning. He was immaculate in a shirt that looked new, a uniform jacket that looked like it had just been ironed, not a hair out of place, and a smile straight from a toothpaste advert. Not for the first time, she thought she might have been interested, a few years ago. But not now. Too smooth by half.

'Anyway, Jane; we need to talk about today's media briefing, yes?'

'Yes, sir -'

'I think we can use first names now, can't we?'

'OK, yes. Well, I was thinking there's no point trying to hide what's happened. We need to find the killer, and we need the public to keep an eye open. But we also need to -'

'- alert them to the potential danger? Agree totally. Difficult balance. How do we do that without immediately spreading fear? You can see the headline yourself, can't you - killer on the roads… that's the last thing we need.'

'Plus, all three of them served in the Armed Forces, and they come a close second to the NHS in the public's list of saints and heroes. And one of them got the Military Cross…'

'Yes … difficult one.' He tapped on his notebook to bring up a file, then studied it for a few seconds. Jane waited. She knew what she would do, but it was his call and she didn't want to push it. But his next comment completely disarmed her.

'OK Jane, I'll be honest. I'm not sure. I don't have an answer and I'm happy to be advised. You're the one with the experience of murder investigation… What do you suggest?'

*****

They were side by side behind a table in the conference room; a line of microphones under their noses.

They were well prepared, though tense. Allan had convinced Jane it was better to lay on the drama right from the start. It would divert the media away from the living in fear angle. It went against all her instincts, but Roy Cooke liked the approach, and thanked her muchly for her input.

Allan had already written his story, but promised he'd look interested, and take notes. The Free Press was ready to go to press the moment he called the printers, so he was looking annoyingly relaxed.

Unlike Jane, who was facing two tv cameras, and six journalists, including Allan. He was cleaning his fingernails to avoid catching the eye of the fearsome Victoria Pleat, chief reporter of the Ashbridge Times, who'd already been on the phone to Roy to make clear her annoyance.

'Our paper has just come out and you call a briefing an hour later? That's grossly unfair and my editor wants to know what possible reason you could have, apart from doing a favour to a certain Allan Askew, who just happens to be living with your top detective.'

Jane had listened on speakerphone as Roy soothed her with impressive ease. 'It was entirely my call, Vickie. We have to do what fits with the investigation, and we have learned new facts that we want and need to share quickly. You'd be the first to call us out if we'd sat on it for a week, just to fit in with a deadline… Anyway, it'll be on tv and radio before the Free Press get to print, so I guess they're not over the moon either. You can still get the news on your website, can't you, and we'll have other briefings which might not fit nicely for the Free Press. So just bear with us this time, ok?'

He'd put the phone down and raised his eyebrows as he glanced at Jane. She just gave him a thumbs up.

She thought now how much the atmosphere had improved between them. There was a feeling of trust, but she wondered how deep it went, and how he'd react when something went wrong, as it surely would.

She could see Allan checking his watch and she caught Roy's eye. The look told him...*let's do it.*

He nodded, sipped sparkling water, and cleared his throat. Jane looked down at her notes.

'We need your help: and your readers', listeners' and viewers' help.' He'd got them on his side already, and he'd got their full attention - especially, Jane noted, the women in the room. Vickie was wearing a fashionably short skirt, and kept her eyes on Roy as she slowly crossed her long legs, and flicked her long brown hair off her face. But if it had any effect on Roy, he didn't show it.

'We're saddened to tell you that three ex-soldiers, including one holder of the Military Cross, have been killed in hit and run accidents that we believe were deliberate, cold blooded murder.'

They clearly weren't expecting him to be this up front. She'd never seen them so quiet, so focussed. She gave a silent thank you to Allan, who was busy pretending to take notes.

'I'll be honest, we don't know why. But we will find out, and we have already made significant progress in tracking down the perpetrator of these cowardly killings. DCI Jane Birchfield, here at my side, will give you more details in a moment, but I just wanted to say one important thing…

'The killer has been driving around in a customised vehicle that bears a resemblance to the Army patrol vehicle now being shown on the screen behind me. A copy of this picture has been included in your folders.

'Someone out there has seen this vehicle, either being driven, or parked somewhere. We're fairly certain it will be painted in a dark colour, but as you can see, it's highly unusual. If you did see it, you'd remember.

'We need to hear from anyone who has seen a vehicle like this, wherever and whenever it was - even if it was weeks ago. Any information will be treated in confidence, so you need have no fear that your details will ever be made known.

Perhaps you have seen it near your home, or place of work… but you can contact us in complete confidence.'

He paused impressively, looking at both cameras in turn like he was born to it.

'You don't need me to tell you how appalling these acts of violence are, and we are counting on the people of Manchester - of Ashbridge - to work with us to make sure the killer is brought to justice.

'Thank you. Now I'll hand over to Jane, who'll give you more details about some of the other pieces of the jigsaw we are putting together.'

Jane took a breath. *Follow that,* she thought…

14.

The news conference lasted over an hour, but the media were eating out of Roy's hand, as Allan had predicted, and the coverage had stuck to the line they'd wanted… three incidents; horrific and tragic, of course, but spread over a month in one of the busiest road traffic areas of Britain; … no reason for undue alarm… but you can help...etc etc

Allan had said the key thing was to emphasise the Army connection before asking for co-operation: 'Just tell them the victims were war heroes, and they'll roll over.'

Roy handled the tv and radio interviews. He'd clearly had the training, and Jane was relieved because she hated doing it.

Back in the office and bonding over cups of tea, Jane was having to fight the urge to tip her Darjeeling into a plant pot.

'So, Jane, about that lunch…'

Jane had prepared for this, and put on her most regretful expression. 'I'm just wondering how it would look… Roy… us being seen at the best restaurant in Manchester, in the middle of a murder investigation… and in working hours…'

He looked genuinely shocked. 'Oh! Yes...You think so? Well … yes, I suppose it would look… Better postpone for a while then.'

'It's a shame, but, yes, I think so. Maybe when this is over?'

'Yes, definitely. Ah well… ' Jane felt miffed about how quickly he seemed to get over it. '...was there anything else?'

*****

Lorry was so absorbed in her notes she didn't notice Jane.

'Oh, sorry ma'am.'

'Great job on your interview with Seymour, Lorry. I'm going to see if we can get more info out of the Army about the incident he talked about. He's right at the centre of this, so we'll have to bring him in… but wait till tomorrow - let him think we've lost interest for a while, ok?... Is Ross around?'

'He's...gone to the shop, ma'am.'

‘OK, can you ask him to come and see me? And well done again, Lorry. You and George can interview him formally tomorrow. Let’s see what a little pressure can do…’

‘Yes! Thank you, ma’am.’

Ross appeared with a full carrier bag and the irresistible smell of fish and chips. Jane stopped at the door. ‘I need a word, Ross, when you’re ready. And if you bring a few chips with you, I shan’t complain. I’m starving.’

Ross smiled. ‘Right you are, ma’am.’ He dropped a greasy parcel on Lorry and George’s desks and left the office carrying his.

Lorry ignored the wooden fork, bit into a large battered cod, and tried to speak at the same time. ‘He gets away with murder… Where’s he going?’

George’s tone was disapproving.’He’s obviously sharing his with the boss. What a creep. And did your mother never tell you not to speak with your mouth full?’’

Lorry wrinkled her nose. ‘She did, regularly… Hang on… Share fish and chips? He must be mad. Pass the salt, will you, George?’

*****

Jane patted the grease off her lips with a tissue and leaned back with a contented puff of the cheeks.

‘God that was good!’ She patted her stomach, then sat up straighter. ‘I suppose we’d better talk about the investigation. I’m intrigued by your account of this guy you met at the garage… Crayford?’

Ross scrunched up the chip wrapper and stuffed it into the carrier bag. ‘He was just a bit too smooth for a bloke in a back street workshop, ma’am. There was nothing definite that would make him a suspect; just an impression.’

‘I’m all in favour of impressions, but I’m interested in what triggered it. Think about it for a minute. What made you suspicious?’

Ross looked up at the ceiling, trying to picture the place again. He remembered feeling there was something that didn’t look right.

Suddenly, it was there. He spoke quickly. 'The shelves at the back. Everything was right in the middle, like it had been arranged. No garage I've ever been in has been that neat.'

Jane nodded. 'Good. Anything else?'

'Welding .... he was looking busy; there were sparks everywhere, but when I looked at the car he was working on, I was thinking ... where's the weld? I wasn't that close, to be honest, but there was no sign of it. Sorry it's so vague.'

'Don't apologise. Remember what I said when you joined us? I don't just want super-efficient note takers; I want people who use their imagination - as well as feed me chips, of course. So ... let's imagine you're right... what could this tell us?'

Ross nodded and leaned forward. He felt more relaxed now. 'What if the garage is just a front? I couldn't find him in the phone book or the trade directory. There's no ad in the local papers. He might not even have any customers. He could be up to anything. No-one would know.'

Jane narrowed her eyes in concentration. 'Go back to the shelves. What's your theory?'

'All I could think of was a movie I saw, where the shelves were just like a... false wall, you know?'

'Was there a side or back entrance?'

'There's an alleyway at the back, but I didn't check it out because I hadn't thought about it then. Want me to go back?'

Jane checked her watch. 'Yes, do it. We need to crack on with the case. It's a bit too vague for us to think about dragging him in now, but if you find anything, call it in and we'll go get him. Take Eric with you. Where does Crayford live?'

Ross swiped through the notes he'd saved on his phone. 'Here we go. Said he's got one of those park homes, out towards Bolton.'

'OK, check that out, too. And Ross..?'

'Yes, ma'am?'

'Are you OK? This is all a bit personal for you, isn't it? You and your grandad...'

'Yeah. I was angry at the start. It was just that Army connection... I'm over it now.''

'That's good.' Jane hesitated. 'You can probably work out why I'm saying this, but ... I need you to hear it. Never forget you're valued here for who you are, as well as for the job you do. I want to know if anyone makes you feel... uncomfortable. Understood? My door is always open.'

'Thank you, ma'am. Understood and appreciated. But it's ok. I feel better for saying it, and everyone's been great since I blurted it out.'

'Best way sometimes. Just jump in at the deep end. So... let's get on. Take no chances tonight, all right? Call in when you get there, and again when you leave. And look after Eric.'

'Yes, ma'am. I will. And thanks again.'

'I should be thanking you. Those chips were a lifesaver. Now, go on... Be off with you.'

Jane flicked her desk lamp on and listened to Ross's footsteps as he walked down the corridor, then the loud footsteps a few minutes later, as they walked down the stone staircase to the car park.

They were laughing now, but they were on their way to a potentially dangerous situation. She remembered finding Jag barely conscious in his car after his beating by Beavis's thug, and said a silent prayer for them both.

*****

Media coverage had the expected impact.

Dozens of calls were coming in from people who said they'd seen the Foxhound replica at various locations, including, George announced with his usual deadpan demeanour, the Scottish Highlands: 'I reckon the lady who called that in had drunk more than a wee dram.'

Jane put in a request for a couple of uniforms to sit by the phones for the rest of the week, and even George was now warming to Roy Cooke, who'd signed it off straight away.

She'd been promised a call back the next day from a high-up in the Royal Lancashire's about Jack Cooper's medal and the incident it was awarded for.

Meanwhile, there was a judgement call to make about Chris Seymour. Bring him in for a formal interview? Send George out to see him with Lorry? Either way was valid. But was it better to keep a discreet eye on him from a distance, on the grounds that he may give himself away?

She day dreamed for a moment about chatting it through with Charles Aston. 'Go with gut instinct, Jane,' he'd say, with a teasing twinkle in his eye. 'And looking at the size of my stomach, I should know all about that.'

She could hear Roy moving about in his office next door. He would never compare with Charles, but he was being supportive now, and Jane wanted to believe they were over the mutual hostility stage. But something told her not to trust it: maybe it just suited them both to hide it. For now…

*****

He'd heard people say that no-one's ever as pleased to see you as your dog. But now he believed it.

It was almost dark when he got home, and Bess was beside herself. He could hear her whining as he walked up to the door. The turn of the key got her yelping, and as soon as he opened it she put her paws on his shoulders and licked his face.

He hugged her face to his chest and calmed her down, then reached for a tin of dog food.

He thought about Susan and how it all went wrong. She used to be all over him too, but she said Afghanistan had changed him, and she was right.

She'd live without him for months on end, counting the days. But they were soon back in the same groove when he came home on leave; her full of chat and smiles; him like a brick wall, to use her words.

So it wasn't a big surprise to come back to an empty house. She'd left a note on the worktop, propped up against the tea caddy. He'd just read it, screwed it up and thrown it in the bin.

The Army did that to people. You got used to being on your own; either living on adrenaline, or bored sick waiting for something to happen. The only time he came alive was when there was action - a patrol, a recon, or a bigwig wearing stripes to drive round.

Some guys were homesick, but he never was. Never missed Susan, if he was honest. Dreaded going home, but then couldn't wait to get back there after those bastards committed murder right in front of him, and got away with it.

It cost him his pension, and it cost him his freedom. He'd never been able to forget what happened; could never move on... He'd devoted two years of his life to planning and executing his punishment. Two more days would be enough for him to close the book forever.

He turned as Bess pawed gently at the door and looked up with her soft dark eyes.

He knelt down and kissed her head. 'Good girl … come on.'

He slipped his jacket on, pulled his cap down, and stepped out into the twilight.

He'd go back to the garage after the walk. But this time, he'd take Bess with him. She'd been on her own too long today.

*****

Brigadier Ronnie Watts was famous for his ebullience.

He was consistently the life and soul of the party, which meant he rarely had a free evening.

Now, much to his beautiful and much younger wife Melanie's delight, he'd stomped through the front door an hour earlier than usual, hugged her so hard she nearly spit out the grape she was eating, and announced that tonight's engagement had been cancelled.

'A free evening? Really?'

'Yes, really! So why don't you get some dinner going, while I change myself into a normal human being?'

She laughed. 'Good grief Ronnie, how long will that take?'

He shouted as he hurried up the stairs. 'You'll pay for that insubordination, young lady…'

Ronnie Watts was a career soldier. He joined up straight from sixth form, got into Sandhurst and fast tracked his way to officer class. His aim was to achieve the rank of Lieutenant General by the time he was 45, and he was only two steps away with four years to go.

He'd proved himself an efficient administrator, and an effective leader both in the office and out in the field of combat. The men loved him for his down to earth, lead from the front mentality. The women loved him because he treated them just the same.

There were times when he wished he hadn't aimed so high. The effort he had put in to stamp his personality wherever he went soaked up a huge amount of nervous energy, and sometimes... well, he just wished he could have a few months out of it, preferably on a beach with Melanie - a former catalogue model who was much in demand among expensive lingerie houses.

Ronnie sluiced his face with cold water and went back into the bedroom where he'd laid out his faded blue denims, a white Oxford shirt and a pair of Timberland loafers.

After dressing, he sat down to pull on the shoes, just as the bedside phone rang out.

He delivered his default greeting, which would not win any customer service awards but did tend to give him the upper hand from the off. 'Watts.'

'Sir. We have Ashbridge police asking questions about Cooper, Fry and Flynn.'

'What sort of questions? Give me the full picture will you, otherwise I'll be constantly having to come up with the right question to get it out of you.'

'Sir...they say the men were deliberately killed in those hit and run accidents, and they want to talk to anyone who knew them.'

Ronnie sat down on the bed. He'd always known that what happened would come back to haunt them all one day. He'd worked his nuts off to protect the regiment's reputation. The key thing was always to make sure it stayed in the family, and there was no room for those who didn't share that view. 'Lots of bloody people knew them, so what do you want with me, Staff Sergeant?'

'Sir... they say they want to speak to the person at the top.'

'They? Who, exactly?'

'DCI Jane Birchfield is expecting a call back, sir. Says it is a murder investigation and to use her own words, sir, it cannot wait.'

Ronnie hid his shock with a loud sigh of annoyance. 'Oh, alright, message me her number will you, Poole?'

'Sir.'

‘And Poole?’

‘Yes sir?’

‘Sorry for biting your head off. Carry on, fella.’

Poole’s expression of gratitude was cut off as Ronnie put the receiver down.

He went out onto the landing and called down, working to keep his tone casual: ‘Just got to make a call Mel. Won’t be long.’

He could hear the resignation in her voice, even from that distance. ‘OK, but I’m opening the sauvignon now.’

He glanced at the number Poole had sent through by text, and made the call.

*****

Crayford’s place was in darkness.

Ross told Eric to keep lookout while he went round the back.

‘First sign of anyone, bell me, ok?’

Eric nodded, and Ross jogged round to the back, counting the premises till he’d reached the workshop.

The alley was wide enough for a vehicle, despite the overflowing wheelie bins to one side, and the workshop had an unmarked double gate. The others just had single gates with their trade names on.

He spoke softly into the radio: ‘All clear Eric?’

‘All clear here.’

‘Ok, sit tight, I’m going into the back yard.’

‘Roger.’

Ross grinned. Roger? He was a nice enough lad, but he took everything so seriously… Still, why not play the game, keep him happy? ‘Roger and out.’

The gate had been locked from the inside, reasonably enough. Ross dragged a discarded pallet into position and leaned it against the gate at an angle. It was just like going up the stairs.

The yard was a total contrast to the front of the premises: clean, with what looked like a new concrete floor, and freshly painted wooden windowless doors that took up most of the back wall. It meant there was no way of getting a glimpse inside.

He looked up. There was a window just below the roof line. If he only had a ladder…

His radio crackled and Eric's voice was not so formal now. 'There's a guy pulling up just outside the workshop.'

'Stay out of sight. I'm on my way.'

The gate was about six feet high. Ross took a running jump and got enough of a grip to pull himself up. His feet fluttered against the smooth surface, as he climbed, and he felt the first stirrings of panic.

He made it just as a light illuminated the yard. He heard the back door opening. There was no time to drag the pallet back where he found it.

He tiptoed away quickly, then nearly called out when Eric's head appeared over the top of one of the wheelie bins.

Ross's voice was a cross between a whisper and a scream. 'Jesus Eric! Don't do that! Did he see you?'

Eric shook his head and whispered. 'No, I hid behind your car.'

Ross groaned. 'If he spotted the car, he'll probably know it doesn't belong here.'

Eric smiled. 'No, it's ok. I wondered about that, so I moved it further down the road.'

'Legend! Come on, let's get out of here…'

'Shouldn't we stay in case we can see what he's up to?'

'It's a good thought, mate, but we can't take a chance in case he sees what we're up to... He's come back at dead of night, and the back of the workshop looks brand new. I reckon that's enough for us to get a search warrant, and grab him for questioning tomorrow. But we'll call it in first, just as Jane wanted.'

Eric nodded, and gestured Ross to follow him down a zig zag route using back streets that led back to the car.

Slightly out of breath, Ross unlocked the car. 'Blimey Eric, you know your way around. How did you work that out?'

'I checked it out on my maps app while I was waiting for you.'

Ross smiled to himself as he started the car and drove gently away, keeping the revs down. He had the feeling Spotty Eric was here to stay.

*****

The call was being recorded, but Jane took notes anyway - she found it helped her to concentrate.

Brigadier Watts briskly summed up the incident that led to Cooper's Military Cross.

'The three of them were part of Operation Forcefield. We'd had reports of the Taliban gathering in numbers in a certain area of Kabul, but we weren't convinced of the veracity of those reports.

'One sure way to flush them out was the sight of the Brits stepping up patrols. And it worked. After that it was easy enough to nail their location. But that was the easy bit. Next question was, how do we take them out? We couldn't go in guns blazing because they're careful to surround themselves with innocent civilians.'

He paused. 'I sometimes wish we weren't so bloody civilised… Anyway, the upshot was, Cooper and his men drove into the street where they were hiding out, and the Taliban opened fire. Our vehicle was out in the open, and a very tricky situation quickly developed.

'Despite being under heavy fire, Cooper led the men out into the open, and neutralised the lot of them.'

'You mean, killed them?'

'Yes exactly. While they were in the mopping up phase, they went into a particular house, and found another gunman. There was an exchange of fire, and that was the end of it.

'If you ask me, he deserved the VC for what he did. Not my decision, though.' The Brigadier paused for breath. 'We're all pretty badly shaken by these road accidents, you know. Like losing family. Not sure what else you need, but … just ask.'

'Thank you, sir, that's appreciated. Were there any casualties on your side?

'No, thank God. One of them - Flynn, I think - got winged by a bullet, but that was it. Very minor. They were obviously shaken up, but who wouldn't be?'

'Of course. Was there anyone else in Cooper's group at the time? We're looking at a range of theories, and with him and two others already dead, we're concerned the killer may have other targets in mind.'

'Yes I see. You have got your work cut out, haven't you? Let me think … I remember the driver of the Foxhound was called Armitage… Thomas Armitage. Definitely. Just the three of them, plus the driver. Plucky chaps, the lot of them.'

'What happened to him? Still in service?' The Brigadier went quiet again. 'Brigadier?'

'Sorry. Just remembering. He bailed out a few months after the others took their pensions. No idea where he is now, but the HR people might be able to help.'

'Did you know him? What was he like?'

'Oh he was a quiet one. Seemed to withdraw even further after that op, to be honest. Not particularly well liked - no warmth in him. Never heard from him since.'

'You said he left a few months later… Do you know why exactly?'

'Sorry, no… can't recall. Look, I'd better go. It's my only night off this month and my wife is going to murder me - oh, sorry - wrong choice of words there.'

'Understood. I may - probably will - need to speak to you again at some stage. Thanks for your time. Have a good evening.'

She put the phone down and looked back through her notes. The Brigadier was a charmer, and most of it was just useful background. There was a subtle change of tone when she asked why the driver had left, though.

Two words stood out from all of it, and she underlined them - *Thomas Armitage.*

Meanwhile, Brigadier Ronnie Watts sat back on the bed and made one more call.

'John? Ronnie… Listen, that Kabul thing with Cooper has reared its head.... Yes I know; eight years... tempus really does fugit, eh? All three of them have been murdered - or so the police believe. Look, I told them about Armitage, and this DCI … Birchfield … will be on to you as soon as, asking her questions. Just play it with a straight bat, all right? Who knows, you might be trying to be helpful, only to find that some fool has lost his personnel file…'

15.

He cleaned and oiled the angle grinder, then put it back in its carry case.

Foxy had been reduced to a stack of irregular size sheets of metal, and plastic boxes of parts that he'd moved into the main workshop.

All that was left now was the chassis of the old Defender he'd bought from a scrapyard in Sheffield, and they'd have a hell of a job tracking that down. But he was always on his guard against over-confidence, and as he sat on one a bench with Bess stretched out on a piece of old blanket, he thought about his next moves.

He'd sprayed Foxy in matt black, but had sanded that off the sheets now, so all he had to do was drop them off at a scrap yard or two tomorrow. He'd have to think about which ones.

The chassis was a link to Foxy, but he planned to strip it right down, sooner rather than later.

Once done, they'd never find the vehicle. So it all came down to the neighbour and his wife; the only people who could put him and Foxy together.

He stroked Bess's head as he considered his options again. He hated himself for even thinking it - after all, they were just innocent bystanders, just like the innocent family those bastards had murdered in Kabul.

If he eradicated them, was he just as bad? Could he live with that old guy and his wife on his conscience? Or was he too late anyway? They could already have told their friends.

Bess was standing at the door, whining. He let her out and unlocked the back gate. Strange. It wasn't swinging out. He pushed against it as hard as he could and he heard a thud.

Bess was nervous in the dark, but she trotted off into the shadows to do her business. He stepped out into the alleyway and froze. Why put a pallet against his gate? It had to have been propped up for it to crash to the ground like that.

It took him a few seconds to work it out. It was unlikely to be kids, but whoever it was had been keen to look over the gate. And possibly climb over. He was being watched.

There was no time to waste. He whistled softly to Bess, stowed the loose metal and boxes, locked up, and drove home the long way round, just in case he was being followed.

He wasn't worried. It was too late for that. He actually welcomed the surge of adrenaline. He'd expected to be easing off now the job was done, but he'd never shied away from a challenge. He smiled as Bess curled herself into a ball on the back seat.

'Nearly there, Bess. Nearly there…'

*****

Jane thanked Ross and Eric for a good night's work and sent them home while she did the paperwork for the search warrant which would be presented to their friendliest magistrate in the morning.

She shared the curiosity about Seymour, and Crayford's garage, but she was more interested in Thomas Armitage now, and Roy Cooke was backing her up.

Calls were still coming in from the public claiming to have seen various weird and wonderful vehicles rocketing through the suburbs, much to the amusement of the uniforms manning the phones in CID, who had a bundle of funny stories, including a guy from Ancoats who claimed to have seen a Batmobile and - their favourite - a woman who saw a vehicle that looked like '*something out of Thunderbirds*' in Newton Heath.

There was no shortage of public interest, as predicted. But Jane was trying to assess progress more rationally, now she'd got a bit of space.

Lining up three suspects at this early stage was not to be sniffed at, but she had a worry at the back of her mind that the Army connection could be leading them down a blind alley. Chatting it through with Roy earlier, they'd agreed they had to pursue it - however many feathers they ruffled.

Jane knew she had an instinctive mistrust of obvious lines of enquiry, and she wanted to keep an open mind. But even she couldn't argue with the weight of evidence pointing in that direction. And the brigadier's show of being eager to help had actually made her more suspicious.

So she'd made no apology for interrupting Phil's evening viewing a few minutes ago - despite his protestation that he was watching the final episode of Law and Order UK on catch up - or for pushing him to phone his Army contact tomorrow morning at the latest.

Her thinking time was punctured by the shrill bleep of her phone. Allan messaged her to say he'd had an improved offer from the media company that was so keen to buy his paper, and he'd just got home after a long Skype chat with them. She replied, promising to be home within the hour and he replied promising he'd still be sober.

She wondered if that meant he was celebrating, or drowning his sorrows.

She found out before she'd even had time to take her jacket off. 'I've turned it down again,' he announced, as she walked into the kitchen.

She was genuinely shocked. 'What? Allan...! Was it a much improved offer?'

'An extra £100k; same salary and expenses, but a promise that I could continue to manage the Free Press.'

Jane did a double take. 'Just an extra hundred thou…? But ... come on, their offer actually sounds like what you wanted.'

'Don't look at me like that… It's closer, yes, but I need to be hands on, not just managing, otherwise the Free Press will just become a rag - full of adverts for perfume and recycled press releases. I told them journalistic standards have to be maintained, and that was my bottom line.'

'Right. And they told you where you could put your bottom line, did they?'

Allan grinned contentedly. 'Not exactly… They said they'd think about it. And I've bought us a really good bottle of red because I stood up for myself, and I think that … maybe… I'll get a result.'

Jane kissed him on the cheek and they chinked glasses …'Well done, and good on you. I love a man with principles… So I might still get that new coat?'

Allan laughed and kissed her hand. 'Play your cards right and I'll buy you a woolly hat to go with it. Now, are you going to tell me what you've been up to today?'

Jane yawned as she took her jacket off, then kicked off her shoes. She walked into the living room and stretched out on the sofa.'Oh nothing much… Just pour me another, and massage my feet, will you?'

*****

Phil called back in the morning, while Jane was munching muesli and staring into space after another restless night.

He told her Armstrong had left the army a few months after the three hit and run victims. He was a driver, but he drove many different patrols so wasn't one of their close pals. He'd left without a pension, which had surprised a few people, but the word was that he must have a good little earner lined up, otherwise it wouldn't make sense. If he'd waited another year, he would have been entitled to a generous package, apparently.

Phil's mate said he'd have a word with the personnel section to see if they had any more info on him, and a current address.

Jane tried to concentrate while Allan was crashing around in the kitchen. He was full of nervous energy, wondering if his bullish approach to negotiation would pay off, or whether they'd pull out. He was putting a brave face on… 'If they back out, I'll just carry on doing what I'm doing, and make a success of it on my own' … but Jane wasn't fooled.He was a big man, but, like so many, he had a sensitive inner layer that only she could see.

She felt guilty as she drove into town. It was one of those life changing moments, for both of them - the opportunity to have a different lifestyle, apart from anything else - and she knew she wasn't giving Allan the attention he needed. Still, she thought, leading a complex murder investigation was a fairly good excuse.

She pulled up at the crossroads. It struck her that, like the case, she could go one of three directions. Left, right, or straight across? Armitage, Seymour or Crayford?

So which way was it to be?

*****

He was grappling with one of the wheel hubs when they came.

'Mr Crayford?' He nodded, wiping his hands on a cloth as the knucklehead read his words off a card. 'We have a warrant to search these premises. You are welcome to observe. Please do not leave these premises until our search is completed. Please do not touch or move any items. Do you understand?'

What a tosser… 'Yes, understood. I don't suppose you'll tell me why -'

He stopped when a young woman stepped out of the Incredible Hulk's shadow. They were doing their best to unsettle him. But at least she looked like she had a brain. He read the ID card she held up… DC Loretta Irons.

She looked him in the eye. 'We're investigating the murder of three men… all former soldiers in the Army. That's why we're here, Mr Crayford.'

She was trying hard, looking for signs of a reaction, but it was too easy. He smiled back. 'I read about that. But what's that got to do with my garage?'

She just turned to one of the uniforms, another bruiser who fancied himself: 'Ok, start over there, will you, and work towards me…'

Three of them got to work, opening boxes, checking every shelf. Lorry took a closer look at the shelving unit at the back. 'Why would you need a false wall in a little place like this, Mr Crayford?'

'It's not a false wall. It's a room divider. It means I can work in the back in peace when it's quiet and get on with stuff, but come out if anyone turns up.'

Lorry wasn't convinced. She looked into the back room.

'What's that?'

'It's an old chassis. Got it off a scrap dealer a few days ago. I'm stripping it down for parts.'

'A chassis of what?'

'An old Isuzu.'

'A what?'

'It's a Japanese make. I'm often asked if I can do repair jobs on them.'

'What happened to the rest of it?'

'Scrapped. It had been in an accident, apparently.'

That got her attention. He smiled to himself as she crouched down, looking for the vehicle ID plate he'd melted down months ago.

He sat down on the bench and checked his phone. There was a message from Mike down the road, thanking him for the sheet metal he'd dropped off earlier, and one from a punter called Seymour wanting a brake job. It was driveable, just, so he told him to drop it in later. Why not? A few more quid would come in very handy and he couldn't risk doing anything silly like shutting up shop straight after this.

*****

Lorry called George when it was over. 'Nothing, George. Big fat zero.'

'Bugger… seriously?'

'Just what you'd expect from a workshop. Loads of spare parts in boxes, an Isuzu chassis he's stripping down…'

'Tell me you got a picture of it?'

'George… I got a picture. For what it's worth.'

'Ok, good. Anyway, don't worry about it. We'll check that out later. Come in, and we'll get cracking on mystery man Armstrong.'

Lorry disconnected and walked back to the workshop, as the uniform lads drove away with a squeal of tyres. He was closing the fake wall with his back to her when she called out. 'Mr Crayford?'

He turned and snapped on a smile, but there was something about the way he moved…

'We're all done. Thanks for your co-operation.'

'No problem. Just doing your job…'

'Which scrap dealer do you use, by the way?'

'Mike, just down the road. Mike Steele.'

'You're kidding me.'

'Nope, that's his real name.'

'Well… be seeing you.'

He shook his head as he watched her walk back to her car. The police think they're so clever, so hard. Their beer bellies and swagger might work in Manchester but they wouldn't last five minutes out on the streets of Kabul. He'd been knocked about a bit when he signed up all those years ago, but he'd got through it, shown his inner strength He had nothing to prove, and nothing to fear - especially from a cocky Goth detective girl.

He chuckled to himself as he walked back inside and put the kettle on, then sat down to think.

He'd just have time to break down that chassis before the brake repair customer came in. Hopefully, the Isuzu lie wouldn't come back to bite him. Once the chassis was dismantled, all traces of the vehicle would be wiped out. He was certain there'd been no witnesses to any of the killings, so there'd be nothing to pin on him.

He poured the boiling water into his coffee mug and slowly stirred.

That just leaves the old man and his wife, and he'd deal with them tonight.

16.

George called in to tell Jane the search had yielded nothing.

She tapped her pen against her teeth. She didn't seem at all bothered. 'OK, well, if nothing else, we gave him a nice surprise.'

He chuckled. 'We all like a nice surprise, ma'am.'

'Do you fancy giving the Army a surprise?'

'The big surprise would be if they came up with a straight answer.'

'That's exactly what's on my mind.'

She talked him through Brigadier Watts' story. 'He was being helpful, on the face of it. But he was a bit too keen to seem helpful for my liking, so I got Phil to check with his mate. He wasn't much help either... I can't shake off the feeling there's more to this. So let's make it official; let them know we're serious. We need chapter and verse on this guy Armitage. See how you get on, ok?'

'The brigadier won't like that. An official approach?'

She laughed. 'That settles it, George. Go for it!'

George gave Lorry the job of trying to get an address for Thomas Armitage. 'Start with any businesses with a motoring connection - driving schools, haulage, car sales, garages. Let's say he's a person of interest, but keep it low-key and no mention of the hit and runs.'

'Any suggestions about the line of questioning then?'

George slurped his coffee noisily and gave her a sly smile. 'I'm sure a woman studying for promotion can come up with something, Lorry.'

She looked down, frowning. 'How about I just say we're looking for a driver for our new Chief Super?'

George leaned forward, looking so serious that Lorry was expecting a telling off. But then he gave her a smile.

'Genius, Lorry. I'm glad I thought of that... Now go and have a break; and for God's sake, grab some grub, you're fading away before my eyes...'

'Cheeky bugger.'

'I know. Sorry. I'm just jealous. Wish I could lose some weight.'

Lorry could have kissed him for noticing. 'George! Was that a compliment?'

'I suppose it was. Now clear off before I start insulting you.'

*****

He heard the car pulling up outside.

The chassis was almost done, just a stubborn shock absorber to dismantle. It had paid dividends doing the oil spray regularly over the last few weeks; even so, there were some bolts that were reluctant to let go.

He watched through the peephole window in the front door as a man walked up. He was wearing a dark padded jacket and a flat cap, and limping quite badly. The Escort looked like it had seen better days, too.

He unbolted the main access doors ready to swing them open, just as the customer came in through the pedestrian door behind him.

He swivelled round, and the greeting froze on his lips.

'So it is you,' said the man.

'Chris Seymour. Christ Almighty! What are you doing here?'

'That's a nice welcome after all these years. I've come to get my car fixed, you berk. What else?'

'Right. So… how are you?'

'I'm good. You doing all right?' He took a few steps, looking round. 'Nice set up.'

'How did you know it was my place?'

'Putting two and two together, that's all mate. As soon as I saw that name Crayford, I thought to meself - that's the fella.'

'You've been looking for me then, have you? What's up? You were the mechanic. I'd have thought you could fix your own car.'

Seymour laughed. 'I'm not as young as I was. And anyway, I wanted to get acquainted again. We go back a long, long way.

'We do. But, anyway, come on… shall I get on and fix your car, or was there another reason you're here?'

Seymour sat down on a bench and took his jacket off. 'How about a nice cup of tea and a sit down for a sec? I noticed you had a visit from the local constabulary this morning. Now what was that all about?'

*****

George could feel a migraine coming on: either that or a really bad temper.

He'd just been stonewalled by a smoothie Army officer who said there was no trace of Armitage's personal record for some reason. Even worse, he'd called him matey… 'It does happen, matey.'

All he'd confirm was that Armitage served for just over 10 years and he was a qualified mechanic. 'Asking round and no-one had a bad word to say. Hope that helps?'

Just as George was muttering obscenities into his now disconnected phone, Ross and Eric returned with the news that they'd failed to find any scrap dealers willing to admit they'd had even a whiff of a Land Rover in the last couple of weeks.

George looked so broken, Ross offered to buy him a fried egg and bacon roll from the canteen.

Martyrdom was written all over him. 'Not sure I'll be able to enjoy it, but go on then.'

While Ross was queueing up for the cholesterol special, Eric suggested to George it might be worth checking out the area around Crayford's workshop.

'Good thinking, lad. You're wondering if he's just dumped the stuff in a back street or something.'

Eric looked sheepish. He had thought about that, but discarded it as highly unlikely. The bottom of a lake maybe, but the nearest stretch of water was a boating lake in a park that was locked up at night. A bit too risky…

He decided it was unwise to share that with George in his present mood, so he opted for diplomacy. 'Hadn't thought of that, sir. It's just that when we were there, I noticed a lot of small businesses, most of them with no names on the door. I just wondered if one of them might be doing scrap. It'd be right on Crayford's doorstep...'

George rewarded him with a grunt that sounded a bit like 'well done', and although Eric couldn't be certain, he took that as permission to go and have a look round.

By the time Ross came back, George was smiling again - a paper towel spread out on the desk, and Eric was nowhere to be seen.

'Fancy a coffee to go with that, George?'

His voice was slightly muffled and there was a dribble of egg yolk on his chin. 'Thought you'd never ask.'

*****

Chris Seymour frowned as he drove away.

Tommy had changed; hardened up. He always was a bit of a loner, standing on the outside, so to speak. But there was an edge to him now; he was shifty, avoiding eye contact... definitely something on his mind.

He'd clearly looked after himself, though. He'd always worked the weights and run the miles to keep himself fit. Looks like he'd never stopped.

Chris had always been keen to keep in touch with what he called his 'brothers in arms', and he'd spent ages trying to track Tommy down. The other boys told him not to bother, God rest their souls. Jack said Tommy was trouble, and Colin clearly hated his guts but never said why.

Chris's hobby was family history. He'd traced his line back to the late 18th century. People were fascinating, and he couldn't understand those who just walked away from work and never looked back. It was good to keep in touch.

It wasn't that difficult to do the detective work. It was all about patience and time, and Chris had plenty of both. He'd been a driver and a mechanic, so it didn't take a genius to guess what trade he'd be in. He'd never shacked up with anyone since his marriage broke down, so chances were he'd stay local, where he knew people. And he always used to go on about his bets on the greyhounds - checking the stats, studying the odds, salting away his winnings... He did well, and it was the only time he seemed happy to talk. He was convinced that the Crayford track brought him the most luck, so what better name for his garage?

Looks like he'd built himself a new life, and you couldn't question his car repair skills. But as Chris drove up past the allotments on Mottram Road, he couldn't shake off an uneasy feeling.

He could trace it back to his reaction when he had peeked behind the shelves and saw the chassis. 'Looks interesting. Looks like new.'

'It's a pile of junk, and you're a nosey bugger.'

'Are you building or cannibalising?'

'Just grabbing spares where I can. Anyway -'

'What's it from?'

'Christ! Give it a rest… It's an old Isuzu, if you must know.'

Chris slowed down to let an old boy cross the road by the pub. He hadn't said it at the time, but that was obviously a Land Rover chassis. He'd worked on them often enough in his time.

It wasn't a big deal in the great scheme of things, but why would Tommy lie?

*****

Jane's earlier optimism was rapidly being replaced by bloody mindedness, as her mum would say.

Three prime suspects, and no progress with two of them. She had to keep the momentum going. More than that, she wasn't going to be defeated: not even by the British Army.

She knew it wouldn't be long before Roy Cooke was telling her nicely how much pressure he was under to get results, and could she kindly get a move on.

She picked up the phone and got through to George.

'Get the uniforms out and bring Seymour in. Now, please George. And tell Lorry I want her in my office in 30 minutes, prepped for the interview.'

George passed on the news. 'She sounds in a mean mood, guys.'

Ross grinned, completely unfazed. 'Maybe I should buy her an egg and bacon roll, too, then.'

Lorry shook her head. 'Don't be stupid. Buy her chocolates. That always works.'

*****

It was dark by the time he'd broken the chassis down.

He decided to dump the parts in stages on the drive back to the residential park. Mike Steele would take them off his hands with no questions asked but that was a non-starter after mentioning his name to that aggressive jerk of a DC. He knew he was taking chances but he couldn't resist the idea of Steele and Irons meeting up at a scrap yard.

He'd regretted it ever since. This was no time to get cocky. The police were on the case now and he needed to stay at least one step ahead.

It had been an easy job cutting through the 2mm steel of the chassis. He'd done uneven sizes and shapes that would make them difficult to identify, especially spread over a route of about seven miles.

He fired up the truck and the gears crunched as he manoeuvred out onto the narrow street, reversing carefully between double parked cars.

PC Eric Sykes was sitting in one of them, noting down the registration number.

He waited till he saw the truck turn right, before deciding to follow.

Eric had spent over an hour trying to find a scrap dealer near Crayford's place, without any success. But maybe his luck was about to turn…

*****

Bob and Maureen Collings celebrated their 46th wedding anniversary with a carvery lunch at the George, and an afternoon at the Ikea store between Ashbridge and Manchester.

Maureen was rapidly filling up the enormous trolley, which Bob was manfully pushing round the one way system that led inexorably to the moment when they took your money at the till, and you wondered if you really needed another toilet brush.

It wasn't his idea of a perfect celebration, but it made her happy, and that was the main thing. He'd loved Maureen from the day they'd met at a cricket match. He was batting number 3, she was the scorer, and it was - as he liked to tell everyone - *'love at first sight screen'*.

She was frail, even then: a slim girl in glasses. She still was. She was the best scorer the Old Paulians had ever had - perfect concentration throughou. And he could tell she was totally absorbed in the bargain hunting now.

He discreetly checked his watch - 5.30pm. They'd been in here two hours and they were still nowhere near the escape hatch. It would be dark soon, too. He hadn't been so keen on driving at night since he had his cataracts done last year. They told him he was fine and nothing to worry about, but he'd lost a bit of confidence, and the headlights were so much brighter these days.

But more importantly, it had been three hours since his last toilet trip and his bladder was complaining.

He patted Maureen's shoulder. 'Sorry, love, are you nearly done? Only it's going dark, and I need to find a loo before we set off.'

'Oh sorry… yes, nearly done. Look, there's one over there. You go, and I'll wait over there; see? At the light fittings.'

Bob groaned as he walked off. What possible need did they have for new light fittings? He had no idea how all the stuff she'd already bought was going to fit into their park home, let alone the car.

He quickly suppressed the thought as the importance of emptying his bladder, and maintaining a happy anniversary mood, began to take over.

Then, standing at the urinal, he started musing about light fittings, and suddenly remembered he wanted a new torch; one of those really bright LED ones. Just the thing for dog walks on dark nights. His only prayer was that they wouldn't have to go round the store again to find one.

*****

He'd clocked the car parked a few yards away when he reversed out, and it was there again before he'd even reached the junction. Bloody amateur.

He dropped speed, and quickly re-evaluated. It had to be one of the plods, keeping an eye on him. No chance of dumping the metal anywhere on this trip, then; and the longer he had the stuff, the higher the risk.

So, options... Head for that new housing estate and use the new road layout to shake him off. Drive out north onto one of the single track roads, pull into a layby and force him to either drive past or make himself obvious by parking up too. Or go straight home, park out front so he could keep an eye on it, walk Bess and sit it out… The plod could wait there all night if he wanted to, but he'd soon get bored. Then dump the stuff early doors tomorrow.

He nodded to himself, checked the mirror, and indicated left.

They were putting the pressure on, but he could cope with that. What they didn't realise was that he didn't care. He had nothing to lose anymore. His aim was to move on and start life all over again where no-one knew him. God knows he'd waited long enough. But, there was one thing the Army had given him, he knew he could face whatever happened.

Some nights he'd lain awake, mentally preparing himself for life in prison; or he'd picture himself standing on the edge of a cliff, steeling himself to jump. Either way, he knew he'd have the strength. He'd done what he'd set out to do. His only worry was who would look after Bess.

*****

Eric gripped the wheel and forced himself to concentrate.

The light was starting to fade, and it was a long time since he'd rung in. If he stopped to phone now, he'd lose the truck. If he didn't phone in, he'd get a kicking for putting himself at risk. If he did phone in and admit what he was doing, he'd still get a kicking for doing it on his own.

He was only supposed to be looking for scrap metal dealers near Crayford's place, and now he was tailing the guy like something out of a cop movie.

He bit his lip as he struggled to come up with the right answer. Had he already made such a big mistake that it wouldn't make any difference what he did now?

The car clock flicked over to 6pm. That clinched it. He'd been out for four hours and if he didn't phone in, or get back soon, he'd get slaughtered.

Eric thumped the steering wheel in frustration, turned into a garage forecourt, drove straight through and headed back into town, as the truck disappeared in the opposite direction.

*****

Bob was pleased with his new torch, and the stash of batteries that came with it on special offer. He wouldn't offend Maureen by saying it, but it had somehow redeemed the afternoon.

Now he wished he could flash it in the faces of all these drivers with their halogen headlamps shining full blast, making him screw up his eyes and slow down.

His arms were aching, he was holding the wheel so tightly. Maureen was studiously looking out of the passenger window, leaving him to it, frightened to speak in case it broke his concentration.

After what seemed an eternity, they reached the dual carriageway, and it got so much easier with street lamps lighting the way. Gradually, he felt the stress leeching out, and he dropped his shoulders and pushed the speed up to 50. It was the legal limit on this road, but some idiots were still blasting past him.

'Look at that Maureen.'

'What is it, dear?'

'A bloomin lorry, overtaking us, going like the clappers.'

'Never mind anyone else. You just get us home safely, love. We're in no rush…'

Bob sighed quietly. He could remember bombing around in his MG a long time ago, when he had hair on his head and none up his nose. Such happy memories. Now he'd joined the inside lane brigade, but at least he'd refused to wear driving gloves. That was a step too far.

He let his mind wander… *People don't want to hear old men's stories. They don't see the person you are, they just see old people. Like that bloke who lives round the corner; the one with the greyhound. You can tell he thinks I'm a boring old git with nothing better to do than stick his nose in.*

Just because I was interested in that ex-Army vehicle he'd hidden under the trees. It's not a crime to be curious, is it? But he went all shifty looking; a bit scary, he was. Maureen told me not to say anything to anyone in case he was working on it for the government. I ask you... as if! I'd love to know what he is up to, though...

Bob turned off the dual carriageway, and into the darkness of the country road that led to Broad Farm residential park. No oncoming headlights here.

He turned to Maureen. 'Soon be home, love.'

But she'd nodded off, her mouth open, her head bouncing gently against the headrest. He slowed down and put the lights on full beam so he could avoid the potholes.

As he drove into the park, the man was there, putting concrete blocks on the back of his truck to weigh down a sheet of tarpaulin.

It was parked right at the front. Bob decided he might take a peek later when he took the dog out to do its business. Good excuse to try out the new torch, too.

17.

Jane looked across the table at the grey haired man sitting opposite, calmly sipping tea.

He was either a consummate performer, or totally innocent. Jane favoured the latter. Even before he'd said a word, she was prepared to take him off the list of suspects, but he might have useful info. She was certainly in need of it, not least because she could tell that Roy Cooke was feeling the pressure.

That was the thing about any crime, let alone murder: everyone expected results and couldn't understand why it took so long. What most people failed to recognise was that most crimes were either completely random or carefully planned. There were no in-betweens, and that made it nigh on impossible to unpick them quickly, unless you got extremely lucky.

She wasn't feeling particularly lucky now, but she smiled as Chris Seymour placed his mug on the coaster and looked up at her. Lorry opened her notebook, and that seemed to add another line to his discomfort. He rubbed his hands together. He moved so slowly, she was almost hypnotised.

'I'm a bit puzzled about why I'm here,' he said, eventually.

'We just want your helpl. You're free to leave at any time, as I'm sure my colleague Lorry has explained.'

He nodded and sat back, his arms folded. Ready to help, but on the defensive, thought Jane. She ran through the preliminaries and gave him the background about the three hit and runs.

'You knew all three of them, didn't you?'

'Yes, we were in the Royals together.'

'And kept in touch ever since?'

'Well, those three did. I only joined them when they started using the Feathers for their Friday night out. I'm a regular there.'

'Did they get on with each other? Any signs of tension in the last few weeks?'

'No, I didn't detect any. Actually, they seemed in high spirits. Jack was celebrating.' He chuckled. 'He called it his *medalversary*… the day he got his Military Cross.'

Jane glanced at Lorry, whose jet black hair had fallen over her eyes as she bent over her notes. 'Do you know the date of that anniversary by any chance?'

'No, sorry. But it was definitely around the time these accidents started happening.'

'Were you involved in the action that led to him getting his medal?'

'Oh no, I was just a mechanic, in the background.'

Jane paused. Was he just a little bit quicker with that answer? She decided to let it go. 'You have a bad limp, I notice.'

'Yes, but that's not a combat wound - tempted as I am to get sympathy. I got mangled in a rugby scrum that went wrong, that's all.. Never been right since.'

Jane switched the line of questioning again, increasing the pace to see if it threw him off balance. 'When Mr Cooper died, were the rest of you… concerned … that it might not be an accident?'

Jane waited as he scratched his head elaborately. 'I got the feeling the other two -'

'That would be Andy Fry and Colin Flynn?'

'Yes. Well, they were obviously upset about it. But … oh I don't know… I can't be sure but I got the feeling they were a bit afraid.'

'And how did that show?'

'They weren't so chatty with me. I mean, I was a bit of an outsider. Not in their gang at the Army and you really bond with the ones you work with. Like you in the police, I suppose…'

Jane saw Lorry nodding out of the corner of her eye. 'Go on…'

'Not much I can say, just the atmosphere changed. When it was my turn to get the drinks in, I could see them … really talking, like something was going on and they were keeping it to themselves.'

Jane hid her irritation. This was going nowhere. He could say what he liked unchallenged. She tried yet another tack.

'Did you ever see anyone else in the pub from those days?'

Seymour just shook his head and took another slow swig of tea.

‘Can you remember any incidents in the Army involving them? Anything that might suggest they’d made enemies?’ She paused for emphasis. ‘You, for instance?’

‘I’m no-one’s enemy… so, sorry, no. I had nothing to do with them in those days.’ He looked so apologetic, Jane almost felt sorry for him. ‘I’m not being much help am I?’

She resisted the temptation to agree with him.

*****

Ross was working his way through a list of Armitages, picking up from where Lorry had left off before she brought Seymour in.

He noticed Eric, staring at his computer. ‘If you’re not too busy watching stuff on iPlayer, how about giving me a hand?’

Eric blushed and Ross felt guilty. But not for long. He’d already told him he needed to toughen up if he was going to make it as a detective. ‘I wasn’t watching tv. Well, I was in a way…’

‘CCTV was it, yeah?’ Eric nodded. ‘Anyway, don’t take me too seriously; no-one else does. Fancy calling a few of these up for me?’

Eric walked over and Ross handed him the last sheet of A4 with 15 Armitages listed. ‘No luck with scrap dealers up at the garage?’

He blushed again. ‘No, no luck at all. Sorry.’

‘You were a long time, though.’ This time, Eric went a deep shade of crimson from his neck to his forehead. ‘Is something wrong?’

Eric just shook his head. Ross went over to him and put a hand on his shoulder. ‘Come on, mate, tell me. George is with Forensic Phil for half an hour, so it’s just you and me. What’s happened?’

Eric took a deep breath and spilled it out at high speed: how he’d given chase, then thought better of it, and thought about phoning in and changing his mind; and wondered if he’d stayed with him he would have caught him up to no good; and how mad George was going to be if he found out …

Ross held his hands up, palms facing Eric. ‘Woah, slow down… You’ve done nothing wrong. Jane would have crucified you if you’d carried on, on your own.’

'But now, we'll never know what he was carrying and where he was going.'

'True. But we do have reason to suspect he was up to something, and that's down to you.'

'What should I do?'

Ross became aware that his hand was still on Eric's shoulder, and they were standing so close he could smell his aftershave. He stepped away, and cleared his throat. 'Just tell George you saw Crayford loading some metal on his truck, and it looked a bit suspicious. Then I'll butt in and tell him we ought to pay him a visit.'

Eric smiled. 'Thanks for looking out for me, Ross.' He paused. 'We...? Does that mean you'd come with me?'

Ross tried to look more casual than he felt. 'It does, Eric. You know what? I think we'll make a good team, you and me.'

*****

Bob sipped the last of his Guinness and stretched out in his recliner chair, warm and full after pie and mash. He liked his food, and the size of his belly proved it, but Maureen ate just as much and never put an ounce on. Like today... she'd had a roast beef lunch, and apple crumble at the pub, then polished off her dinner tonight. He chuckled to himself. He'd always told her she must have hollow legs.

They'd sat close together at the table after dinner, doing their anniversary ritual, looking through the photo album; cruise pictures, the kids, their wedding; rueful smiles at how young they looked; wondering where the years went, and raising a glass to each other.

Archie was waiting at the door, giving the occasional whine in case Bob hadn't noticed, but he could wait a bit longer for once. It had been Maureen's idea to get a dog. 'It'll be company for us,' she said. Well it was company, but it was also hard work, and he was usually the one doing it.

Up early to feed him and let him out for a tiddle; the main walk with Maureen around 10; cleaning up the hairs and the messy footprints when they got back; out for Archie's afternoon loo break on their bit of lawn; feeding time; then - just when you felt like snoozing, the night time walk.

Bob yawned and forced himself up. At least this time he could try out the new torch, and have a nose round that man's truck if the coast was clear.

'I'll take Archie out now, love.'

Maureen was putting their new pillowcases on the bed, and most of the other stuff they'd bought under it, because there was no room anywhere else.

'Ok Bob.'

Archie rose onto his back legs and pawed the air as Bob fastened his coat and reached for the lead from the hook on the back door.

*****

He stood under a tree at the side of the static caravan, wearing black.

The old fella was running a bit late. Normally, he'd have been out with his dog 20 minutes ago. Didn't matter that much, though: there'd be no witnesses at this time of night.

He'd drawn the curtains and left a low light on inside, so anyone would assume he was nicely tucked away staring at crap tv like everyone else.

He kept his eyes on the dim outline of the old boy's park home. And there it was… the rectangle of light as the door opened; the soft click as it closed; the sound of shuffling steps on the gravel.

He felt the weight of the brick in his hand and eased behind the tree.

*****

'Where are we Eric?'

Ross was weary of narrow, winding roads that meant he restricted him to doing 40mph at most.

'It's a couple of miles down here, then a right and we're on the access road to Broad Farm residential park.'

'Two miles, promise?'

'Promise.'

Eric gazed ahead as the headlamps gave fleeting glimpses of farm gates, and barns and dark trees. He loved being out in the country, even though this bit of countryside was just a narrow strip keeping Manchester and Bolton apart.

He was loving his job too, especially since Ross seemed to have latched onto him. He was really cool, and funny with it. Eric's mind was made up: he was going to become a detective, and if that meant spending more time with Ross, even better.

He checked the maps app on his phone. 'Ok, look out for the turning, just after this barn.'

'Ok Chalkie, flaps down, we're going in.'

They were laughing right up to the first bend, until Ross hit the brakes to avoid a tree that had fallen across the road.

Eric got out and took a closer look, then tapped at the window. Ross lowered it and felt the cold air on his face. It didn't seem to bother Eric, who was out there in his shirt sleeves. 'Don't worry, I can move this enough for you to drive through.''

'What are you? Superman?'

Eric laughed. 'Nah. I work out at home. Anyway, it's only a young tree...should be easy to just pull it a bit. I'd best get on.'

'Want a hand?'

'No, it's fine, thanks.'

Ross shrugged and shut the window to keep the draught out.

*****

He was in luck. The light was on and the curtains were drawn. He decided to take a closer look. He pulled the torch out of his pocket.

'Come on Archie.' He crossed the road to get a closer look at the truck. The torch picked out the blue tarpaulin, and a couple of concrete blocks that were holding it down. There wasn't much of a bulge underneath, so what was it?

He was right up against the back of the truck now, but cursed as Archie suddenly pulled strongly against the lead, which he always did when he picked up a scent.

'Stop it, Archie!'

He heard a scuffling noise behind him, but he was intent on lifting up a section of the tarpaulin so he could look underneath.

Archie tugged again, and he turned, hissing angrily.

'Stop it, Archie!'

It was the last thing he remembered before he felt a heavy thud against his head, and everything went dark.

*****

Ross was enjoying First Aid Kit and the heater was on full when Eric finally got back in the car.

He winked. 'You took your time. And you've got leaves in your hair.'

Eric smiled shyly, and Ross had to force himself back into work mode. 'Ok let's go.'

It proved easier than expected to find Crayford. He was outside a park home, not far beyond the entrance barrier, wearing a white t shirt, kneeling next to someone lying motionless.

Ross pulled up next to the barrier. 'Stay here a sec. Let me check this out.'

The old man was bleeding from a head wound, and Crayford was trying to stem the flow with a tea towel.

He nodded as Ross showed his ID, though he showed no sign of recognition. 'I didn't know who he was. I saw this bloke snooping around the truck. He had a torch. We've had problems round here with robberies. I came out and he turned on me with the torch in his hand like a weapon. I thought he was going to clobber me. His dog was all over me too. Bloody thing bit me on the leg. I just hit him with one of the bricks on the back of the truck...'

Ross probed the man's neck till he found a pulse. 'He's alive, anyway.' He gestured to Eric to get out of the car, then called over. 'Call an ambulance, Eric. Old man, in his 70s at a guess, unconscious but alive, bleeding from a head wound.'

Crayford stood and leaned against the truck. 'He's just a neighbour. Don't know his name. Christ, I'm so sorry. But I didn't know... Pardon my French, but what the fuck was he doing?'

Ross knelt down and felt the man's warm breath against his cheek. The heart beat was irregular but that wasn't unusual for people his age. 'It's ok. I think he'll live.'

Crayford pointed out the man's home and Eric stayed with him as Ross went over to break the news. They heard her crying and watched as she hurried over in a dressing gown and slippers, with Ross holding onto her arm.

She was hysterical. 'Bob! Bob! What have you done?...' She grabbed Ross. 'Is he all right? Is he?' Then she turned on Crayford. 'Why did you hit him? You could have killed him? He's just an old man… What harm was he doing?'

Ross stepped between them. 'Please calm down, Maureen. The ambulance will be here soon. This was an accident. I'm sure he'll be fine.'

He and Eric separated and took statements from Maureen and Crayford, as the paramedics treated Bob. Maureen wept as one of them put an oxygen mask over Bob's face and gave him an injection.

She told Eric: 'He was so keen to buy a torch today. I should have known he'd go snooping. He got it in his head that man was up to no good.'

'Why did he think that?'

She dabbed at her eyes with a tissue but her voice was loud and angry. 'Bob saw an odd looking vehicle under a tree behind his place. The man said he was working on it for someone. It was supposed to be a surprise. I thought nothing more about it, but Bob wouldn't shut up about it.'

'Did he describe the vehicle at all?'

'Oh I don't know. I wasn't interested. He just said it had a funny shaped bonnet. Like the prow of a ship, he said.'

*****

Ross studied Crayford through the one way glass as he waited for George to lead the interview.

He'd called in for instructions after Eric told him about the vehicle, but George wanted to save that for later. Eric was keen to stay, but George sent him home. Ross caught him on the stairs on his way out, and he looked downcast. 'Don't let it get to you.

George is just trying to go easy on you. It's early days. You did great today, so get some kip and see you tomorrow, all right nipper?'

Eric summoned up a weak smile and nodded his thanks. Ross jogged back up the stairs, unnerved by how much he cared about the new boy. He'd been a star all day, too, even had the sense to sneak a look under the tarpaulin while Crayford was getting his coat. 'It's just a few pieces of scrap metal,' he'd whispered, looking disappointed.

Crayford sat still and straight in the chair, moving only to sip the water he'd asked for. He'd got through half the jug before George lumbered in and gestured through the glass for Ross to join him.

George asked Ross to take notes.

'Mr Crayford, you are being interviewed informally in connection with the injuries sustained by Mr Robert Collings. We're grateful for your co-operation and your frankness in explaining what happened. Of course, you understand that we still need to go through the motions, otherwise our superiors would have our guts, see what I mean?'

'Yeah, no problem. I feel really bad about it. Is he ok?'

George looked at Ross for the answer. 'He's conscious, but very weak. They think he'll pull out of it.'

George gave his best impression of sympathy. 'Why don't you tell us again, exactly what happened?'

Crayford ran through his story, and Ross was struck by how close he stuck to the wording he'd used at the scene. He wrote a reminder to himself and underlined it; *'It's like he's rehearsed his story'*

He was told he was going to be released without charge, pending further investigation, and advised not to approach Mrs Collings until it was over.

George smiled. 'She's very upset about it, as you can imagine. Thinks you overdid it. And you can understand that, can't you? He was in his 70s, you're a lot younger and stronger. So that's what we need to clarify… was it excessive force, or was it - as you say - self defence?'

Crayford didn't break stride, nor did he show any emotion. 'I told you what happened. I can't really add anything else. He was on my property, and he raised his hand which was holding a heavy looking object. I didn't have time to check who he was. I had to defend myself.'

George nodded and began bundling his papers, then stopped. 'Oh, one thing, Mr Crayford...'

'Yeah?'

'You were hiding a vehicle under the trees behind your property a few weeks ago; a vehicle with a very distinctive bonnet shape - very similar in fact to this...'

He kept his eyes on Crayford as he slid a photograph of the Foxhound across the table.

Ross watched closely, but Crayford didn't move a muscle or change his expression.

Crayford answered straight away. 'Oh, that thing... Yeah, I was doing it up for a customer. I brought it back home once to do some work on it out of hours. Needed to catch up. He wanted it kept a secret, so I made sure it was out of sight. That was it.'

'And who was this customer, Mr Crayford?'

'His name was Simpson: Chris Simpson.'

George and Ross exchanged glances. 'Contact details?'

Crayford frowned. 'He just came to check on progress every week. Paid me in cash. Said the quicker I worked, the bigger the bonus. I wasn't complaining.'

Ross cleared his throat and George nodded. 'So you'd never seen him before? He wasn't a regular?' Crayford shook his head. 'Where's the vehicle now?'

'No idea, sorry. He drove it away and I never saw it again.'

'Why haven't you come forward about this? You know we're investigating the deaths of three men, who were knocked down and killed by a vehicle matching this one?'

He looked shocked. 'Bloody hell! I didn't know. No, sorry, it's just that... well, I don't buy newspapers, don't bother with the news.'

'OK... Can you describe the man who paid for this vehicle?'

'Yeah. Middle aged. Grey hair. Fairly tall. Had a bad limp.'

*****

Crayford accepted the offer of a lift home.

George and Ross slumped into their desk chairs, and George automatically reached into a drawer for his wine gums. 'Want one?'

Ross nodded his thanks and pulled off a good overhead catch as George threw one over.

He chewed thoughtfully, relishing the restorative powers of sugar and unhealthy chemicals. 'We should get him to sketch the car he built for Simpson. Shall I go round to see him tomorrow?'

George nodded. 'You'd think he'd have a photo of it, wouldn't you?'

'Maybe he has. Did you trust him?'

'Not much. Too cool for my taste.'

'Yeah, and the answers were almost word for word what he told us at the scene. I told you, he's just too smooth for my liking.'

George sighed. 'Jane'll be pleased we've got another name to track down.'

'Eric will help. I bet he'd enjoy having a go at that.'

George winked. 'You two are getting on all right, aren't you? Getting a bit cosy?' He yawned with studied indifference. 'Don't tell me... just good friends, eh?'

Ross felt his face get warm. 'I like him. We get on ...'

George smiled. 'I know. I'm only winding you up. You did a good job today. You both did. Now bugger off and leave me in peace so I can write a note for Jane.'

'Love letter?'

George laughed and threw another wine gum at him. 'Cheeky sod.'

18.

He sat in the back as the copper drove him home, and reflected that sometimes, a plan B isn't enough. You need to be ready for anything, and have the guts to go with your instincts.

That's what they'd taught him as a new Army recruit. They'd yelled and screamed and brought him close to mental and physical collapse, but then they'd brought him back from the brink.

It taught you to abandon yourself to the mission, to be willing to sacrifice yourself. It also made you understand your own strength; gave you self belief.

He allowed himself a smile. He'd certainly needed that tonight.

It had all been going to plan… the surprise attack on the old man; smack around the head with a brick, enough to knock him out, not enough to kill; quick change, then dash round to his place to tell his missus … *I just stepped out with Bess and there he was; looks like he must have banged his head when he fell.*

The car slowed as it approached the barrier. He tapped the copper on the shoulder. 'Just drop me off here, mate, ta.'

The dog bite was beginning to hurt with every step. Little bastard…

The main thing, though, was that he'd bought some time. The police weren't stupid: they'd work it out eventually. But at least he'd created a little diversion for them. He could imagine them sweating over who this guy 'Chris Simpson' was; the one with the limp. How long before they connected it to Seymour, then wasted a few more hours interrogating him?

He felt a bit bad about that; but what's that phrase? - all's fair in love and war.

By the time they'd worked it all out, he'd be long gone, and the extra bit of insurance was that the old man - the only person who could place him with Foxy - would be in no state to talk for a while.

He took the keys out of his pocket. There was a faint glow from the waning moon now, and the trees were alive with sound as the wind picked up from the west.

The old woman's light was still on. Probably forgot to switch off when she went with him in the ambulance.

He opened his door and laughed as Bess jumped up and licked his neck, then cursed as pain shot up his leg when he stepped back.

He let her out, and slowly pulled the sock off. The bite was on the shin bone, and the wound was red and swollen. He knew he should get it treated, but there'd be time for that in a few days. He poured boiled water from the kettle into a jug, and added salt, then dabbed the wound with a paper towel, before strapping it up with a torn-off strip of tea towel.

Bess was waiting outside, looking eager for a romp. 'Not tonight, girl. Come and have a lie down with me, eh?'

He poured a large vodka, drank it in one, and stretched out on the sofa.

'It's not right, is it?' He said to Bess, who closed her eyes as he stroked her head. 'That old bastard gets a hospital bed and a nurse. Still, you'll look after me, won't you, girl?'

*****

Jane sipped coffee as she read George's notes.

She wondered if she was losing focus. She'd been happy enough to let George take the lead up to now, and she knew she could trust him. But a little voice was telling her she needed to move things along. It was drifting rather than being steered, and that was down to her. It was time to step in.

Maybe she'd got distracted by the long wait for the promotion she'd been promised: that, and the small matter of agreeing to get married. Her mum had been buzzing about it when she called round last night. She'd obviously fallen for Allan, big time… 'You're a very lucky lady,' she'd told her. 'He's quite a catch.'

There was no question of Allan being a very lucky man, of course…

Jane shook her head. It was time to do what she was good at; namely, putting all the personal stuff into a dark room, shutting the door and bolting it.

She'd told Doreen to hold her calls for an hour, and stuck the 'do not disturb, or else' sign on her door with a bit of sticky tape. Roy Cooke would be horrified because, a) the sign wasn't exactly centred, b) it was handwritten, and c) you could see where she'd torn the printer paper in half. She was expecting an email from him any minute now asking her to maintain professional standards by getting a printed sign made up.

She clicked on the log entries for the hit and runs, and began reading. She was looking for loopholes, missing links… anything that didn't stack up. And especially anything that *did* stack up.

Half an hour later, she looked back over the one liners she'd written …

Three soldiers, only one medal - jealousy, rivalry; the patrol/incident, what really happened; why kill by car - why not shoot; they die - who benefits; Seymour - soldier, knows more, man with a limp; Simpson - named by Crayford, man with a limp; GET SEYMOUR IN; Army - covering up, why; Foxhound replica - has to be found; forensics - feather, tyre tracks - need more; Crayford - keeps cropping up - 24/7 obs; interview old man; revisit Feathers.

She closed her eyes, relaxing back into her chair, letting the words filter and swirl and combine, hoping something would fall into place.

Suddenly, she blinked her eyes open and stared at the sheet...Crayford! The vehicle under the tree… the old man in hospital … Simpson …

She picked up the phone. 'George? I want you and Phil in here, now!'

*****

Chris Seymour poured his third cup of tea of the morning.

Breakfast was always in threes: three dessert spoons of cereal, three small slices of toast with honey, and three mugs of tea.

He'd stuck with it ever since he'd read the Latin phrase *omne trium perfectum - everything that is three is perfect.* Even though he lived alone, there were always three chairs at the kitchen table, three books on the coffee table…

Today, though, his mind was on his three drinking buddies; all dead. There was nothing at all perfect about that.

Chris knew who did it, but something was holding him back and he was such a perfectionist that he wanted to understand why he was reluctant to speak out.

The police suspected him, he was sure of that. If he came forward, they'd think it was a clumsy attempt to divert attention. But if he didn't tell them, he was abdicating his responsibility as a law-abiding citizen, and as a former soldier in Her Majesty's Armed Services. Standards were slipping badly enough as it was. If he couldn't set an example, could you blame anyone else when they fell below expectations?

He stood by the sink and looked out of the kitchen window. The grey morning sky was streaked with a hint of yellow as the sun began its inexorable climb above the high horizon of the distant hills. He loved the view of the Pennines, but he always felt a little bit cheated that their height kept the sun at bay a few minutes longer every morning.

He sat down again. His diary was open at today's date, made ready the night before so it was there to challenge him each morning. Now was the time he always put down the three things he was going to achieve today.

He made his mind up there was one more step to take before he went to the police. One more day wouldn't hurt. That would go on tomorrow's list.

He picked up the pen and wrote … *1. check intruder alarm settings; 2. 20 mins bike ride; 3. See Tommy.*

*****

George had asked Jane if she wanted to brief the team after their meeting with Phil, but she'd said he ought to do it. And he wasn't sure why.

But, as he walked into CID and saw Ross, Lorry and Eric looking up at him like eager puppies, he wondered if Jane was playing it clever; delegating more, making him feel more involved, figuring it would make him less likely to want to retire… Whatever it was, she'd changed a bit. And it seemed to date back to her trip to Lyme Regis. He couldn't escape the feeling that something was going on.

'Penny for them, George.'

Lorry's voice intruded, and he gathered himself to pass on the news.

'Right, you lot. Four things, all top priority. One - search warrant for Crayford and Seymour's homes; then get Crayford back here. Two - get what we can from Mr Collings about last night, the minute he comes round. Three - find that bloody vehicle, or what's left of it. And four - get back to the Feathers, show them Crayford's mugshot; has he been in there, did he ever work there?'

He gave them time to catch up with their note taking. 'Lorry - can you sort the warrants, and keep checking with the hospital? We want to know as soon as we can have a chat. Don't wait to be told, just go if you get the ok.'

Lorry nodded, clearly pleased she was being trusted.

'Ross and Eric - go back to Crayford's place and check inside every business in the area. We want to know if he's been offloading scrap metal… yes, I know you've been round, Eric, but Jane wants this nailed down. So if the door is shut and no-one's home, you have my permission to take a look anyway, all right Ross?'

Ross winked at Eric. 'Yes, George, understood. And do you want us to pay the Feathers a visit, too?'

'Only if you promise to behave... '

'I will, but I can't speak for Eric.'

George and Lorry laughed, but Eric turned bright red.

George walked over to him and patted him on the back. 'Take no notice of us, mate. You're doing great. Keep it up.'

He watched them as they settled down to their tasks, and wondered if Jane's strategy was working: retirement was the last thing he wanted right now, and the team was responding to the extra responsibility.

He reached into his desk drawer for a wine gum, and wondered how he could have doubted her. Jane knew exactly what she was doing. She always did.

*****

Mike Steele was built like a wrestler, but had a voice like a naughty child who's been found out.

'Crayford's always dropping off bits of stuff.'

Eric kept a straight face and got his notebook out to make it look more official, though he knew he'd remember every word. 'What about the last couple of weeks?'

Mr Steele's chair creaked ominously as he leaned back, his head resting on a pinboard featuring a gallery of footballers in light blue shirts. 'He came in once, I reckons. A few bits of sheet metal, nothing special.'

'Have you still got them?'

He wheezed out a high pitched giggle that almost set Eric off, too. 'You're kidding, aren't you? Have I still got them? Oh yeah, I like to hang on to bits of scrap, keep 'em filed away, I do.' He laughed again and now Eric was starting to blush.

'Sorry, daft question…'

'It was. Thing about my little business is - I reckons stock is just money, and I'd rather have money, so if you was to walk into the yard at the back, you'd find it nearly empty. I get rid quick, me. Only way. Business is tough, these days.'

'Who do you sell to?'

'Anyone. I don't have to raise sweat either. People round here are looking for deals; they're like scavengers. They're the ones you see at car boots in their white vans. They call in here on spec, then try and make a few quid for themselves selling it on. Suits me. Crayford's bits of metal could be anywhere by now.' He raised a hand. 'And no, I don't keep bloody records.'

Eric decided to give it a go. 'So you haven't got any by the Beatles, then?'

Steele started giggling again, and, this time, Eric was powerless to resist, but Ross was not amused when they met back at the car and he was still chuckling.

'Well, I'm glad you had a good time. I got nowhere. None of them touch scrap metal, and none of them have a sense of humour. Anyway, we've checked them all out now, so it looks like you win first prize: your Mr Steele is our only hope.'

'What do you mean?'

'Duh. Come on Eric… If Crayford's a regular, he might sneak back in there, mightn't he? I'll ask George if he'll authorise a watch for a few days.'

Eric nodded. It had been a good start to the day: interviewing on his own, making Mister Steele laugh, and coming up with a lead.

Ross saw the satisfied smile as Eric climbed into the passenger seat. He was a good looking lad, so shy and modest, too, and it was great to see him coming out of his shell. George had joked about them becoming an item.

Eric was a really nice guy, but … nah; he just wasn't his type.

*****

While Lorry waited for the warrants to be signed off by the magistrate, she decided to go to Ashbridge General to check on Bob Collings, rather than trust it to a phone call where she could easily be brushed off.

The first nurse she met had the demeanour of a prison guard, but the ward sister was a bundle of angelic joy by comparison.

She looked up from a desk littered with manila folders - every one a patient demanding their full attention. Lorry felt guilty about ever complaining about her own caseload. 'You're here about Robert, are you?'

'Yeah, sorry to bother you. But we need a word so we can find out exactly what happened to him. It's suspicious, and he's our only witness.'

She picked out a folder and quickly read the notes on the back, then shook her head. 'He's not out of it yet, poor soul. We're keeping him under for a while. Doctor wants more tests to check for internal damage. He took quite a whack.'

'Any idea how long?'

'He's down for an MRI later this morning, and it'll take time to evaluate the results. Hmmm… to be honest, I'm not sure he'll be in a fit state anytime today. Maybe try again tomorrow?'

Lorry cursed under her breath but kept the smile on her face. 'MRI… that's a scan, isn't it?'

'Yes, love. Doctor wants to know if there is any damage to the brain.'

'Is there any chance you could call me if he comes round? Sorry, but - '

'Course I will, love. Just doing your job like the rest of us... His wife went home last night and I promised I'd phone her, so I'll add you to the list.'

A loud alarm drowned out Lorry's thanks. The ward sister checked the flashing light on the console next to her, and yelled: 'Bed 6, come on!' Within seconds, she was on her way, and Lorry counted seven nurses hurrying to join her.

She put a pound in the Friends of Ashbridge Hospital box on her way out, and drove extra carefully back to the station.

*****

Three ibuprofen and strong coffee took the edge off the pain, but he couldn't face walking Bess this morning.

She went wild when he'd opened the door, and instantly downcast when she realised he wasn't coming, too. She looked happy enough, though - nose to the ground, gliding along - when he checked on her through the window at the sink.

He took time out to collect his thoughts. He'd woken up sweating and fearful after dreaming he was driving Foxy off the cliff at Beachy Head. It was either too much vodka or the dog bite spreading infection. Either way, it wasn't a good sign. He'd lain awake for over an hour, turning things over.

He knew the dog bite was the least of his worries. The police would catch up with him sooner or later, and he'd be stuffed if that old man had enough brain left to remember seeing Foxy that day. He just had to trust he'd hit him in the right spot, and with enough force.

Lying awake listening to the freshening breeze disturbing the trees, he'd regretted taking pity on him, giving him a chance.

It had been a show of mercy for someone who had become an innocent bystander - and it was important because it showed he was better than Cooper and his mates. But he knew it could come back to bite him.

He managed a trace of a smile at his choice of words, then rattled Bess's treat box to lure her back in.

Jobs for today were getting rid of the bits off the back of the lorry, doing a deep clean here and at the workshop. All being well, he'd throw the bag in the boot tonight and head South where no-one would find him. He'd take the old car, of course. He was pretty sure the police didn't know about that.

His plan had always been to look for a small plot of land, in Devon or Dorset, somewhere remote, get an old caravan on there, and live off grid for a while. After that, who knows? Abroad maybe, as long as he could take Bess with him. Money was no problem. He'd been putting it to one side ever since he left the Army - all in cash, neatly stacked under his clothes at the bottom of the bag.

He grimaced as a flash of pain moved up his leg. Making his escape would have been a lot easier if that bastard dog hadn't bitten him. He'd have to take it slowly. He'd decided to dump the metal in the woods, and cover them with leaves.

He let Bess back in and let her chomp away on the treats while he checked the wound. It was even more swollen, and the puncture wounds were leaking fluid. It needed disinfecting. While he was lying awake, he'd remembered a tip he picked up in the Army. There was wild garlic growing on the edge of the woods, so he'd need his knife. He strapped up with another strip of tea towel, took a tablet and put the bottle in his pocket, then whistled Bess to come with him.

He checked his watch. 1015. He was running late.

The truck turned over slowly, but started at the third attempt. Bess was sitting regally beside him. Neither of them noticed Maureen Collings, watching from behind the hedge.

19.

The old guy at the bar was the only customer. He looked out of it already, and it was only 11.30.

Ross could tell from Amy's face that she was having a hard time, and who could blame her; stuck in here being forced to smile and listen to drunken old farts with nothing better to do than reminisce, and convince themselves they were great conversationalists.

He was gratified to note that her face lit up when she saw him. 'Two glasses of tap water please, bar person.'

She grinned and gave Eric the eye, much to his embarrassment. 'It must be your round then...welcome back, big spender. And who's your friend?'

Ross did the introductions, and nodded as the old fella looked in his general direction through glazed eyes. Then he turned to Amy and pointed at a table by the window. 'All right if we park ourselves? And will you join us?'

Amy put on a posh voice. 'Oh, yes, one would be delighted.' Then, as they sat together, she was a northern barmaid again: 'So, what's this in aid of?'

Ross nodded at Eric, who handed her a photograph of Crayford. Ross gave her a few seconds. 'Do you know him?'

Amy frowned slightly. 'I'm not sure… he looks sort of familiar, but - no, I don't know.'

Eric interpreted Ross's glance as permission to join in. 'Do you think he might have been here recently? Is that why he looks familiar?'

She kept staring at the picture. 'That's the problem. I don't know…' She suddenly slapped the picture onto the table. 'Wait a minute! I couldn't swear to it, but he looks like a bloke I saw a couple of times during my break.'

Ross leaned forward and flashed a look at Eric that meant *'don't say anything'*.

Amy looked round, checking no-one was listening. 'I'll have to be quick, the landlord would go mad if he saw me sitting here. But I think this is the man who gave me the creeps a few times...

If it's not too cold, sometimes I'll stand out at the front, just to get some air. I usually get a break just after last orders - you know, five minutes before I have to help with the clearing up. Anyway, a few times I was out there, and I kept seeing this bloke, standing opposite, just sort of watching…'

'Watching?'

'Yeah, not moving. Like he was waiting. It just freaked me out a bit, and I used to sneak a look through the window before I went home.' She turned to Eric. 'I walk, you see.'

Ross was writing in his notebook. Eric cleared his throat and flushed slightly as she turned to look at him. 'You were checking he was still there…' Amy nodded. '... and was he?'

'Sorry?'

'Was he ever there when you left?'

'Oh no.'

'So do you think he was waiting for someone else?'

Ross looked up. 'He could have been waiting for anyone, but, for the sake of argument, was he only there on some days, or every time you nipped outside?'

Amy wrinkled her nose slightly. 'Well, now you mention it, I'm pretty sure it only happened on a Friday night.'

'And - out of interest - which punters would be last to leave on a Friday?'

'That's easy… the Army gang.'

Eric thought for a moment, and Ross gave him time. 'Have we checked CCTV for this area?'

Ross winked at Amy. 'This boy is going straight to the top, I'm telling you.'

Amy smiled and her eyes held Eric's gaze for a few seconds. Suddenly, Ross felt left out. He scraped his chair back, and Eric quickly stood up.

He apologised as Amy's shoulder brushed against him as she stepped towards the bar. She smiled: 'Oh don't worry… you can bump into me any time.'

She laughed as she saw his embarrassment and put a hand on his arm. 'Sorry, only kidding.'

Eric could do nothing to disguise his very uncool soppy grin, but it didn't last long. He was brought swiftly back to earth by

Ross calling impatiently from the door. 'Break it up you two. Come on Eric!'

Amy whispered as he turned away: 'I think he's jealous…' Then, as Eric hesitated. 'Come back sometime, ok?'

Ross could tell Eric was distracted by the way he was making a meal of fastening his seat belt. 'You fancy Amy then?'

He didn't need to think about it. What's more, to his own surprise, he didn't even blush. 'Yeah, I do…. Amy said she thought you were jealous.'

'She should know better.'

'What do you mean?'

'I'm gay, and she knows it.'

Eric just nodded. 'Oh. Right, yeah…'

Ross shrugged, fired up the engine and headed back to the station with a squeal of tyres, thinking that if he'd known coming out would produce such a muted response, he'd have done it years ago.

*****

Lorry's day was not improving.

She had the search warrants signed, but Seymour's place was locked up, and he was too canny to leave a key under the pot of geraniums outside the front door.

Alex, the duty sergeant, had volunteered to break in, but George refused permission. 'Yeah, I know I said you could, but I also said just get on with it, so it's your own fault for phoning in. Get round to Crayford's gaff instead. Hopefully he'll be out, and you can use explosives to get into his place for all I care.'

Lorry knew it was going to be about an hour's drive to the other side of Manchester, and driving wasn't high on her list of favourite activities, but she decided to go with the flow. At least Alex was good company, even if he was a bit too good at I Spy. So much so that Lorry had been forced to look for victory in obscurity. 'I spy with my little eye, something beginning with A.' She was quietly confident he'd never get this one.

Alex closed his eyes, which she thought was a curious tactic in this game. 'Alex?' he said.

'Nope.'

He opened his eyes and looked at her. It was as if he could see into her soul.

'Air.'

She thumped the steering wheel in frustration. 'For Christ's sake, Alex! How the hell did you get that?'

He punched the air and laughed. 'Intuition, mate. I reckon I know how your mind works; you and all the other devious detectives.'

'Devious? That's nice.'

He made it up to her by buying coffees from a coach converted into a cafe, parked in a layby.

'Where's my egg and bacon bap, then?'

Alex sighed. 'Ye gods! You don't ask much, do you?'

'Well if you will wipe the floor with me at I Spy, what do you expect?'

Lorry smiled winningly as Alex returned with two paper bags and handed one to her, then produced a sachet of brown sauce. 'You know how to treat a woman, Alex…'

He grunted as he bit into a hot dog the size of his forearm. 'Huh… take more than that to please the wife.'

'I don't want to know any more, thank you.'

Half an hour later, they pulled up at the entrance to Broad Farm residential park. Alex used his phone to send a signal that raised the barrier and pointed to Crayford's park home. Lorry parked on the grass verge and they walked slowly to the side door. She waited as Alex checked round the back. He came back, and gave the thumbs up.

Lorry was tense. 'Stay on your toes, Alex. I've got a feeling about this guy.'

Alex nodded, then started as he saw an older lady over Lorry's shoulder. He spoke quietly. 'Yes, ma'am?'

'I'm Mrs Collings. That man assaulted my husband and he's still in hospital. I saw him go off in his lorry to the woods, that way.' She pointed off to the left where a narrow track led into the trees.

'How long ago, Mrs Collings?'

'Only about half an hour, I think. He hasn't come back yet, and as far as I know this is the only way out.'

Lorry stepped closer, keeping her voice to just above a whisper. 'Was he alone?'

The woman instinctively lowered her voice too. 'Yes. Just him and his dog - a greyhound, Bess. A man like him shouldn't be allowed to have a lovely dog like that…'

They heard the sound of an engine getting closer and Alex was first to react. He took Mrs Collings by the arm and led her away. 'Just get home, please, quickly, so we can do what we need to do.'

Her last words as she disappeared behind the hedge were: 'Bang him up!'

As Alex turned, he saw Lorry step in front of a red truck with her arms stretched out as if she was going to rugby tackle it.

The cab rocked as the driver slammed on the brakes, and climbed out. He was built like a scrum half and limping badly. He moved belligerently towards Lorry, then stopped as he caught sight of Alex's uniform.

'What's going on?'

Lorry was totally unfazed, and Alex was impressed. 'Mr Crayford, is it?'

'What of it?'

'We have a search warrant. Will you open the door of your property for us, please.'

He stared at the document she held out for him, then shook his head in apparent disbelief and walked up to his door.

Alex called out. 'What happened to your leg, Mr Crayford?'

He ranted as he unlocked the door. 'That woman's bloody dog bit me. I was trying to help her bloody husband and it bit me. Next thing I know, she's having a go at me!'

Lorry took her notebook out. 'Can you tell me what you were doing in the woods just now, Mr Crayford?'

'Taking the bloody dog for a romp, that's what! I have to drive up there now because I can't bloody well walk! Satisfied?'

Lorry winked at Alex as Crayford thumped the door open, then called out. 'Well come and do your search then. I have got work to do, you know!'

*****

He watched from the window as they drove away.

They were putting the pressure on, hoping he'd crack. But he wasn't about to surrender.

He'd had a moment's anxiety about the search until he remembered he'd stowed his bag in a hidden compartment behind the cab of his truck. Now they'd gone, he was angry with himself again. He shouldn't be forgetting stuff like that. It joined a growing list of potential cock-ups - like not finishing the old man off, and delaying getting rid of the scrap metal.

Still, they'd gone away empty-handed, and he was still on track. But he'd lost more time, and doubts were creeping in. Was he losing his edge?

He winced as the pain flared again. Out in the woods, he'd crushed wild garlic with his knife and spread it over the bite like margarine, then folded a few leaves round the wound, and strapped them on with a piece of cloth. It would help tackle any infection, but there was no sign of the swelling going down.

He slowly climbed into the cab, and shared a shortbread biscuit with Bess before driving away.

*****

Lorry and Alex were parked up round the corner near Mrs Collings' place. They watched the truck until it disappeared, then Lorry drove back and followed the track into the woods.

Alex called her to stop after five minutes bouncing around on the uneven surface. 'He obviously stopped here.'

They were in an open area, with trees on each side, about 20 yards away, and no obvious footprints. Lorry checked her watch. 'He's been up to something.' She thought for a moment. 'Let's split up. Give it ten minutes then head back to the car. Call me if you get anything.'

Alex grinned. 'What, like Dutch Elm disease?'

Lorry faked hilarity. 'Oh, please, no, I can't take any more.'

'All right, please yourself. I'm off.'

He moved quickly across the grass, and Lorry immediately regretted wearing leather boots with heels. She was only halfway to the trees when her phone rang.

Alex was pleased with himself. 'Bingo!'

‘What is it Alex?’

‘Well he definitely came this way. Come and have a look.’

Lorry hesitated. ‘I’ve got to ask. You haven’t trampled all over the evidence, have you?’

Alex was indignant. ‘No I have not!’

Lorry was cursing by the time she’d made it across the squelchy field. Her one-week-old boots were soaked and muddy, and just to make it worse, there was nothing to see when she got there.

She glared at him. ‘Well? What’s with the bingo? I can’t see a bloody thing.’

Alex smiled annoyingly. ‘You should have been in the scouts, mate. Look. There.’

He pointed to a patch of undergrowth at the base of a tree that had been flattened. ‘I reckon he sat down there.’ He pointed at some leaves on the ground. ‘And look, these have been cut off at the base.’ He crouched down and reached out so he could carefully pick up a leaf. He held it to his nose and sniffed. ‘Yeah. Wild garlic.’

Lorry raised her eyebrows, and strived to maintain control. ‘Alex. Anyone could have sat there and inhaled wild garlic, or smoked it, whatever. How do you know it was him?’

Alex smiled again, and Lorry knew he was enjoying this as much as beating her at I Spy. ‘Because, matey, you can tell it’s only recently been flattened. If it had been done a few days ago, the vegetation would be bouncing back, but it’s still got a bit of green to it.’

Lorry sighed. ‘OK, so if he sat here, that suggests that apart from harvesting garlic for some reason, he may well have dumped the metal nearby.’ She looked round at the dense woodland, and reached for her phone.

She smiled at Alex. ‘Well done, my man. Gold star for you. I’m calling in the troops. We need a search team and forensics here.’ She looked down at her shoes sulkily as she pressed the speed dial. ‘And a pair of wellies for me.’

20.

Chris Seymour parked a few streets away. He thought a short walk might help clear his head. He hoped he was doing the right thing, but was by no means sure.

And even if he was right, what then?

He picked up the pace as he walked over the uneven pavement. Well, he'd just have to trust his instincts, as always. He was a believer in being prepared, but the best organisers also trusted their ability to react in the right way whatever happened.

Chris was an optimist, believing that if you showed support and understanding, people would respond. So many of his friends called him naive. 'You're far too trusting,' they'd say. But 'good will prevail' was one of his mantras, and it was no coincidence that it consisted of three words.

He breathed in deeply, and out slowly, feeling his body begin to respond to the exercise. The air tasted clean, considering he was in a back street just off the main road between Manchester and Stockport.

He could remember his mum talking about the old days when chimneys belched out smoke from coal fires and factory furnaces, and the fog, or smog, was so thick it caught in your throat.

The government finally legislated and the smoke and fog slowly disappeared. How long before the roads are silent and fume free with electric vehicles, he wondered.

He heard the grinding of gears as a truck lurched past him, everything rattling as it bounced over the cobbles. It struck him how things connect in strange ways. He'd been thinking about the hit and runs, and then about the old days, and both came together in the image of the big vehicle and a cobbled street.

He stopped at the corner, and those two connections suddenly formed a perfect three. The truck had parked outside Crayfords workshop.

It gave him the reassurance he needed that he was doing the right thing.

*****

George was briefing Jane on today's progress.

'No chance of interviewing Mr Collings today, says Lorry. Nothing turned up on the search at Crayford's, either. But, some good news -'

'Spit it out George.'

'Yes, well… First off, the barmaid at the Feathers reckons our man Crayford has been lurking outside the pub. And, Lorry and Alex got a tip off that Crayford drove off into the woods this morning. He said he was just taking his dog out, but they followed the track after he'd gone to work, and found where he'd parked up. Lorry is sure he went there to dump the metal sheets he'd loaded onto the truck.'

Jane held her hand up, a look of disbelief on her face. 'Wait. Are you telling me they knew he had the metal on his truck? The metal that very likely links him to the vehicle that killed three people? They had a search warrant in their hands, and they didn't think to check it out? Jesus wept, George!'

George spoke slowly and carefully. 'Lorry followed her instinct, ma'am. She was tipped off by Mrs Collings, and decided they'd have more chance of nailing him if they could prove he was trying to hide the stuff. Like she said, he could easily come up with a good explanation for a few bits of metal on his truck.'

Jane nodded briefly, a signal that she was willing to concede that point. George ploughed on a bit more confidently.

'So they waited till he left, and followed his tracks into the woods. She seems sure we'll find the sheets near there. So, first question ma'am: are you happy for me to send out Phil's team and a few uniforms to do a search?'

Jane just nodded again. Inside, she was fuming. She'd have to discipline Lorry. She should have called it in, not made the judgement herself. Her instructions were to carry out a search warrant, which she hadn't done thoroughly, and bring Crayford in, which she hadn't done at all. And how do they even know he was going to work? Their top suspect could be anywhere by now.

George chewed his lip as he waited. Her annoyance was written all over her face, and he decided silence was his best tactic. Eventually, she turned to him, with a shrug of her shoulders.

'Ok George. Yes, go ahead with the search and forensics. But for God's sake get Crayford in here for questioning, which is what I asked for this morning.' She stood and walked quickly to the door, then turned. 'You'd all better pray that he hasn't already done a runner. I want him in here within the hour.'

It was George's turn to nod. He preferred not to say anything, in case it worsened her mood.

But she wasn't finished. She stepped towards him. 'And I want an update from you on where we are in our search for this guy Armitage, and what the hell is going on with Seymour, or Simpson, whatever his bloody name is.'

She pointed at the whiteboard where the names were underlined in red. 'Couldn't be clearer could it? Now come on, George; let's get our act together.'

She turned and walked out. George leaned back against his desk. He'd never seen her so angry, so aggressive. What was that about? Maybe Cooke is putting her under pressure. That might explain it. But then again, Jane wouldn't be intimidated by a creep like him, would she?

He thought for a few seconds, decided it was a mystery he couldn't solve, then punched numbers on his desk phone. 'Lorry? Search team and forensics are on their way, and I'm going to Crayford's workshop to bring him in. Now do you want the bad news?'

*****

Jane took out her frustration on the computer keyboard, tapping out a record of George's report so she could give Lorry the mother of all bollockings later.

Then she stopped, and stood to look out of the window. She'd been shaky with anger, but, really, was this entirely Lorry's fault? Or was the error of judgement her own? After all, she'd been so self-satisfied about encouraging people to take responsibility. She'd given the team more slack than ever since she got back from Lyme Regis. But was that not so much a strategic management tactic, as a convenience, because she was so preoccupied with her personal life?

It was the second time this week that she'd had that feeling. And if it was true, it was unforgivable, and she should be the one getting the bollocking. Whatever happened next, she'd have to apologise to George. Losing her rag like that was unacceptable.

She sat down again, and deleted the note, replacing it with a reminder to get the team together for a briefing tomorrow.

She put her elbows on the desk and slowly massaged her temples. Her lack of leadership was creating the conditions in which mistakes and lazy thinking were flourishing, and there was no more room for excuses.

It was time for her to take charge; to live up to her own standards.

*****.

Across town, Allan was also in self-analysis mode.

To his complete surprise, his demands had been met. NW Media had changed the job description to include a clause that he would be director in day to day control of the Ashbridge Free Press, on a salary of £35,000 a year, and a brand new car. Not forgetting the £250,000 buy out. He would lead the appointment of a new editor, and he would be responsible for steering the paper's development.

And now it was his moment of truth. He'd got what he wanted. He'd be richer than he'd ever been. All he had to do was send an acceptance by email and a new life would begin. The email was still there, on his screen, the cursor blinking as it waited patiently.

So why was he holding back; standing at the window, looking down at shoppers trudging past in their rain-soaked coats?

He knew why. He was afraid. It would take him right out of his comfort zone, and he wouldn't just be signing up for money and the prestige. He'd be taking responsibility, and living with the pressure of the company's investment in him.

They'd want a return on their money, which meant the Free Press turning in a profit .

He turned back to the desk, and stared at the screen, rendered motionless by indecision. Jane would be horrified, he knew that. Strong, decisive Jane, who led murder hunts, caught criminals, managed a team. She was brave. So brave that she wanted more and more responsibility.

So much braver than him.

That thought stuck and began to burn inside. He could almost feel his reaction building up; the indignation growing; the voices within: *Hang on a minute! Why should I be afraid? I've got nothing to prove. I've negotiated with them, and won!*

He felt the beginnings of a smile, which soon became a wide grin. His mind was made up, and there was no going back this time.

He was still smiling to himself as he sat at his desk, tapped out his reply, and hit 'send'.

21.

Ross stifled a yawn as he read the memo George had posted on the online message board.

'Work your way through the Armitage list. See what you can come up with. Quick as you can.'

Ross ran a hand through his hair and stood up to stretch. If there was anything he hated, it was desk work. It was a waste of time anyway. Why not send him out to bring Seymour in? Just to rub it in, George had taken Eric with him to pick up Crayford, and Lorry was out there hugging trees and metal detecting with Alex.

He looked at the list on his desk, and decided he'd never be able to face it without caffeine. He walked across the room and flicked the kettle on. The sound of hissing told him that the last person to use it hadn't topped up the water.

He sighed and set off down the corridor towards the kitchen, almost colliding with Jane as she left her office in a hurry.

She smiled as he leaned back heavily against the wall. 'Sorry Ross, didn't mean to run you over.'

They laughed and stopped laughing at the same time. Jane gave him a rueful smile: 'Sorry, bad choice of words in the circumstances.'

Ross grinned. 'That's ok, ma'am. Can I make you a cup of anything?'

'Nice of you, but - oh, what the hell, yes! Thanks. I'll come and get it in a minute, all right?'

'Tea, no sugar?'

'Just the job. Thanks Ross. Just got to run and congratulate my other half. See you in a minute.'

It was tempting to change direction and spy on them from the window, but Ross resisted.

Had he done so, he would have seen Jane running up to Allan's car, which had just pulled into the car park, him stepping out and lifting Jane off her feet in a bear hug. He would have seen him talking to her for a few seconds, then Jane holding a hand to her mouth in shock before snogging him ferociously.

Instead, he saw Jane two minutes later, looking very pleased, a little flushed, and a little out of breath.

Ross didn't dare ask what she'd been doing.

She sipped her tea appreciatively, trying desperately to concentrate after almost screaming with delight at Allan's news. 'What have you got on at the moment, Ross?'

'I'm checking through the Armitages, ma'am, and not having any joy.'

She shook her head. ''It's a thankless task, I know, but these routine jobs are so important. More often than not, that's where the breakthrough comes.'

'Any news on Jag?'

Jane smiled. 'Yes, actually. I've agreed he can come in for an hour tomorrow, just to say hello. He can't stay long this time. The important thing is to take it slowly.'

'It'll be great to see him.'

'It will. And he can't wait to see you all. I rearranged the briefing till then, so he can start to feel he's part of something again.'

Ross nodded his approval. 'Nice touch, boss.'

Jane smiled briefly as she put her cup down. Time to get back to business. 'So, tell me more about Crayford loitering outside the Feathers.'

*****

'Hello again, Tommy.'

Seymour watched his face closely as he turned, and saw a glimpse of uncertainty that was quickly suppressed. 'Chris. Back again?'

Seymour had no idea how this would end. He bent down to stroke Bess's head, and it was if he was speaking to her. 'Thought it was time we had a proper conversation, Tommy.'

Crayford opened the padlock and the big metal door screeched in protest as he hoisted it up. Bess trotted in happily, and flopped down on her blanket.

Crayford walked in and kept his back to Seymour, pretending to check connections at the fuse box, while he tried to anticipate what was coming. If it was what he was expecting, this wasn't going to end well for either of them.

He turned, a cold smile on his face. 'Tea, Chris?'

'Why not? White without for me, thanks.' Seymour wasn't fazed. 'Mind if I look round?'

'Help yourself.'

Seymour walked round, feigning interest in the gear on the shelves, and stood beside a brown Ford Capri that looked new, though its registration plate showed it was 40 years old. 'New motor, Tommy?'

'Not so new. Nice isn't she?'

'Is it the three litre?'

'Close. 2.8 V6 injection.'

'What a beauty.' He smiled and looked him in the eye. 'I suppose that's the getaway car, is it?'

Crayford's hand clenched as he lifted the kettle. But he simply poured the boiling water into a mug and squeezed the tea bag against the side with a spoon. 'That strong enough for you?'

'Perfect, thanks.'

He spoke slowly as he handed him the mug. 'You'd better get it off your chest. I've got a lot to get on with. So let's have a nice cup of tea, and then you can fuck off. How's that?'

Seymour shrugged. 'Sorry, I know you must be busy. I've just got a few things on my mind, and - look, I'm saying this as a friend, ok?' The only response he got was a stony-faced stare. 'I know you did it, Tommy. It was you, wasn't it? It's been troubling me. I tried to think who might have. I mean, it had to be someone who knew what happened back then. That's the only connection between them. And what they did was wrong, we both know that.'

His voice was a whisper. 'You knew?'

Seymour nodded. 'They got drunk one night. The pub was empty apart from us, so the landlord locked the door and dimmed the lights so we could carry on. Jack said it was the anniversary of him getting his medal. The medalversary, he called it.

'Tommy, you have to understand … none of them were proud of what they did. Jack was a bit teary that night, remembering. They'd just had to learn to live with it. Eight years is a long time.

I just sat and listened. They talked about you, Tommy. They knew how you felt, and they were scared.

'One of them - I think it was Andy, said he was sure he'd seen you outside the pub one night, just standing there in the shadows. That freaked them out so much, you wouldn't believe.'

He looked up and saw the smile. 'Yes, I thought you'd like that. But they'd felt safe till then. No-one had heard from you, or seen your name anywhere.

'Anyway, to get to the point. I've always been keen to keep in touch with the boys from the old days, so I started ferreting around, checking garages. It gave me something to do. And when I came down here and saw Crayford on the door, I knew it was you. Crayford stadium greyhound racing... I remembered, see? You always were a big fan.

'I had to be sure, though, after Jack died. Andy and Colin just gave up after that. They tried to hide it, but they were shocked. Andy especially. They knew they'd be next, and in a strange way they were ready. Resigned to it, you might say. Colin said on his way home one night: '*We knew the past would catch up with us one day.'*

'So, like I said, it didn't take a genius to work out it was you. And it won't take the police much longer. And the more you hide away, the worse it's going to be for you.'

Seymour shook his head. 'You shouldn't have lied to me about that chassis. I knew it wasn't an Isuzu. That was the clincher for me. There's only one reason you'd lie about that, isn't there… Tommy Armitage?'

He stepped back as Armitage picked up a heavy duty screwdriver and hefted it in his hand.

'Don't be daft, Tommy.'

Armitage laughed. 'Nice story, Chris. But I don't know what you're on about. You always were good at talking bollocks. So, if you're finished, I need to get on.'

Seymour had gone too far to back down now, and the words spilled out. 'Tommy, all I wanted to say was, give yourself up! You don't need to worry about me. I'm not going to say a word to anyone. I just want you to do what's best; what's right. People will understand why you did it.' He held his hands up in surrender. 'It's entirely up to you. But it's time to face up to what you've done. it's the only way. If you don't turn yourself in now, you'll be running for the rest of your life.'

Armitage laughed harshly, glancing down at his leg. 'Run? I can't even bloody walk. Anyway, you can spin your story to whoever you like. My name's Tommy Crayford, a humble garage mechanic. Who the hell's Tommy Armitage?'

They both turned as a car pulled up outside the door. They heard doors slam, and a voice. 'Move along, please, sir. Ashbridge Police.'

Armitage put the screwdriver down and sneered. 'You said you weren't going to say a word, Chris. I'm really surprised at you.'

Seymour shook his head in dismay, then stepped back as a bulky figure walked in, holding up his ID.

'Mr Crayford, you're wanted for questioning in connection with the deaths of Jack Cooper, Andy Fry and Colin Flynn. You do not have to say anything but anything you do say may be taken down in evidence. Do you understand?'

Armitage nodded, and George turned to Seymour. 'Mr Seymour. Fancy meeting you here. Met up for a cosy chat have you? Tell you what, why don't you join us too?'

'Why? I've already told you I don't know anything.'

'It's voluntary. This time. You don't have to come with us, but...'

'Ok, no problem.'

'Excellent.' George turned to Eric. 'Eric, will you be good enough to escort Mr Seymour to our limo, please? I'll bring Mr Crayford along after I've helped him lock up.' He stopped and pointed at Bess. 'You can bring your dog with you, if you like.'

Armitage just sniffed. 'Just as well. I'm not going anywhere without her.'

*****

The dark silhouetted trees stood like monoliths against the orange-grey sky as the sun slowly, reluctantly, gave way to twilight.

But Lorry was shivering too much to appreciate the wonders of nature.

Alex had told her to keep moving to get the circulation going, but she'd dismissed that crazy idea and was now sitting in the car crunching mints and watching three people sweep the woodland floor with metal detectors.

She could see Alex laughing and joking with a couple of uniforms, his face half lit by the emergency lighting.

Lorry sighed. How could anyone possibly enjoy this? It was at times like these that she envied Mark. He'd be sipping coffee and shoving shortbread down his neck, served by Adrian Cheshire's lovely PA Chloe, while reclining in his luxury leather reclining desk chair in his fully carpeted - and heated - office.

She jumped as Alex tapped the windscreen and gestured her to follow him.

She stepped out, wincing as the cold air went straight up her skirt.

Alex called over his shoulder. 'They've found something. Come on!'

22.

Ross wasn't prone to self-doubt, but even he was feeling the strain.

Jane had asked him to come up with an interview plan for Crayford as part of his development, and George had just called to say they were bringing him in, with Seymour.

He'd checked through online resources, and reminded himself of the PEACE process: planning and prep; engage and explain; account clarification and challenge; closure; and evaluation.

That was all well and good, but Ross was suspicious of neat procedures that weren't designed to cope with difficult people. Like Crayford.

Ross had suspected him from the start. He remembered being struck by how smoothly he dealt with his first visit, when he was faking a welding job.

Jane had told him the key tonight was being clear about the information they wanted, and how it would help plug the gaps in their knowledge. Ross's job was to convert that into a timed programme that would fit within the dreaded detention clock. That meant aiming to make significant progress in the first 24 hours, and hoping Roy Cooke would sign it off for another 12 hours. After that, it would be up to a magistrate whether they could keep Crayford for further questioning.

So it was in his interest to stonewall them for 24 hours. And Ross had no doubt he was capable of doing just that.

It didn't help that this was part of his training. Jane was working on it, too. But Ross wanted to impress her. He wasn't sure how she did it, but she always made him feel like he wanted to shine for her.

And he had no intention of letting Crayford stop that happening.

*****

Jane was buzzing.

The search team had found a stash of metal sheets that had been scattered over a patch of woodland where Crayford was known to have taken his truck. They were on their way back and it was up to Phil to identify them.

Bob Collings had been given the all clear at hospital. The scans showed there was no critical damage, and although he would be confused and unclear for a day or two, they expected him to make a full recovery.

And Crayford and Seymour were on their way in for questioning. Was it too much to hope that they could crack the case tonight?

Roy Cooke was bordering on ecstatic when she told him. He was striding briskly down the corridor, apologising for being in a hurry because he was on his way out to a Chamber of Commerce networking event.

'Fabulous news, thanks muchly Jane. I'll mention to Simon next time we chat. I told him it wouldn't take long once you got involved.'

Jane had smiled, despite the pointed remark. She knew she'd *got involved* a little late in the proceedings. Was that his way of letting her know he had the ammunition to fire if the investigation went pear-shaped? And did he have to namedrop the Chief Constable in the same breath?

She shrugged. That was for another day. And the consolation was that he was going to have to smile at a load of pompous windbags while chewing curled up ham sandwiches, and not her.

Jane checked her watch and messaged Allan. *Late night tonight, sorry. Stay awake for me, tho... jxxx*

His reply pinged back as she was pulling her interview notes together. *Save you some wine! Take care xx*

She smiled and sent back a heart emoji, but somehow she had connected drinking wine to celebrating promotion. She was still waiting to hear from Simon Hopkirk, yet Allan's life was already changing. His new salary would more than double their income, and that was without the six figure sum he'd get for selling his newspaper.

She'd told herself many times she was pleased for him. And she was.

But she could feel a tiny knot of anxiety chafing inside. All this was bound to lead to change; even more so if Jane was to get that promotion.

She started walking towards the interview rooms, and wondered: *is our relationship strong enough to survive it?*

She heard doors slam and George's voice as he shepherded Crayford and Seymour up the stairs. She straightened her back, remembering the doctor at the crash scene. She needed to match his professionalism right now. There was no room for distractions. This could be a very long night.

And a very significant one.

*****

Forensic Phil held both hands round a mug of hot tea and sized up the task.

It was certainly an unusual one, and reinforced his conviction that he never stopped learning. He'd told Lorry earlier that he was much happier dissecting bodies than inanimate objects, and he could honestly say that he'd never had sheet metal laid out on his slab before.

He watched as his new trainee, Claire Pearce, carefully cleaned them with a set of paint brushes.

She was in her second week and Phil was impressed. He particularly liked the fact that she took her time, and also took care in the way she treated equipment, and people. She took care of herself, too, he noted. Her uniform of choice was dark trousers and a light coloured blouse, and Phil was grateful she wasn't turning up in ripped jeans and tattoos like one or two of her predecessors.

She was pretty too, with her red hair and a dusting of freckles on her cheekbones. He knew he'd be in trouble for even thinking it, but he'd found himself wishing he was a lot younger, just lately.

He nodded his approval as she stepped to one side. It was good to see young people coming through the system. Eric Sykes and Claire were great examples of what the next generation could offer. Not that he was ready to give way to them, just yet, though his increasingly frequent headaches were giving him pause for thought.

At least burying those sheets under leaves had not fouled them up too much, so there was still a chance of getting something that would help the investigation. He was hoping for DNA traces, but maybe that was a shade optimistic. A partial fingerprint, maybe.

Phil flicked on the fluorescent lamps and wriggled his hands into a pair of blue nitril gloves.

'Right Claire, will you take notes for me, please? I'll talk you through it as I go.'

She smiled but looked around, unsure.

Phil pointed to his desk. 'It's ok. You can sit there. You'll find pen and paper. But whatever you do, don't drink my tea.'

She smiled. 'I wouldn't dare, sir.'

'I keep telling you, call me Phil - everyone else does.'

'Okay, Phil.' She nodded, walked over to sit down, and crossed her legs as she picked a pen from the pot.

Normally, he'd be talking to the body he was examining. It helped him to focus on the person, reminding him of the responsibility to get justice for a victim. The thought made him chuckle happily to himself as he lined up the first piece on the bench. He pulled the magnifier into the position.

'Now then number 1, what can you tell me about yourself?' He stopped, smiling at Claire. 'Please don't write that bit down.'

*****

'So tell us what it was like, serving in Afghanistan, Mr Crayford.'

Ross followed instructions, keeping watch for the slightest break in Crayford's composure; any sign that a line of questioning was getting through his defences. But so far, Jane might as well have been interviewing a brick wall.

He had one or two questions of his own, and he felt confident enough to step in, if Jane gave the word.

She'd given him the honour of doing the intro and explanation stuff: *this is why you're here, this is what we want to ask you about, you do not have to say anything, but....* Etc etc

Crayford had just stared at him, unblinking, as he'd gone through the formalities. He was tough, for sure, and Ross was more than happy to press record and stay in the background, watching and learning as Jane worked through her questions.

Now, she wanted to bring it round to the Army connection.

'So, Mr Crayford... Afghanistan?'

'What about it?'

Jane had decided early on that she would play along, let him think he was winning, see if he got over-confident and started making mistakes. She sighed in apparent frustration. 'Did you serve there?'

'I run a garage. What would I be doing in Afghanistan?'

'Oh, I see. So you were never in the Army, then?'

'Correct.'

Jane took a chance. Fabrication wasn't recommended in the interview bible, but what the hell... 'So Mr Seymour, who is being interviewed in the next room, is mistaken, is he?'

Ross noted a moment's hesitation, the trace of a rapid eye movement. Crayford was obviously having to think quickly. Ross made a meal of writing a note, hoping to add a bit more pressure: *'You're giving yourself away, mate.'*

Crayford recovered, and gave them both a cool smile. 'To be honest, I'm not really interested in what Mr Seymour says. He'll say anything to put the blame on someone else, won't he? Anyway, how do you know what he said in the next room? I can't hear them.'

Jane returned the smile. 'You'd be surprised how much we know, Mr Crayford. For instance, we know you misled us last time we met.' She turned to Ross. 'We never did find a Mr Simpson, driving around in a customised vehicle, did we?'

Ross shook his head regretfully. 'No, ma'am. We didn't.'

Crayford sighed. 'You need to try harder.'

Jane sat back and chewed on a small piece of digestive biscuit. 'So you built a special vehicle for someone called Simpson, are you? The one that you had hidden under a tree behind your home?'

He nodded, looking bored.

'And yet you can't produce any paperwork - any evidence, in fact - to support that claim?'

'Some people don't want paperwork.' He sneered at Ross. 'We leave that to junior pen pushers like yourselves.'

'But you remember that Mr Simpson had a bad limp. Correct?'

'Yeah, that's right, he did.'

'Mr Seymour has a limp, doesn't he?'

Crayford feigned astonishment. 'No way! Does he?'

Jane and Ross exchanged wry smiles, as Jane dug out a photograph and carelessly pushed it across the table to Crayford. 'This is a photograph of Mr Seymour's current vehicle. I believe it is a Ford Mondeo. So, for the record, is that the one you worked on?'

Crayford kept his face blank as he took his time studying the picture. He'd fixed the brakes on a car looking a bit like this, but they didn't know that. If he confirmed it, it could suggest to them that maybe Simpson really was Seymour, and also put doubt in their mind about what the old man says he saw. Trouble was, he couldn't remember what he'd told them last time he was in here, when they'd shown him a picture of a Foxhound.

To hell with it. He looked Jane in the eye. 'I work on a lot of cars, but yeah, that looks like the one.'

He saw her trying to hide her surprise, but she couldn't quite manage it. He decided to go for broke. The more confusion he could spread, the better. 'He wanted me to give it a facelift. Make it a head turner. That's what he said. Brought it home to work on a few times cos I had a lot on.' He paused, then smiled. 'Any chance of a cup of tea?'

*****

Jane sat on the edge of her desk. Ross was standing at the door, pushing up onto his toes to stretch his legs; much needed after an hour in an uncomfortable plastic chair.

'The only time he got chatty was when you showed him the car, ma'am.'

Jane nodded. 'And what do you make of that, Ross?'

'He thinks he's caught us out?'

'Exactly right.' Jane stretched to pull open a drawer, and grabbed a folder which she handed to Ross. 'Take a look. Tell me what catches your eye.'

Ross flicked through the papers, then stopped at a picture of Seymour. He was standing outside the Feathers with Amy, in front of a car. He turned to Jane with a knowing look.

'That wasn't his car, was it?'

'Nope. That picture I showed him was my mum's old car.' She smiled as Ross snorted with laughter. 'He saw an opportunity to get one over on us, and he couldn't resist it. He likes playing games. He wants to make us look stupid. And he got so blinded by it, he couldn't see the trap he was walking into.'

'Genius, ma'am.'

She shrugged her shoulders and sipped more sparkling water. 'Hardly. What's that old phrase? Give him enough rope and he'll hang himself…'

Ross frowned. 'I get that, but how does that help us now, ma'am? We still can't prove he worked on the vehicle that killed those people, or that he was driving it.'

Jane checked her watch and stood up. 'One step at a time, Ross. We've caught him out with a deception. We can use that. It's a little chink in his armour. Phil is checking those bits of metal he dumped, and who knows what George will get out of Seymour.'

Ross stepped back and pushed the door open for her. She smiled her thanks.

'Ready for Round 2?'

'Yes, ma'am. I'd put money on this being a knockout in the third round.'

Jane stopped, her smile fading. 'Keep your focus, Ross. Let's not make the same mistake as him, ok?'

0

23.

George felt as though Seymour was draining the life out of him.

He never changed his expression, never changed his dull flat voice, and he definitely never hurried an answer.

He felt sorry for Eric. It was his first experience of the interview, and he'd certainly get more excitement listening to the shipping forecast.

George heard the chairs scraping and the door opening next door, so he guessed they were taking a break. But he had no intention of letting Seymour off the hook.

He changed tack. 'How long have you known Mr Crayford?'

Seymour looked thrown for a second, and George could see that Eric had noticed it too. A glimmer of hope, at last. 'Oh, let me see… yes, well… I can't say I know him at all really.'

George sighed and Seymour looked alarmed. 'Mr Seymour. I think you're withholding information. You're here voluntarily, as I said, but if I have reasonable grounds to believe that you are not telling us the truth, or the full story, you need to be aware that is a serious offence. We are conducting a murder inquiry, and believe me, you don't want to get on the wrong side of us.'

Seymour's eyes flicked between them, and he licked his lips. But, for the first time, he didn't reply.

George kept up the pressure. 'What are you afraid of, Mr Seymour?' He just shook his head, but George wasn't letting go. 'Look, mate. You're not a criminal. But whatever's going on between you and Crayford, I guarantee you're going to end up worse off. He doesn't care about you. He'll let you take the blame. Is he really worth it? Just talk to us…'

Seymour sat back and made a gesture that resembled someone zipping their lips shut.

George slammed his hand on the table with such force that Eric had to grab his paper cup to stop it spilling. George turned to him.

'Eric, would you be so kind as to formally suspend our little chat? Oh, and Mr Seymour ... ' He leaned in close. 'You need to talk soon. You're not going anywhere until you do.'

Seymour looked indignant. 'You said this was voluntary.'

'It was. Until I decided to arrest you.'

The colour drained from Seymour's face. 'On what charge?'

'Conspiracy to commit murder.' George held a hand to stop Seymour speaking. 'But I am going to give you one last chance. You have 15 minutes to think about what you're doing. When I come back, you need to start talking, because if you do not, I promise you, I will be formally charging you and it will be a long time before you get home to Mottram. Is that clear?'

Seymour looked straight ahead, and nodded once.

*****

Phil was regretting thinking he was young and fit enough to jog from the lab to see Jane.

His heart was thudding when he caught up with her and Ross just before they reached Interview Room 1.

He put a hand on the wall and bent over, catching his breath.

Jane put a hand on his shoulder. 'Are you ok, Phil?'

'Yeah... I made the mistake of forgetting I'm an old timer... Just give me a minute... ' He pulled himself upright slowly, to avoid any dizziness from his low blood pressure, but he was still feeling breathless. 'Wanted to catch you... update...'

Ross caught Jane's eye, flicking his head towards the chair in the corridor outside CID. She nodded and he brought it over for Phil, who said his thanks and sat down.

He looked up, ready to talk but only able to do so in short spurts. 'Sorry, folks. Not as young as I was... Wanted to tell you...The metal sheets. I've done the best I can. There's no chance of confirming which vehicle they were from. Though there were traces of black paint -'

Jane nodded, looking towards the interview room door and keeping her voice just above a whisper. 'Okay, but that's not going to help us, Phil.'

He took a deep breath. 'I've got hopes I can get DNA off a few of the sheets.'

'But that will only show us what we already know, won't it? That he handled them before he dumped them in the woods. We need more.'

'I know. I'm just updating you. But there is more. I put every sheet under the microscope, and I found lettering etched on two of them. I've got pictures for you here.' He handed Jane two large prints, heavily magnified, and noticed his arm felt heavy and his hand was shaking slightly.

Jane frowned as she scrutinised the prints, which showed the neatly engraved letters Y, F, and X. 'Are these meant to mean something to me? Something to do with the Land Rover base vehicle?'

Ross looked over her shoulder and shook his head. 'Doesn't make any sense to me.'

Jane nodded her agreement. 'Sorry, Phil, but it's not enough. This wouldn't stand up as evidence. We're still looking for that key piece of the puzzle. I appreciate what you've done, but I think that's enough for one day. Get off home and take it easy tonight. I can't afford to lose you.'

'I'm ok.'

'No, you're not. You've overdone it, Phil, and I can't let you take any chances with your health, alright? Now go home. That's an order. We can catch up tomorrow.'

Phil pushed himself out of the chair, and immediately felt dizzy. He fell back against the wall, and Ross grabbed his arm and helped steady him.

Jane's tone was businesslike. 'Right. Ross. Call 111 right now. Phil, stay there. I'll get you some water.'

'What about Crayford?'

'I don't care about Crayford, Phil. I care about you. Now stay still, try to relax, and let us look after you.'

Ross was already on his way to CID.

Jane pushed the interview room door open slightly and nodded to the constable standing guard. She called out: 'There'll be a short delay, Mr Crayford. Back with you in a few minutes.'

She let the door close, then winked at Phil. 'Let's hope that worries him even more than you're worrying me.'

Phil smiled weakly. He knew something was wrong but his brain didn't seem able to tell him what it was. It was as if he was seeing Jane through water; his breath was coming in ragged gasps; and his chest felt like it was in the grip of a powerful vice. He wanted to speak but the words wouldn't come.

Then he felt himself falling into darkness.

24.

‘Jesus Jane! What’s happened?’

Allan was sprawled on the settee, with his eyes closed and his mouth open, when Jane got home just after midnight.

He jerked awake when he heard the front door shut, and the moment he saw her face, he knew something was wrong.

Jane moved away as he reached out to hold her. Her voice was flat as she headed for the stairs. ‘Just give me a minute. Get me a tea with sugar, will you?’

She came down the stairs wearing a white bathrobe over her pyjamas, and they sat at the kitchen table, sipping tea and holding hands. Jane quietly told the story of her day.

‘I’m so late because I went to see Phil at the hospital. He’d had a heart attack, but they got to him quickly so he’ll recover, in time.’

‘That’s good. But what about you? You look wiped out.’

‘That’s because I am wiped out.’

Allan put the mugs in the sink and poured a glass of water. ‘Sorry. Stupid thing to say. We’d best get to bed.’

Jane managed a smile. ‘I’m sorry too. You go. I’ll be up in a minute.’

He kissed her head and squeezed her shoulder gently, but she didn’t react.

He lay awake, fighting down the old resentment. Yes, she’d had a shock. Yes, she’d had a bad day. She was worried about Phil. But did that make it acceptable to blank him out?

He’d been sat alone all night again, waiting, bursting to tell her that he’d finally signed up to the deal; that he’d been to the bank and opened an investment account and the money would be transferred by the end of the week. For the first time in his life, his hard work had been recognised, and he was financially secure.

And Jane didn’t even know. She hadn’t asked him. It was all about her, again, and his brain was travelling round the same loop.

He'd never loved anyone the way he loved her, and yet he'd never felt so alone.

The stairs creaked and a streak of light widened as she pushed open the bedroom door. He closed his eyes, pretending to be asleep. He could hear a drawer opening and closing, the rustle of clothes, and the door closing gently behind her.

He sat up, listening. Every sound seemed magnified in the stillness of the night. The tap running, a cupboard door closing, keys rattling.

Then the light went out, and the front door clicked shut.

*****

It was 3 in the morning, but Jane was wired and ready to attack the case notes.

She'd nodded as the duty sergeant greeted her with raised eyebrows and a sleepy 'good morning, ma'am'.

Allan would be cheesed off, but she'd made her mind up over several mugs of tea that hard work was the only way she was going to get through this, with her sanity more or less intact.

Allan would get over it, Phil was going to recover, and she'd always miss Charles Aston. What really mattered now was nailing the bastard who'd killed three people.

The question in her mind as she'd driven in through the empty streets of Ashbridge was whether they'd already got the killer in the overnight cells. Was it Crayford, or Seymour? Or were they both in on it, working together to lay false trails?

Having the place to herself seemed like the ideal opportunity to study George's notes and the audio from his interview with Seymour, and go back over her chat with Crayford.

She switched the desk lamp on. She needed to be clear about where the gaps were, and what she wanted done, in time for the team brief. And, she remembered, Jag was coming in, so she'd have to run through things with him to tick all the health and safety boxes.

A 3am start and she was already wondering how she was going to fit everything in.

She put her mobile phone on the desk, thought about scheduling a reminder to phone Allan and mum, then shook her head and switched it to *do not disturb.*

Time seemed to stand still as she forced herself to concentrate, feeding her brain with water and a couple of apples taken from the deserted canteen in exchange for a scribbled apology and a £1 coin.

Explaining her job to mum a few days ago, she'd compared it to finding the right pieces to start off a jigsaw. Mum loved jigsaws, and she jumped in straight away: 'Well, I just look for the straight edges.' Jane had nodded. 'That's right. But the corners come first usually, don't they? That's what I mean - trying to solve a crime is mainly about being methodical. But it's easy to get sidetracked, like doing a jigsaw when you see a piece that you recognise and you move to a different part of the picture because it's more exciting than doing the sky. And one thing you learn from tackling crime is that there are usually a million pieces, and lots of them don't even belong in the same box - they're from a different jigsaw.'

Mum nodded, understanding growing in her eyes. She'd patted Jane's hand. 'Yes dear. But the worst thing is when you get a jigsaw with a piece missing.'

Jane stared at the screen, and said a silent thank you to her mum. That's the whole problem: there's a piece missing!

She scrolled quickly through Phil's copious notes on the crime scenes, the property search, and the sheet metal. She looked again at interview notes from one of the victims, Fry, and from Crayford, Seymour, Amy at the pub.

Jane remembered thinking there was something that didn't quite add up. But what was it?

*****

'It suits you.'

Moraji grinned and kissed Jag on the cheek as she helped him slide the eye patch into place. 'Very distinguished.'

Jag felt it digging in when he smiled, so he hugged her close and grunted instead. 'It's as well my vision is blurry. Anyway, I'd better go.'

Moraji brushed away a tear as she led the way down the hall.

They'd always been hard workers, out all hours and tired when they got home, so she'd not been surprised how difficult it was to adjust to being with him round the clock - '*under your feet*' as her school colleagues described it.

Theirs was an arranged marriage, and, in the awkward beginnings, it was impossible to know whether the bond would remain as strong as the sense of duty.

But life with Jahangir had been a joy, despite the difficult few months when he got his wish of joining CID and was working even longer hours. She'd taken maternity leave, and then just as Aarav was born, Jag had to work on his first murder case and she'd hardly seen him, let alone felt supported. She'd felt bitter about that, but it had soon passed, as her mother told her it would: '*aapako bas dhairy rakhana hoga'; 'you just have to be patient'*.

And then, when he was beaten up so badly by that man, Moraji had feared Jag would lose the spark and the vitality she had grown to love. Having him home and seeing him fight back, had filled her with pride. And now he was going back to the station, and although she admired him, a big part of her wanted to keep him to herself.

In the last few weeks, they'd talked like never before; about their childhoods, she from a family with money and a house with a walled garden, Jag working from the age of 12; and about the future. She was hoping to become a deputy head teacher at her school, but it would be long hours and she was worried about leaving Jag alone in the house. He'd told her she had to do it, that he would not hesitate if he were in her shoes, and she had tenderly kissed his eyes and said a silent prayer of thanks to Kamadeva.

Reading was almost impossible, so Jag had listened to podcasts about crime and policing and used a big magnifying sheet for short sessions looking at case notes that Jane had brought round. He was determined to stay focussed, hoping against all odds that he would be able to retain a job in the police force. Moraji didn't have the heart to discourage him, but neither did she have the heart to build his hopes up.

And now the police car was waiting outside, and a bright eyed young man in a uniform was standing in the doorway holding out a hand for Jag.

Moraji's voice broke a little: 'Be very careful. Aarav and I will be here when you get back.'

Jag smiled and squeezed her hand. 'Don't worry. I'll be fine. I'll probably crack the case for them, you wait and see.'

*****

George's eyes were glazing over as Seymour droned on about Afghanistan.

But orders were orders. Jane had told him this morning that the key to everything was hidden in that history, and when she had that gleam in her eye, you knew better than to argue.

He sneaked a look at his watch: an hour to go before he and Lorry could escape to the briefing. He'd never been one for meetings, but he was more than ready for this one.

Seymour paused to sip water, then carried on: 'Well, what happened was, the international military campaign - and it was truly international, you know; people think it was just us and the US, but, oh no - anyway, it reduced the terrorist threat. That's what it set out to do, pure and simple.'

He took a breath, and George raised an eyebrow towards Lorry, who looked as if she'd lost a pound and found a penny.

Seymour seemed to upping the pace now, getting more enthusiastic. 'And there was another strand to the job: to help train a 350,000 strong Afghan National Security Force. Afghanistan has about 30 million citizens, you know, so that's a tough job keeping that lot in check.'

He smiled, but getting no response, he carried on. 'I think there are still a few hundred UK troops over there, but I can't be sure. It's not in the news so much now, is it? Well, anyway, we all know what happened on the 11th September 2001 …'

He paused, looking at them both in turn. Lorry sat up like a school pupil not paying attention. 'Sorry, what?'

'9/11... about 3,000 people were killed in terrorist attacks against the United States; and 67 were British. It was the work of Al-Qaeda terrorists, led by Osama bin Laden. At that time they had bases in Afghanistan, under the protection of the Taliban.

'The UK government stood with other countries in condemnation of Al-Qaeda's actions. When the Taliban refused to hand over Osama bin Laden, we joined the US to bring Al-Qaeda's leaders to justice, remove the Taliban from control in Afghanistan and prevent the country from becoming a safe haven for international terrorists.'

He sat back, as if expecting questions at the end of his lecture.

George cleared his throat. 'Well, thank you Mr Seymour. That was very helpful background. Now, I need to bring you back to the present day, and the situation you are in is this… I think you are holding something back, and I think it has to do with Mr Crayford, who, let me remind you, is also being interviewed in the next room.

'My boss has got a feeling about this, and Loretta and I can tell you she is rarely wrong. Now if it is true, and you do have some information about Crayford from the past, then you really need to share it with us.

'This is serious, Mr Seymour. We are looking at three murders, and I think you know how serious that is. If you continue to withhold information which may help us in our enquiries, well… what more can I say?'

Loretta smiled. 'We don't think you're a criminal Mr Seymour. But you're in danger of making yourself one. And if you are doing that for Mr Crayford's benefit, let me tell you now that he won't be returning the favour. He's already mentioned your name in connection with the murders.'

Seymour kept his voice steady. 'What do you mean?'

George leaned forward. 'He's dragging you into the picture, Chris. Classic technique. Trying to blindside us, send us the wrong way; well, if I'm honest, blame you, basically.'

'What's he saying?'

'You can't expect us to tell you that, can you? It's very simple, Chris. If you tell us the truth and tell us everything, you can't really go wrong, can you? And if you are in it with Crayford, helping us now will do you a lot of good.' George leaned back. 'Now, you've given us a bit of history. How about giving us the whole story? You and Crayford were both there, weren't you?'

Seymour stared at the table, frowning, and nodded to himself. George smiled as Lorry gave him a crossed fingers gesture from below table level, and kept it there as he turned back to face Seymour.

‘When you’re ready. Nice and clearly for the recorder, please Chris.’

25.

Jag felt a lump in his throat as he walked into the station. Everyone on duty was there, waiting for him, and to his intense embarrassment, they applauded him.

Jane stepped forward and linked his arm. 'Welcome back, Jag.' She thanked everyone and led him towards the lift, but Jag shook his head.

'Let's walk up, ma'am.' He turned back and waved. 'Thanks everyone. It is very good to be back.'

He took it slowly, but made it up the stairs, then smiled like a kid at Christmas when he saw his desk, a red balloon tied to his computer screen. Lorry pointed to the mug of tea waiting for him on his Manchester City coaster. 'I've made you one, just for a change, mate.'

Jag covered his emotions by giving her the thumbs up, then he nodded at everyone, and sat down as Jane tapped the whiteboard with her fingernails. Everything felt so familiar, but so blurred. He could see the whiteboard and Jane's shape, but no detail. He knew he was a long way from being able to report for duty.

'OK everyone. Jag's back with us, thank God. But, at his request and mine, we're carrying on as normal. We've made massive progress the last couple of days, but time is of the essence, so pay attention.' She smiled. 'Including you, Jag.'

'I'm keeping an eye on things, ma'am.'

Ross groaned. 'I suppose someone had to say it Jag, but I never thought it would be you.'

Jane cleared her throat. 'Come on, you lot. There'll be time to chat after. Let's crack on… First: Seymour has confirmed that Crayford's real name is Armitage.'

'The driver of the Foxhound in Afghanistan.'

'Yes, Ross. So now we can definitely place our Mr Crayford, or Armitage, at the scene of the incident in Kabul in which Cooper was awarded a medal. Second: Seymour tells us that the chassis in Armitage's workshop was definitely not an Isuzu - it was a Land Rover.'

Jane glanced down at her notes and checked her watch. She'd done an eight hour shift already, and it was only 11am. 'Seymour is remaining with us a while longer, voluntarily, and we will have to decide whether to press charges against him for withholding information. George thinks there is more to come from Seymour, so the longer that's a possibility in his mind, the more likely he'll deliver.'

She paused because Ross looked as if he was about to say something, but carried on when he shook his head by way of an apology.

'It's a big step forward, but we're not there yet. We have a lot to do if we're going to pin the murders on Armitage. A big part of that work is forensics, and as you know, Phil is out of action for the foreseeable. I've got the ok to borrow some help, but fortunately, we have Claire, who is doing a great job holding things together in the meantime.'

She paused and pointed to Claire, not that you could miss her, with her red hair, red cardigan and white blouse.. 'Do you want to share your news, Claire?'

Claire flicked her hair behind one ear as she studied her notebook. 'With the information from Mr Seymour about the chassis, I did a quick check to see if the sheets left in the woods could be identified. They were all cut from 1.2 mm mild steel, which is standard for the Land Rover Defender, and one of the pieces is part of a footwell which we can definitely say was from a Defender. We can also see traces of black paint on some of the samples.'

She stopped and looked at Jane... 'Do you want me to talk about the search at the workshop, too, ma'am?'

Jane nodded, and she carried on. Jag was instantly impressed, and he could tell from her voice that she was getting more confident by the second. 'So, we went to his workshop after Mr Seymour talked about a Capri motor car that Armitage seemed to be working on. The car didn't tell us much. But we did find black paint residue in a spray gun, and a lot of bolts, wing nuts and screws that are Defender spare parts.'

George held his hand up and Jane nodded to him, feeling much like a teacher in class. 'How can you be so sure, Claire?'

Jag smiled appreciatively as Claire responded to big George as if she was stating the obvious. 'I checked them with a Land Rover specialist in Manchester, sir.'

Jane gave them time for a few more questions, before summing up.

'We're making fantastic progress. But Armitage knows nothing of any of this, and I don't propose telling him just yet. As far as he's concerned, we still think he's called Crayford.'

She paused before delivering the punchline. 'I'm letting him go later today.'

The room went quiet, but she'd expected that. 'Yes, I know. Brave or foolish? We'll soon find out. But it's all part of the plan. You all know that we haven't got enough evidence. The CPS wouldn't give us the time of day. There's at least one piece of the jigsaw missing, possibly more, and I'm hoping Armitage will help us find it. So there's a little bit of method in my madness. So here's what's going to happen next...'

*****

'So how does it feel, coming back?'

Jane looked across her desk at Jag. The adrenaline was beginning to fade slightly, and she'd finally given in to George's offer of a large coffee and a chocolate bar. Jag was carefully sipping green tea, holding the mug with both hands as he guided it towards his face and put it down again.

She felt guilty, just looking at him.

'It feels very good, ma'am. I'm very grateful for all you are doing.'

'What's the latest from the specialist?'

'She says I'll never get sight back in this eye.' He pointed to the patch. 'But there is some hope that the other will improve. She says there's no damage to the optic nerve in that one, but things have been dislodged. I have to be patient. It can take months for everything to settle down, and even then she doesn't know how good my sight will be.'

'How do you feel about that?'

Jag smiled and held his hands together as if in prayer. 'I am going to be ok. I tell Moraji not to worry; that I can manage, whatever happens. There are many things that can help me to have more like normal life - computers, voice assist, text to speech, all these things.'

Jane nodded. She'd become something of an expert on making the workplace accessible for people with visual impairment, and she wasn't surprised Jag had been doing his own research. 'Well, you know I want you back, and I'll support you. In fact, I have a little surprise for you...'

Jag sat up a little straighter, smiling. 'Ma'am?'

'I asked someone from the RNIB to come and see me. I explained your situation, and they are going to help us. I thought you'd like to get more involved, even if you are stuck at home, so you'll soon be able to access the case notes at home. They'll install software so you can have them magnified on screen, and converted to speech, too, if you want. That way, you'll be bang up to date, and knowing you, you'll spot something we've all missed.'

She remembered his ecstatic response an hour later as she was attacking a cheese and tomato sandwich and a slab of chocolate cake. If Jag did retain a reasonable amount of sight in one eye, there was just a chance of being able to resume his career, or a semblance of it, at least.

He was counting on it, and the RNIB had made her think it was feasible, though she was having doubts. It depended how well he recovered, and how strong - and patient - he was.

She stood up to stretch. This was her 11th hour at work, but the calories and the caffeine were doing their job, and she was ready for the next instalment: another interview with Armitage/Crayford, or AC as he was now being referred to.

Ten minutes to go.

She closed her eyes, trying to snatch a few moments of relaxation. Allan's reaction to his lucrative deal came into her thoughts. She understood now why he had shied away from it. Any minute now, her phone could ring and the Chief Constable could offer her the job opportunity of a lifetime. But she was so absorbed in leading a murder investigation that she found it hard to picture herself leaving it behind for a desk job. Would she really accept the offer?

Meanwhile, work had opened up a gulf between her and Allan. They kept patching it up, but the repairs didn't seem to last long. They'd only just decided to get married, and yet work was building a wall between them, causing resentment on Allan's part, and guilt on hers.

Problem was, if she did get a promotion, that would make it worse. And if she didn't, wasn't there a chance that she'd be the one feeling resentful? It occurred to her, not for the first time, that she was far better at handling murder investigations than relationships.

Loud knocking on the door made her jump. George half opened the door.

'Sorry to disturb ma'am. AC says he wants to talk.'

26.

Clouds were gathering outside, and the first drops of rain sounded like pins as they hit the window.

Jane welcomed the background noise as she sat back with her eyes closed, listening to a replay of the interview with the now departed AC.

She had to give him credit, it had been a good performance. But then again, he'd been given plenty of time to prepare.

He'd done all the things he'd refused to do yesterday: looking her in the eye, appearing to think carefully about his answers, and exuding an air of injured innocence.

He was obviously keyed up because he'd gone into overdrive as soon as the questioning began.

'I'm the innocent one, here. Seymour's framing me. He's the man you should be talking to. Ask him about the vehicle he asked me to build for him. It was like a monster truck. Showed me a picture of the Foxhound. Said he wanted one like that...

'No, I didn't ask him why. He was paying good money for it, and I needed the work. He was in the Army, and I suppose it was like a nostalgia trip for him. I don't know. Ask him...

'Yes, ok, I made that bit up about Simpson. I was worried what he'd do if I went to the police. If he's killed them, he wouldn't think twice about topping me as well, would he?...

'So what? Yeah, there are Land Rover bits all over the workshop....

Jane remembered he'd made eye contact with Ross at this point. *'I didn't own up to it when you came round that time because I guessed how it might look, you know? I know I should have, but I was scared. It sunk in what Seymour must have done....*

'I've got no idea where it is now. I suppose he's had it crushed somewhere, or it's hidden. He lives near the moors: he could have hidden it anywhere up there...

'If you wanna do me for something, charge me with fly tipping. I own up to that. I couldn't be arsed to drive back with

that pile of metal. My leg's bad and I thought a trip to the woods would be quicker. That's all...

'So what if some of it was from a Land Rover? Look, I run a workshop. I collect parts that might come in handy. People bring me stuff hoping I'll buy it off them - like scrap dealers. It happens. Doesn't mean anything...

'The Capri; that's a project, yeah. Beautiful motor. I drive it sometimes. Goes a bit quicker than the truck, know what I mean?'

Jane had been content to let him talk, because the more he said, the more likely it was that he'd give something away, say the wrong thing. He was still denying ever being in the Army, and, much to her annoyance, Ross had confirmed that the Army was still apparently unable to find an HR file for Armitage.

Towards the end of the session, she had leaned forward with her elbows on the table; her chin resting on her fist.

She hated the sound of her own voice, but there it was on the tape, sounding soft and a bit whiny...

'So, tell me Mr Crayford, why would Seymour want to kill those three men? And why now?'

He'd come up with the usual response. *'You should be asking him, not me. But, if you want my opinion, he was jealous of them.'*

'Why?'

'Because they were heroes, getting all the glory. It must have stuck in his throat, listening to them in the pub every Friday -'

He'd stopped suddenly, realising his mistake. It wasn't a secret that the three victims met at the pub on a Friday, but how did AC know Seymour was with them? Amy's testimony would confirm he was watching the place, and now he'd pretty much confirmed it.

It was another box ticked, but it still wasn't anywhere near enough.

Even so, she'd stuck to her plan to release him, but wiped the smile off his face right at the end, just when he thought he'd got it all his own way.

'Thanks for your cooperation. You're free to go. But I'm worried about that leg, so I am going to make sure you get treatment at Ashbridge Hospital. One of my officers will escort you, stay with you, and take you home after. How's that?'

The smirk remained in place, maybe with a bit less conviction, but he didn't kick up a fuss, except to ask about his dog yet again.

She reached out to switch off the tape, and swivelled to face the window. The predicted storm had settled over Manchester. The way the rain was battering the window it felt like her office was going through the car wash.

She thought about AC and what would happen to his dog if - or when - he was sent down. She'd been to the kennels at the back of the station a couple of times, and had rather taken to Bess, though she'd never admit it to anyone - and especially not to Allan, who'd sworn he'd never have a '*hairy flea infested four legged poop machine in the house'*. Jane had jokingly told him he needed to make his mind up, but he was adamant.

She'd loved dogs as a child, but mum wouldn't allow it. She'd wondered briefly if Bess's liquid brown eyes and gentle nuzzling would win Allan over, but she wasn't betting on it. And anyway, their lifestyle and a dog would definitely not mix.

Her daydream was interrupted by scraping sounds from Roy Cooke's office. Jane shook her head, smiling. More new furniture? George had already likened his office to an IKeA showroom.

She checked her watch. It was nearly time to get Roy's approval for her decision to let Armitage go. And then, she was going home via Ashbridge Hospital to see how Phil was getting on, and to check on AC.

She'd be home by 7. She hoped she'd have the energy to clear the air with Allan. Something had to change, but the big doubt in her mind was whether either of them actually cared enough to make it happen.

Jane checked herself in the mirror, and frowned at the sight of the dark rings under her eyes. She reached for the eye serum in her handbag, then, while that was drying, applied a touch of lip pencil.

She smiled at the mirror. 'Right, Roy. Let's see if I look as good as your office, eh?'

*****

He winced as the nurse slowly peeled away the cloth from his leg.

She muttered to herself. 'Dear oh dear. What a mess.' She raised her eyebrows as she straightened up to look at him. 'You should have come in straight away, Mr Armitage.'

'It's Crayford.'

She chuckled, glancing over to the ward reception desk. 'Well, that's between you and the police, isn't it? You can call yourself Paul McCartney if you like. We don't mind. I'll just get some supplies so I can clean this up, all right?'

He nodded, having to work hard to stop the pain showing, now the wound was exposed to the air.

He was resigned to staying here for a few hours, but that was ok. At least he wasn't being questioned by that smart arse DCI. And when he'd got his leg fixed, he'd be heading south in no time. Whichever way he looked at it, he'd won the battle today.

The key word was time. He knew he didn't have much of it left. He'd given it his best shot with his story about Seymour, but the best he could hope for was that he'd bought himself a few more hours to clear up and get away.

The cops had driven him to the hospital, so he'd be needing a lift back to collect Beth. And he had no idea if the truck or the Capri, or both, had been impounded.

The nurse came ambling back, looking light on her feet for a big woman. She was carrying a box which she tipped out onto his side table.

'Right, my love. The doctor wants to see you in a minute, so I need to clean the wound, then he can have a proper look, alright?'

He grimaced as she raised his leg to tuck a paper sheet underneath, then stared at the ceiling as she got to work.

An idea was forming. He closed his eyes and concentrated hard, blotting out the groans and bleeps and chatter of the ward.

He could see no reason why he couldn't pull it off. It wasn't what he'd planned, but it was his best hope.

He felt a hand on his chest. The doctor looked about 16 and he spoke with a Liverpool accent. 'Alright fella? Got yourself in a mess, haven't you? You're going to need a tetanus booster; it's been a while since you had one. We'll need to do a couple of blood tests. And an X ray, just to be on the safe side, ok?'

'Whatever you say, doc.'

'Good man. We'll keep you in tonight, just to be on the safe side, like. But if the blood results are ok, we'll kick you out after your brekkie in the morning. How's that?'

He smiled. 'Perfect.'

*****

Chief Supt Roy Cooke was in a mellow mood.

He'd nodded affably when Jane announced she'd let AC go. 'Good call, Jane. As long as you've put in place the follow-up we talked about, which no doubt you already have.'

He poured them a cup of Darjeeling, which Jane had no intention of drinking, and looked pleased with himself.

'Are you still hanging on to Seymour?'

'Yes, sir. I think he feels safer, now that AC's out there. I was hoping he could tell us more about Armitage because we're still getting nothing from the Army.'

Jane could see Roy counting the money in his head. 'But we can't keep him here indefinitely. It's not a creche, Jane.'

'No sir. Shall we let him go tomorrow? AC is getting hospital treatment for his dog bite tonight, and I've told the guys to bring him back here to collect his dog. After that, he is a free man -'

'- except he's going to be watched.'

'Exactly. So Seymour should be ok. He lives out in the sticks anyway - miles away from AC's place.'

Roy gave her a hurt expression, which made her laugh. 'Mottram is not out in the sticks, Jane. I live in Glossop, you know.'

'Ah, so you're one of the woollybacks, then, sir?'

He shook his head, and they smiled at each other. Jane found herself liking him again, though he was at least ten years younger. It amazed her how we can judge other people without even meeting them. She made a mental note to ignore the grapevine in future.

Roy stirred his tea before sipping it delicately. 'And, in other news, I have found you a perfect replacement for Forensic Phil.'

Jane was suspicious but maintained a smile. 'That was quick.'

'Well, I do have quite a full contacts book, Jane. And I know you'll be pleased. Her name is Sue Conroy. Top notch. Persuaded a former colleague to let us borrow her from Worcester.' He grinned. 'But it's alright - she is from Manchester, originally.'

Jane narrowed her eyes, as she ran a brain search. 'Can't say I've heard of her, but that's very good news. Thank you, Roy. When can she start?'

He clicked his fingers as if summoning a waiter. He'd done well to get someone in so fast, but Jane found his smugness grating on her again. She wasn't surprised at all when he announced she'd be starting tomorrow.

'You'll get on well, Jane. She's very jolly, and very good at her job, not necessarily in that order.'

'Jolly' sounded like damning someone with faint praise. Jane was preparing to gush her grateful thanks, but he held up a hand. 'One other thing. I think it's time we called the media in, don't you? We can feed them the script we discussed now that AC is out there, and it would also be a good opportunity to introduce Sue. I've asked her to report to you tomorrow at 8.30, all right? Then I suggest we call a briefing for around 5.'

Jane declined his offer to buy her a drink, took her still full teacup into her office and fed it to the Swiss Cheese plant.

Now she sat in the car with her phone, looking up Sue Conroy's profiles on Facebook and LinkedIn.

She was plump and attractive, with big blond hair and a wide smile. That explained the 'jolly' tag.

She got a Masters in forensic science at Leicester, then went into a job as a border control officer. Only a year later, she switched to become a college lecturer in Wolverhampton, before joining the police seven years ago as a crime scene investigator.

She wasn't giving her age away on social media, and she was vague about her employment dates, but Jane guessed she must be late 30s/early 40s. She'd recently worked on some high profile cases, including a mother of two who was strangled, and a disabled woman who was hit on the head, then gassed in her home.

Jane frowned. Sue would do things her own way. But she had nowhere near Phil's experience, and she was joining a tight knit team in the middle of a tricky investigation.

Jane took a last look at Sue's profile picture. Would her arrival mark the end of the road for Phil?

27.

Allan sipped a glass of La Begude Chardonnay and wondered why he'd been so nervous.

NW Media board members had welcomed him like an old friend, with handshakes, pats on the back, a rather fine buffet, and an endless supply of wine which he knew he was drinking too quickly.

He'd felt itchy and uncomfortable in the back of the cab, his new shirt chafing his neck. But it was the sight of the buffet that had got to him when he first walked into the penthouse boardroom. He'd groaned inside at the thought of making conversation while juggling plate and glass, and trying not to mess up the suit he'd bought at Slaters that morning.

But the atmosphere was relaxed and, to his amazement, he not only felt at home, he felt confident. Though two large wines may have had something to do with that.

The chairman, Roger, had laughed at his occasional jokey remarks; the finance director was eager to chat about his projections for the Ashbridge Free Press; and the marketing director … well, she looked like Halle Berry, had the sexiest laugh he'd ever heard, and wasn't wearing any rings.

Sue was with him now, looking amazing in a yellow dress, sipping fizz, exchanging ideas about how to promote the paper without breaking the bank..

'I don't know about you, Allan, but I really think we need to do a reboot for the Free Press. I mean, its title says it all, doesn't it? People are tired of reading the same stuff from papers with vested interests, aren't they? So, we should be marketing what sets your paper apart.'

Allan nodded enthusiastically, careful not to spill any wine. ''I'm glad to hear you say that. We should meet up sometime, to talk it through.'

'Whenever you're ready, Allan.' She flashed him a smile and although he tried his best to smile back without blushing like a schoolboy, he was certain he looked like a halfwit.

Thankfully, a waiter appeared from nowhere offering him another large glass, just as Roger tapped his glass with a teaspoon. The high decibel chatter immediately stopped, and Allan hid behind Sue to sneak a look at the notes he'd written on an index card.

'Good evening to you all, and a big welcome to Allan Askew, our new director!' Allan hastily looked up as everyone applauded. 'As you know, it's been a sticky old year and it's challenged us in new ways. Thanks to you, the company is in a fairly good state, so we've been able to keep going, but I don't mind admitting within these four walls that if NW Media was my car, I'd be tempted to call the AA.' He winked at Allan as he got the laughs they'd hoped for when they planned the speech. 'And here is the AA… in the form of Allan Askew!'

He waved Allan over and put a hand on his shoulder. 'We've got the best of all worlds here, ladies and gentlemen: a newspaper man with years of experience, and a businessman with an eye to the future, a keen eye to a profit, and - I can assure you from bitter experience - an eye for a good deal! So, I give you a toast. To Allan! Welcome aboard!

His name echoed round the room. Allan felt the wine relaxing him, and his speech was word perfect. As he said his goodbyes an hour later, it felt like he was already part of the family.

Even better, he'd got a kiss on the cheek and a date in the diary from Sue.

He settled into the back of the Mercedes private hire car, paid for by the company. The driver smiled: 'Where to sir?'

Allan felt like he'd won the lottery. He gave him the address and smiled to himself. It was the first time a cab driver had ever called him sir.

*****

Bob Collings was sitting up and taking notice, as his wife Maureen quaintly put it.

Jane sat next to her in a corner of the ward that had been fitted out with a sofa and a coffee table. There was a vase of flowers on top of a bookcase, and a flat screen television with a scattered jumble of DVDs on a shelf underneath.

'I'm sure he'd be happy to talk to you, but he still can't remember.'

'What do the doctors say?'

'They think it will all come back to him eventually.' Maureen's voice broke slightly. 'But they can't make any promises.'

Jane reached out to hold her hand. 'Does he know you?'

Maureeen smiled and dabbed her eyes with a tissue from the box on the table. 'Oh yes. I just get so cross about that man and what he did.'

'Well, let's just hope Bob makes a full recovery. That's the important thing. And if he can tell us anymore about what he saw, that would be a bonus.'

She decided not to tell Maureen that AC was on the same floor of the hospital.

'I'll call in again soon, Maureen. But if he does start to remember, please call me, anytime.'

'I will. Thank you, dear. It's nice to talk to someone. We know lots of people at the site, but none of them have been in touch.'

'People are so busy, these days.'

'Do you think so? I just think they don't care enough.'

Jane reflected on that as she walked slowly down the gleaming greyness of a corridor the width of an A road. She and Allan had lived in their three up, two down terraced in the old part of Ashbridge for two years or so, and they'd only had a few conversations with the neighbours in all that time.

What had happened to community spirit? Was social interaction now limited to Facebook and WhatsApp and work? Work had become her whole life. She couldn't think of any friends outside that circle, and that was certainly true for Allan. Was that the price you paid for 12 hour days, or did she actually prefer it that way?

She felt the old guilt feeling returning as she thought about mum. She'd had minimal contact with her, even though she'd lived alone for 15 years since dad died. It had made her bitter, and Jane's visits had tailed off because she couldn't stand the accusations… *'don't suppose you can stay long, you being so busy'; 'got to go now, have you?'; 'oh don't worry about me, I'm all right on my own'.*

Things were ok again now but Jane knew she could have tried harder to make time for mum. Maybe Maureen was right; she just didn't care enough about other people.

Yet here she was, paying another visit to Phil. She'd been working for 16 hours, and no-one would have blamed her for going straight home. She was willing to put in the effort for a workmate, so why couldn't she do it for mum, or the neighbours?

Or even Allan?

*****

Eric Sykes was on his third hour of guard duty.

The nurses had been great; offering him cups of tea and sandwiches, letting him use the staff toilets, and setting him up in the perfect spot so he could watch the door to AC's ward with a screen he could hide behind if needed.

Three hours of zero activity was a tough assignment, but Eric was determined not to relax for a minute. He was still hurting from Jane's bollocking for not staying alert when he was watching Gonzales' room during the last murder inquiry.

He thought he'd blown it completely, but she'd given him an official reprimand and a final warning. He'd got away with it because they caught the guy eventually, and he'd been dressed as a doctor, so he probably wouldn't have attracted attention anyway.

He'd knuckled down since then, determined to make amends, and been rewarded with a temp transfer to CID, which he was loving.

He heard footsteps, and stood so he could hide behind the screen. Peering round, he almost laughed when he saw Jane about to push the ward door open.

He stepped out so she could see him. 'Good evening, ma'am.'

She turned and waved, then walked towards him. 'Hi Eric! All quiet?'

'Yes, ma'am. Nothing so far.'

'Good. What time are you on till?'

Eric checked his watch. 'Another 40 minutes, ma'am.'

‘OK. I’m going in to check with the medical staff. Stay on the ball. And can you pass on a message to the next officer for me?’

Eric nodded and got his notebook and pen ready. ‘Yes, ma’am.’

Jane smiled. Her doubts about whether she should have been stricter with Eric after his cock-up had disappeared. His enthusiasm for the job, and his utter dejection at his mistake, had saved him. And now, he was doing his prospects no harm at all.

‘Tell him, or her, that if AC tries to discharge himself, let him do it. I’m putting a car out front to follow him if necessary, so the procedure is to radio message control, then follow AC at a distance, just until he is off the premises. The patrol car will take it from there. Got that?’

‘Yes, ma’am.’

‘Ok. Well, I’m here for the next 10 minutes, so why don’t you go and get a coffee, stretch your legs?’

Eric smiled. ‘I will, thanks.’ He turned to go, then stopped. ‘Can I get you anything, ma’am?’

‘You know what, Eric? I could murder a caramel latte.’ She laughed as Eric shuffled awkwardly. ‘I don’t suppose Costa Coffee is open, is it? Don’t worry, I’ll leave it, thanks.’

She watched as he jogged down the corridor, suddenly feeling her age.

The ward sister told her AC was behaving himself. ‘He’s a bit weird, isn’t he?’

‘How do you mean?’

‘You can’t have a normal conversation with him. I can understand him being cool with me, but he doesn’t even try to chat up the young nurses. And believe me, that is unusual!’

They laughed and Jane sat down with her at the reception desk. It looked more like the bridge of a warship, with flashing lights, CCTV screens, and banks of switches; not forgetting the paperwork. There were folders everywhere.

She saw Jane looking and sighed. ‘That’s the world we’re all in now, isn’t it? Everything in triplicate. Everything we do recorded, signed off, and stored.’

Jane nodded sympathetically. 'Tell me about it. But, anyway, what's the verdict on our patient. I mean, you must have it written down somewhere.'

'Ha! We have, but I'll spare you the detail. The wound was quite badly infected, and we were worried about sepsis, but his bloods came back fairly ok.

We've got him on some strong antibiotics, and - ' She winked. ' - we're keeping him overnight, as requested. To be honest, we'd have to anyway. He's been a bit restless so we've given him a mild sedative, to relax him. He needs sleep more than anything else, I think. The poor lad's shattered.'

Jane thanked her and stood to leave. 'Sleep sounds a very good idea to me. What about you?'

'It's a lovely thought. I've been on since 6 this morning, and I won't be home till about 11 tonight.'

'Good grief. Well, you take care, and we'll be on stand by for when you let him go tomorrow. Just call us when you're ready.'

Jane walked past Eric's lookout post on her way to see Phil and nearly jumped out of her skin when he stepped out in front of her, holding a takeaway coffee cup.

'One caramel latte, ma'am.'

She could have kissed him, but he was blushing enough already, so she decided to spare him.

'Eric Sykes. You are going to go a long way. A long way.'

His eyes crinkled as he smiled. 'I did go a long way, ma'am. There's a Costa at the garage down the road.'

*****

There was something about Chris Seymour that Ross couldn't work out.

He looked and talked like he was a pen pusher, but he'd seen active Army service. It was also strange that he was a regular at the Feathers, even though he lived miles away in Mottram.

Ross mentioned it to Lorry and her response was spot on, as usual. 'Ooooh, we are being a detective today, aren't we? But you're right. Who in their right minds would drive all that way to that dump. He was driving, so he couldn't even drink, could he?'

Jane had told everyone Seymour was in the clear for the road killings, but he wanted to stay in custody. That had stayed in Ross's mind ever since. What was that about? Did he seriously think that AC would take him out? Or was he afraid of something else?

Ross had a theory, explained it to George and asked if it would be ok to go and have a chat with Mr Seymour, since everyone else was busy.

'Go ahead, son. I'll clear it with Jane. Just make sure you've got a uniform with you. Good call, Ross. Worth a try.'

So there they were, enjoying the warmth of the empty canteen, sipping vending machine coffee, with a bored PC at a table by the door, pretending not to be looking at his phone.

Ross had his notebook on the table - 'I always make notes. Just a habit, really. You don't mind, do you?'

Seymour smiled weakly. 'No, no. Whatever you think. What is it you want to talk about?'

'Why you're so scared.'

Seymour flinched. 'What are you talking about? I'm just a bit worried about Armitage, now he knows I told you about him.'

'There's more to it than that, isn't there? I mean, it's got to be a first, someone wanting to stay in custody when they've not committed an offence.'

'I told you, I'm scared.'

'Right. I thought you just said you were a bit worried. So now you're scared?' He leaned forward, with a friendly smile. 'What exactly are you scared of?'

Seymour's eyes flicked around the room before settling on Ross. 'I've already told you.'

Ross sat back and sipped the lukewarm dishwater that passed for an Americano here. He stared at Seymour, letting the seconds tick away. 'Ok. I'll tell you why you're so scared. You don't have to say anything. You can just nod if I'm right. OK?'

Seymour nodded and attempted a smile, but failed completely this time.

Ross flicked his notebook open and Seymour stiffened. Time to test out the theory. 'You've given away an Army secret, haven't you?'

'What?'

‘We’ve been trying to get info out of the Army about Armitage for days.’ Ross reverted to his default sarcasm. ‘But they can’t find any record of him. They admit he was there, in Afghanistan, but isn’t it amazing they’ve lost all his personal details? I know! Gobsmacking. Why would they say that, Mr Seymour? Because if the truth came out, it might look bad?

‘But now, all thanks to you, we know Armitage was in Kabul, and he was driving the vehicle used on their patrol, on the day Jack Cooper got his medal.

Ross was almost enjoying his impersonation of a court prosecutor. He pointed at Seymour. ‘You’ve given us the info the Army didn’t want us to have. The info that proves he was there, and means we can identify Crayford as Armitage. And that’s why you’re scared.’ He paused to sip water. ‘What’s it all about, Chris? Is the Army threatening you?’

Seymour shook his head and stood up to leave. ‘No, no, no. This is rubbish.’

Ross didn’t move. ‘Sit down, Mr Seymour. Please. Thank you. Let me finish, and then you can go back to your cell. Just for tonight.

‘You see, I’m wondering how Brigadier Ronnie Watts feels about you being here with us.’ Seymour’s body language was a dead giveaway. He instantly folded his arms and looked down at the table. ‘You do know Brigadier Watts, don’t you, Chris?’

He just nodded.

‘He lives up the road from you, doesn’t he?’

He waited till Seymour nodded again. ‘OK, good. And you being very keen on keeping in touch with Army mates, well, I’m sure you’ve met him recently, haven’t you? Or did he call you?’

For the first time that night, Seymour looked him in the eye. It told Ross everything he needed to know.

The obvious thing to do was to leave him to stew overnight, and get the full story in the morning. Option 2 was to tell him he was being released, and see if that prospect loosened his tongue.

Fired up as he was, Ross had the presence of mind to remember his rank, and decided to play it by the book. He left Seymour alone with the PC for ten minutes while he consulted George. George phoned Jane and they agreed Ross should keep pushing.

But he didn't need to. When he came back, Seymour was ready to talk. He just nodded resignedly when Ross suggested they went to the interview room so they could record his statement.

Ross waved the relieved PC out of the room and poured Seymour a glass of water.

He took a deep breath. 'OK, you win. It's my own fault. I was working on my history of the regiment, and the Brigadier invited me over; said he wanted to help.'

'For the tape, Chris. You are talking about Brigadier Ronnie Watts?'

He nodded. 'Yes, Brigadier Watts. He was fine, very chatty, until I got to the bit about Jack Cooper's medal. I told him people had said that Armitage raised concerns about what happened, even claiming the medal should never have been awarded. I asked him if there had ever been an inquiry, and he went ballistic.'

Ross tried to keep a neutral expression, despite the bubble of excitement he felt. His hunch had been correct. 'What did he say, Chris?'

'He said Armitage was a troublemaker who was set on destroying the regiment's good name, and anyone who repeated his allegations would face consequences.'

'What consequences?'

'Let's just say the gesture he made left no doubt in my mind.'

'What did he do?'

Seymour swiped his hand across his throat.

Ross interrupted. 'For the tape, Mr Seymour is making a throat slitting gesture. .. Carry on, Chris.'

'He said he knew I was a loyal soldier who had more sense than to peddle malicious gossip.' Seymour hesitated. 'He asked me what I knew about it, and I told him. I said the word in the camp was that they had executed a family by mistake, and then Cooper shot the one surviving child in the head.'

Seymour's voice dropped to a whisper, and Ross leaned forward, horrified and yet impatient to hear more.

'I said I heard that the child was injured and could have been saved, but that Cooper and the others wanted to eliminate any witnesses. I said they had murdered an innocent child, and

Armitage had seen it and reported it, and that's why he had been drummed out, forced to leave.'

Ross sat back. He felt he should be punching the air celebrating a major breakthrough. But he just felt disgusted. 'And what did he say to that?'

Seymour licked his lips. He looked tired. 'I asked him if any of it was true, and he just nodded. He ordered me to forget what I'd been told. He told me if I repeated one word of it, he would deal with me personally.

'I was so shocked that this was coming from him. We all respected him as an excellent officer. I couldn't believe it - that he was covering it up. I didn't want to believe it. I just nodded like a coward and told him I was loyal to the regiment. But later... when I got back home, the murders all made sense. Armitage was getting his revenge.'

He looked up, and this time Ross could see his inner strength. 'The murders are dreadful. But I understood. I understood...'

Ross spoke quietly. 'What did you understand, Chris?'

'It was retribution. He did it for those innocent people. That child was eight years old.' His voice was getting louder, stronger. 'I was so torn, you see? I love the Army and it gave me a deep sense of loyalty. I don't expect you to understand.'

Ross nodded. His grandad used to say just the same. He thought how angry he would be if he was sitting here now. And he wondered if his sympathies might have been with Armitage. Grandad always told him: '*People get what they deserve, son.*'

Seymour's voice was hoarse. Ross poured more water. He sipped, and carried on. 'Armitage was wrong to do what he did. Murder is wrong, and two wrongs don't make a right. I just wanted to do the right thing.'

'So, what...? You told him you knew it was him? What did he say?'

'He threatened me as well. Put a screwdriver to my throat, just before you lot came round to do a search. So maybe now you know why I feel safer here.'

Later, as Ross was updating the case log, he suddenly remembered his grandad. He always said the Army had made a man of him. Ross had listened, rapt, as he talked about the war, the heroes, the battles, the pain, and the fear. It occurred to him now that he always associated the Army with heroes.

As he listened again to Seymour's account of what happened in Kabul, he realised that there are probably as many villains as heroes, wherever you look. And a very fine line between the two.

28.

Jane took the call as she was pouring herself a glass of Malbec at the kitchen table.

She'd come home, ready to have a heart to heart with Allan, only to find him crashed out on the bed in his boxer shorts, snoring loudly.

She tiptoed round the room, easing open the top drawer for her joggers and sweatshirt, breathing in the slightly stale scent of booze. She changed in the bathroom, splashed cold water on her face and went downstairs muttering four letter words she hadn't used for a while.

Ross's call gave her a lift. It was a reminder of how much she depended on work for her fulfilment, not to mention the social life. She and Allan wouldn't be talking tonight, that was for sure.

She'd had to gently bring Ross down to earth, though. 'You've done brilliantly, Ross. Top marks. We are another big step nearer nailing him. But we're not there yet. Get home and chill out. You deserve it. Speak first thing tomorrow, ok?'

It was true. They still couldn't prove it. She'd be thinking seriously about recommending Ross goes for a promotion, but they still needed that missing piece, and she was hoping AC would lead them to it when he was out of hospital tomorrow.

Roy had been great, again. He'd signed off a request to HQ to keep a watch at Manchester Airport and to motorway patrols, just in case he made a run for it.

Her hopes rested on his attention to detail. She'd put herself in his mind as best she could - another of her DCI uncle's tips. AC had planned a complex and very risky series of murders, but the police had got onto him quickly, so she was depending on the fact that he still had loose ends to tie up.

She was fairly sure he would be planning to move out of the area, but hopefully not yet.

She poured out another glassful, got stuck into a jar of black and green olives and stared at the kitchen units.

Suddenly, the day caught up with her. She felt light headed from the wine; and tired, emotional and indignant that she was feeling lonely in her own house. She told herself off, just as her mum used to: *Stop feeling sorry for yourself.* It didn't help.

Jane stirred herself into action, reasoning that a few more calories and a bit less alcohol might help. She grabbed a couple of slices of bread, clicked them into the toaster and grunted as she wrestled with the lid of the new peanut butter jar. She was so wound up about her life, and angry with Allan, that it didn't stand a chance.

With an effort of will, she left her wine in the kitchen and settled on the sofa with toast and a mug of hot chocolate, flicking through online news channels on her tablet and finding nothing to interest her.

Still, the food and drink was helping her to relax. She put her head back on the cushion and stretched out with a comfortable sigh.

Her eyes were beginning to close when she heard a phone ringtone. She recognised the stupid tune. 'Jingle Bells' was Allan's favoured message alert, for some completely unknown reason.

She got up, even more irritable now. He was annoying her even when he wasn't in the room.

His phone was in his jacket pocket that was slung on the back of an armchair. The jacket looked new, with dark blue cloth and a bright grey lining. She checked the label. It was a brand name that spelled expensive and there was a faint whiff of cigar.

Jane read the message. '*Thanks for tonight. Looking forward to tomorrow. Sue x*'

*****

Sue Conroy smiled as Roy Cooke poured another glass of prosecco.

'Steady on!'

'Hey, it's not much stronger than apple juice, you know.'

She laughed, and they clinked glasses together. Roy was good looking, charming, and about the same age. She'd touched up her lipstick in the ladies earlier, and smiled into the mirror. A handsome boss, a posh meal at Salvi's, and, tomorrow, walking into Ashbridge nick as head of forensics. What's not to like?

The waiter approached their table, his head tilted to one side, with that knowing smirk they have after the main course. 'You have room for naughty dessert? You must try our tiramisu. Best in Manchester.'

Roy nodded and looked at Sue, admiringly. She was full of life, obviously raring to get started, and very attractive with it. It could turn out to be a great appointment, and who knows what else?

'I'll give it a try if you will.'

She laughed, and that was something else he liked about her. She had a great earthy sense of humour. The complete opposite to straight laced Jane. 'Are we talking about tiramisu?'

The waiter raised his eyebrows, and Roy smiled at him. 'That's tiramisu for two then, please.' He turned back to Sue, trying not to look at the subtle and beguiling hint of cleavage as she leaned towards him. 'You'll like Jane Birchfield, by the way. She's very efficient, good with her team.'

Sue's eyes narrowed slightly. 'That's good. It reminds me of something I wanted to check. I am reporting direct to you, aren't I?'

Roy thought quickly as he sipped his drink. He hadn't discussed it with Jane, and she'd probably go ape. But he'd soothe her ego by assuring her it was a temporary appointment. And she'd be leaving soon anyway when Hopkirk got his re-organisation finished. 'Yes, of course you are, Sue.'

'Great. It's just that, looking at Jane's background, it appears I've got more experience of serious crime investigations, and as I said when we talked about it, I think it works better to have forensics as an autonomous unit.' She blew out her cheeks. 'Gosh, sorry! Talking shop again.'

'Don't worry. Anyway, let me top you up, and then you can tell me a bit more about yourself.'

She smiled again, the soft lighting reflecting in her eyes. 'If I have much more, I'll tell you everything, and you wouldn't want that!'

Roy found himself glancing at her, as they were eating dessert. It was delicious, and so was she. He reluctantly decided to skip the coffee and get an early night. Alone.

*****

Bob Collings woke suddenly. The night lights were on, and the ward looked moonlit.

He could hear the nurses chattering and laughing down the corridor. His fingers scrabbled over the sheet to grab the reassuring unit that would summon help if he pressed the button. It calmed him no end, just holding it. Made him feel safe.

The feel of it reminded him of something that was on the fringe of his memory. He'd been struggling to make the connection since he'd had his evening meal - cottage pie and peas, and rice pudding… He could remember that, but what was it about that plastic control unit?

He closed his eyes. Think Bob! Think! The nurses told him not to try too hard; that it would come back one day. But how did they know? They were lovely - especially that student nurse, Stan; funny accent but so cheerful - but he wasn't going to lie here forever. He wanted to get home, to - oh God! What was she called? She wrote it on a piece of paper for him. Where is it?

He raised the angle of the bed with his remote control and reached across to his bedside unit. There it was, but it was too dark to read. Ah, that's alright - there's a button on this thing to put a reading light on.

Bob pressed it, and suddenly, it came back. The little spotlight reminded him of the torch. The torch! He bought it when they went to that store with the funny name.

He smiled, lying there, alone in the semi-darkness. He could remember!

A few things started falling into place. It was like a series of connectors had been pushed together on a circuit board. Bob used to work for a telephone company so he knew all about networks and wiring.

The torch… he'd gone out to spy on that man … what did he have on his truck? But before that, there was something.... He had his other torch and he'd gone out into the night when he couldn't sleep… the light came from the moon, just like now!

But why had he gone out? What was he looking for? Yes! A tree! There was something hidden under it, something big. It was covered up. It was dark, but not completely dark, like now.

That's why it's coming back… the little lights from the caravans … walking with the dog … feeling the torch in his hand.

Bob slumped back onto the pillow, exhausted. He couldn't remember any more. Tired, so tired …

He didn't hear the staff nurse when she came in for her hourly check. She tiptoed up to Bob's bed and gently slid his finger off the control unit so she could switch his light off.

She smiled as he twitched gently. 'Sweet dreams Bob', she whispered.

*****

The Foxhound was rolling slowly through the dusty, ruined streets of Kabul; its brown and khaki paintwork standing out against the white skeletons of wrecked buildings, and the gaudy litter of scattered lives.

Men in dark waistcoats and loose white trousers stood and stared with blank eyes. Dirty faced children squatted in the dust, pausing their games to watch.

He drove on in the eerie silence. There was no sound from the engine or the suspension, though the road was rough and potholed.

The quiet was anything but soothing. He knew they were out there somewhere, waiting for their moment; their retribution.

Suddenly, he saw them. Cooper, Fry and Flynn screamed like devils as they jumped out in front of him; their faces distorted by fury.

He shouted through the windscreen: 'It's ok. I won't say anything!'

Cooper sneered as he raised the SA80. He was fifty yards away, and he wouldn't miss from there.

He pushed down on the accelerator pedal but the brakes came on instead.

He scrabbled at the door handle, but it wouldn't open. They were walking towards him in slow motion.

Cooper shouted: 'Start running. Go on. That's what cowards do, isn't it?'

He kicked the door open and ran, faster than he'd ever run before; zig zagging as shots fizzed around him, the bullets thudding into house walls, sending shards into his face, kicking up dust. He couldn't see. The shouting was getting louder.

He tripped and fell and turned. They were standing over him, the barrel of the combat weapon looking wide open like a black tunnel inches from his head.

He shouted: 'No! No!'

Cooper squeezed the trigger, and he cried out in terror...

His eyes snapped open. Three nurses were looking down at him. 'It's all right, Mr Armitage. Just breathe normally. You were having a bad dream. It sometimes happens when the sedation is wearing off. You're ok. Do you know where you are?'

He nodded. He was breathing hard, but his heart rate was settling down already. 'It's fine. I know where I am.'

One of them wrote notes on the clipboard at the end of his bed while the others checked on a couple of grumbling patients. They said he'd woken up most of the hospital with his shouting.

'What was I saying?'

The younger one smiled. 'You kept saying: don't shoot, don't shoot. Sounds like a scary dream.'

'Yeah, you could say that.'

He lay there patiently while they did the usual tests - temperature, blood pressure, pulse. They left him to rest, but it wouldn't be for long: he could hear the distant rattle of the tea trolley, and the dark rectangle of the window was slowly turning light grey.

It was the start of his last day in Manchester. He'd put an end to it today.

The nightmare would soon be over.

29.

'Sleep well?'

The sun was shining in through the kitchen window at the back, but Jane's tone was a warning to Allan he was in for a frosty start to the day. He tried an old joke. Jane liked his old jokes. 'Like a log. Woke up in the fireplace.'

It didn't work. 'You had a good night, by the looks of it.'

'Yeah, sorry. I couldn't keep my eyes open when I got back, so I just crashed out. Thought I'd wake up when you got home. Sorry, love. You ok?'

The apology didn't seem to thaw the atmosphere. She looked at him steadily over her mug of tea. 'So how did it go, your initiation?'

Allan poured his tea and sat down, wondering what had upset her so much. 'It went well. They're nice people. Made me feel welcome. Anyway, how about you? How's the investigation going?'

Jane put her mug down, and looked towards the window. 'I'm planning on starting a new one, actually.'

'Really? What's that?'

She twisted in her chair to face him. 'You tell me.'

Allan could cope with confrontation, but this was turning into a game of chess

in which he had no idea what her next move would be. As if that wasn't enough, his head felt like it was full of cotton wool and his stomach was growling at him.

'Jane, if you've got something to say, just say it, ok? And while you're saying it, do you mind if I make a boiled egg?'

Jane was knackered after a restless night sleeping in the spare room. It was freezing in there, and the mattress was lumpy, but she did it because she didn't want to disturb him. Now she was annoyed with herself for being so soft.

So she stuck with her blank face interview room technique. 'You got a message on your phone last night. It woke me up just as I was nodding off on the sofa.'

She knew from Allan's face that he got it now. He tried to sound unconcerned, but failed. 'Oh yeah? Who from?'

'Someone called Sue.' She held his phone out. 'Why don't you read it?'

Allan leaned on the table, his face close to hers. 'From the way you're carrying on, I bet you can't wait to tell me, so can you stop mucking about and let's get this over with, shall we?'

Jane leaned back nonchalantly and flicked to his messages. She read it out:

'*Thanks for tonight. Looking forward to tomorrow. Sue x'* Notice the kiss at the end. So, tell me all about Sue, Allan. Why is she so looking forward to today?'

She backed out of her chair as he thumped the table viciously.

'For God's sake Jane! What is this? You're not interviewing one of your suspects! Sue is the marketing director, and we met at the board meeting and she's going to put together a marketing plan for the paper. I'm meeting her today to talk about. It's a business meeting, all right?.' He stopped, breathing heavily, staring at her.

'What's happened to you, Jane? Yesterday was my big day. New suit, new future, money in the pocket. I finally made it.' He threw his hands up to his face. 'Oh, of course! That's the problem, isn't it? You don't like it, do you? Of course! You don't want me to succeed because I'll be working longer hours and you won't have a pet poodle waiting at home to cook your tea and tell you how bloody wonderful you are. Well, tell you what, Jane, let's remove the problem, shall we? You don't need me, and I can't stand this any more.'

Jane flinched as he stamped past her. 'I hope you get your promotion, because that's obviously the only thing you bloody care about!'

Jane felt cold, unable to move. She stared at the space he'd just occupied, listening as he thudded around upstairs. She could hear drawers opening and closing; the wardrobe door refusing to shut properly; the scrape of the suitcase on the floorboards as he dragged it from under the bed.

It seemed to go on forever. But she was still standing there when he came back down, picked up his phone and keys and walked out without a word.

The last trace of Allan was the faint scent of his aftershave, the gentle click of the front door as he closed it behind him, and the faint squeak of the iron gate as he walked away.

*****

'Excuse me, boss, but have you heard from Jane at all?'

Roy looked up from his computer, taking in George's creased shirt, the tie loosely knotted, his paunch hanging over his denim jeans. He made a mental note to remind staff of the dress standards he expected. 'No, sorry, George. Presume you've tried all the usual numbers, and the radio?'

George nodded. 'She is never late. Ever. There has to be something wrong, sir.'

Roy checked his Tag Heuer and pursed his lips. 'Yes, I see what you mean. The new forensic head will be here soon. It won't look good.'

George hid his irritation. He wanted to tell him he didn't give a toss if it looked good or not. Instead he replied. 'No sir. With your permission, I'd like to send a uniform round to her place.'

Roy nodded. 'Good, yes. Do it. Keep me posted. Thanks muchly, George.'

'And in the meantime, sir, we're supposed to be letting Seymour go this morning. Presume you're still happy for that to happen.'

'Yes, yes. Well, it's what Jane wanted.'

George cursed as he went down the stairs to find the desk sergeant. *'It's what Jane wanted...' 'So it's all her fault if it goes wrong. Spineless bastard.'*

Sgt Alex Gledhill took a message to the control room as soon as George briefed him, and came back looking anxious.

'We've got a patrol car about 10 minutes from her place. Bloody hell, George. I hope she's ok.'

George sighed. 'She'll be fine. She's probably knackered. She did a long day yesterday.'

Alex raised his eyebrows. 'When did that ever stop her being first one in?'

They both turned as they heard her voice. 'Have you two got nothing better to do than stand there gassing?'

*****

Bess was stretched out on a thin blanket on the concrete floor.

Lorry and Ross shook the cage door slightly, but she didn't respond.

'Poor little thing. What's going to happen to her, Ross?'

'Maybe AC will come and get her. They're letting him out of hospital today, aren't they?'

'But what kind of life will Bess have? He'll be going down for a long time.'

'We've got to nail him first. Anyway, I'd have her.'

Lorry laughed. 'You? A dog? In your designer pad? Come off it, mate.'

Ross winked. 'Ah you'd be surprised if you saw my place. It's just a little terraced, tweaked up a bit.'

She snorted. 'Tweaked? I bet everything's white and spotless.'

'Nah. It's just cosy. But the sofa's far too posh for Bess, and no way would I let her upstairs -'

'Cramp your style would it?'

'I wish. I'm living a pure life, me.' He stopped, suddenly indignant. 'Anyways, what's all this? I'd love a dog.' He reached into his pocket, produced a piece of biscuit and pushed it through the wire grill.

'Bess! Come on girl! Look! She's coming.' Bess's nose twitched and she lazily twisted her head to gaze at them. The sweet scent was obviously too much for her, and she walked slowly over to gently take it from Ross's fingers.

'Awww, look. Good girl…'

Lorry smiled at him. 'It's love, I can see that. Come on, you, stop being so soppy. Back to work. We were supposed to be getting the bacon butties, remember?'

She nudged his arm and grinned annoyingly. 'You could always get lickle Bess some lickle treats from the pet shop next door.'

Ross rolled his eyes. 'I was planning on going actually - to get you a bloody muzzle. Anyway, hurry up. You're paying today, remember?'

His laughter echoed as he jogged up the stairs, leaving her trailing slowly behind.

She caught her breath and called out. 'Ross! Wait for me! I don't do running.'

*****

'We were worried about you, ma'am.'

'Yeah, sorry George. I should have phoned. I wasn't thinking straight this morning. Bit of a domestic incident.'

'Sorry to hear that. Serious?'

George noticed that, though her face was pale, her eyes were bright. She was going to be ok. She smiled ruefully. 'Terminal.'

'Right. Erm ...'

'It's OK. I'm fine. Just shocked, but... Allan just lost it with me. He's walked out. And he's not coming back.'

'He said that? Bloody hell!'

'No, he didn't say it. I did. So... come on, what's happening?'

Seymour was on his way home, and the ward sister had confirmed AC was now in a patrol car on his way to collect Bess. Phil's consultant was going to tell him whether he needed surgery or not; Sue was starting today; Jane was leading a team brief at 11; then sitting alongside Roy at a news conference at 1.

Jane frowned. 'Let's drop the AC now shall we? From now on, his name is Thomas Armitage. That's his identity, and we'll be telling the press later that a man with that name is our prime suspect. He'll think he's conned us. And that's just what we want.'

George grimaced. 'He's a smug bastard - pardon my French, ma'am. I can't wait to bring him in again.'

'Soon George, soon.'

Jane thanked him and put a hand on his shoulder. 'Get everyone together for 11, please, George. I'll see you then.'

George shook his head as she walked into her office. Who in their right mind would ditch a woman like that? He'd been surprised how angry he felt when she told him the news, and though he couldn't quite understand why, he knew one thing for sure.

No way was he going to cause her any more problems by retiring.

*****

He couldn't complain about the service.

Leg fixed up nice and neat, and sent on his way with a paper bag full of antibiotics and antiseptic wipes. He'd felt like royalty when one of the nurses waved him off.

Now he was in a police van with Bess in the cage at the back so they could drop him off at the workshop.

Bess had gone mental when he tiptoed up to her cage at the station and called her name to wake her up. She was agitating now, whining and snuffling and scratching; impatient to get out.

Great minds think alike.

*****

Allan walked into the lift and pressed the button for floor 8.

He'd been nervous about starting his new job, until this morning. All he could think about now was where he was going to live after walking out on Jane.

He knew he'd never go back. He'd had a few doubts at first, but he'd pushed those away while sitting in his car near Piccadilly for over an hour, waiting for the senior managers' underground car park to open.

It wasn't as if living alone was anything new. He'd just had his heart set on using the money to get a much bigger place in what mum and dad would call 'a nicer area'. Living the good life with Jane had been the plan.

But she was married to work. And if he was honest, he was, too. Nothing mattered more than building on his success, and harnessing NW Media's muscle to make the Ashbridge Free Press a flagship publication. After that, well, Roger - the chairman - said they were in acquisition mode, so who knows what other papers he'd get the chance to revitalise.

He'd never been so excited. And, he reflected now, as the lift doors slid open, he'd never been so well off. So much so that he hadn't thought twice about booking online for a week at

Malmaison. He'd look like a sad backpacker when he arrived at hotel reception, but he didn't care. He could buy some new luggage anytime. It was amazing what confidence a bit of financial solvency gave a chap.

He smiled as a tall, dark haired woman stepped out from behind a glossy white desk to meet him. Allan took in the tight fitting blue top and the equally snug black trousers, and forced his eyes upwards to meet her smile of welcome.

'Hi. You must be Allan. I'm Ruby. I'll be your PA. I hope that's ok. I'm very pleased to meet you.'

*****

Jane drank the last of the Lucozade Sport. She'd regret the sugar and caffeine overdose later, but it was a price she was prepared to pay for being alert when her body and mind was telling her to find a beach and lie on it for the rest of her life.

Roy had introduced her to Sue rather formally. He seemed awkward, and it made her wonder if the two of them had a bit of history. But she seemed friendly enough, and certainly not short of self confidence. Another strong woman on the team might stir things up a bit.

She'd spared Roy's blushes by not kicking up a fuss when he took her to one side and said Sue would be reporting direct to him. She just looked him in the eye: 'That's fine, as long as it doesn't get in the way of the investigation. We're a team, sir.'

He'd smiled, relieved. 'Of course, and thanks muchly, Jane. You must let me know straight away if it's not working between the two of you.'

The others would meet her in about five minutes at the team briefing. Jane wondered what they'd make of her.

She slid some loose pages into her A4 notebook and held it under her arm as she stepped out into the corridor.

It struck her again how like a hospital it felt. The grey polished floor, the neutral paintwork on the walls, the slight aroma of disinfectant and body odour. It was like a memory trigger, taking her back to the hospice where Charles Aston spent his last days wired up to computers, and she felt completely alone.

She tried to brush it away, but she suddenly felt a weight pressing down on her. It was like a storm cloud had settled on her shoulders, and she couldn't lift it. Her mind began to race; thoughts streaming through so quickly she couldn't hold onto them. She missed Charles... Phil was in hospital...George was going to retire... Allan had walked out… Her head felt as if a steel tourniquet was being tightened. Her vision was blurry. She leaned back against the wall and her notebook fell and she watched as the loose pages slid away across the shiny floor.

She stared at the stark white rectangles of paper. What were they doing there? Litter. Must pick it up.

Then, a voice. Echoing. Her name, over and over. 'Jane, Jane.'

Everything clicked back into place again, as if someone had flicked a switch. Her vision cleared; she took a calming breath; and felt her heartbeat slowing. Roy was walking up to her with Sue.

'Are you alright, Jane? Want a hand?' He bent down to pick up the notebook and the extra pages and smiled as she took them off him.

'Thanks Roy. Butterfingers, me. Shall we go in?'

All eyes were on Sue, which suited Jane. The remaining fuzziness in her head cleared as Roy did the introductions, and she had a moment to analyse what happened. Was that a panic attack? Surely depression doesn't just click in and out quickly like that… Or was it something else? A warning of a problem? Her dad had died suddenly, slumped in his armchair while everyone was watching television. No-one knew what had happened until the programme ended… 'Blackadder'? Apparently, he had a brain aneurysm....

Jane felt a bubble in her stomach as she tried to dismiss the possibility that it was hereditary. She made a point of studying her notes as Roy began winding up. '... with that, I'll hand over to Jane. All the best everyone, and welcome aboard, Sue.'

There was a smattering of applause as he left the room.

Jane moved next to Sue and cleared her throat. 'Let's remind ourselves where we are. Armitage is now at his workshop, being observed by uniform branch. Seymour is at home, no doubt hiding under the table.' She got a laugh for what sounded like an ad lib even though she'd written it down.

'We are assuming Armitage's next move will be to get home, pack up and clear off, but somewhere along the way, we're hoping he'll lead us to the missing bit of evidence that will nail him. It's a long shot, but a risk worth taking. You don't need me to tell you that this is proving very difficult to prove. We need a lucky break, or a stroke of genius, and I have no doubt that we'll come up with something.

'Meanwhile, we've got Sue with us, I'm very pleased to say, and she'll be going over the forensics with Claire to see if we've missed anything.' She smiled. 'As if such a thing was possible.'

'I've put all the info on the log, including the rota for keeping a permanent watch on Armitage. We are following wherever he goes. No switching off. No exceptions.

'I can also tell you that Roy and the courts have given us the ok to monitor phone traffic and to plant listening devices at his home and workshop.

'And we are still hoping for something from Mr Collings, who - for Sue's benefit - we think was attacked by Armitage because he was being a nosey neighbour.

'I know this is a big ask. There aren't many of you, but Roy has at least secured a few uniforms to help us with the surveillance.'

Ross held his hand up. 'What is it that we are looking for, ma'am? What's the missing piece?'

'No idea. We'll know it when we find it. Anyone else? Yes, Lorry…'

'What happens if Armitage makes a run for it, out of our area?'

'Good point. Region have agreed to monitor all transport hubs.

They have his image so we can use face recognition on CCTV systems etc. We've also got the co-operation of security at the regional airports, and motorway patrols.'

George sounded angry. 'We have got to nail this scumbag. Sorry, ma'am.'

Jane laughed with the others, and was pleased to see Sue joining in. 'Couldn't have put it better myself, George. So, Sue… anything you want to add?'

Sue would have been a few inches shorter than Jane's 5'7", had it not been for her high heels. She scattered a bright smile to all corners of the room as if she was a stage performer.

'Just to say I will be going through all the notes in great detail. I'm confident I will find something that has been missed. No reflection on anyone here, of course. It happens all the time.'

Jane watched their faces. They weren't impressed. They'd be resenting the implied criticism of Phil. She'd have to nip this in the bud. But Sue was on a roll, 'My approach is to check, check again, and check again. That's what I'll be doing now, and I'm sure I'll be able to bring my experience to bear to bring this case to a successful conclusion.'

Jane could see George chewing wine gums ferociously. What was Sue thinking?

Jane decided to bring it to an end. 'Yeah, thanks Sue. I'm sure we'll all be using our considerable experience to crack this. Anyway, folks, it's going to be a long day, so don't count on getting any sleep. Thanks everyone. Come on! Let's get this done.'

She stepped out into the corridor with Sue. 'I sent a message to Phil to say you were covering, and he said to give you his best wishes.'

Sue smiled. She really was annoyingly pretty. 'Bless. I hope he gets the rest he needs.' Then, as she walked away, she turned: 'He needs to think about whether it's wise to carry on, don't you think?'

30.

Doreen on the switchboard had left a message on Jane's desk.

'Jag called. Said could you call him back' Love, Dor.'

Jane smiled briefly. Doreen didn't know what businesslike meant, but she called everyone love, and was unfailingly happy every single day. So much so that Jane told her mum one day that she wanted to be more like Doreen. Mum was typically cutting. 'No you don't. She's a drip.'

But anyway, Jag would have to wait. She needed a head massage and a paracetamol or two. The massage was out of the question, so she called Doreen and asked if she had any tablets in her bag, knowing full well that she always carried a stash.

'Yes, of course, my love. I'll bring you a few.'

'No, no, it's ok. I'll pick them up on my way out.'

'Going anywhere nice?'

Jane laughed. Doreen had that uncanny ability to cheer people up without trying. 'Doreen! I'm doing the news conference with Roy!'

'Oooooh! We saw you both on telly last time and Shirley said you looked like a really nice couple.'

'Did she indeed. Anyway, you've got to stop. I've got to get ready. And thanks for the pills, Doreen. You're a star.'

Jane felt herself welling up. She recognised the signs. She was more prone to weeping at 'Call the Midwife' if she'd had a tough week, and this certainly fell into the category of tough.

She got her mirror out of her handbag and cursed under her breath. '*Christ, Jane. You look like a disaster.*' She quickly applied eyeliner and blusher. She finished off with pink lip pencil to add a bit of definition, just as Roy tapped on her door.

'Ready to roll, Jane,' he called out.

She decided she didn't want him to know Doreen was her drug supplier. Or that she needed make up to hide her face. 'I'll just be a minute. See you there, ok?'

It took her a few minutes to realise that Allan's paper would be represented at the briefing. She was certain he wouldn't be there. He'd find an excuse to avoid facing her. But she steeled herself just in case.

Jane practised her Pilates breathing as she walked the last few steps to the conference room door. There was half an hour to go but she could hear a hum of chatter already.

The local papers had gone to town with the story, but although the locals had played ball and opted against spreading fear, one or two of the nationals hadn't been so responsible.

'Roadkiller terrorises city'. 'Army heroes mown down on streets of Manchester.': 'Cops baffled by triple murder.'

With headlines like that, she knew it was only a matter of time before Simon Hopkirk started turning the screw. He was probably already getting it in the neck from the politicians. He certainly wouldn't be so keen to offer her promotion if it went on much longer.

Jane stopped with her hand on the door handle, and reminded herself that what mattered the most was nailing Armitage.

The way she felt right now, she knew that if she didn't get that promotion for whatever reason, she'd walk.

After all, there was nothing to keep her here any longer.

*****

Jag turned up the volume on the radio and leaned forward in his armchair.

He'd sat at Jane's side at a news conference only a few weeks ago. It seemed a distant memory now.

She and Roy Cooke were handling it well, he thought. There was just enough to make the real Armitage think he may have got away with it, and yet enough to convince the media and the public that they were close to bringing the killer to justice.

Jag wondered how Armitage would be feeling if he was listening. He guessed he wouldn't be totally fooled. From what he'd heard from the interviews, he was no fool.

It felt good to keep up with the case. The text to speech software had worked really well. The voice was robotic and lifeless, but in a way that helped Jag to concentrate on the words, and he found he was able to soak up the details pretty well.

He gave Moraji a page to test him on last night, and she'd given him a distinction. She'd kissed him on the cheek. 'You could do that subject on Mastermind.'

Jag remembered how childishly proud he'd been. But he was encouraged. His brain was working.

He turned the volume up as a lorry rattled over the speed bumps. The news report ended with Jane issuing an appeal for anyone who knows Thomas Armitage, an ex soldier, to contact any police station in Manchester, and not to approach him as he may be dangerous.

Jag sat down again at the dining room table that had become his work station.

The next set of notes he wanted to study was the forensic stuff. Phil had done a lot of work, as usual, and Jag would never normally get to know all of it. He was hoping he'd learn something.

31.

Sue was honest enough to admit it.

'Phil is bloody good, I've got to hand it to him. I haven't got anything to add.' She smiled playfully. 'Yet.'

Jane wanted to say that Phil was the best forensic guy in Britain, but she decided on discretion. 'Phil's good, but he'd be the first to say there's always something new to find. That's why he decided not to retire when he had the chance.'

Sue frowned. 'I'm sure you're really fond of him, but he's going to have to think again. He's not going to bounce right back is he? Not at his age.'

Jane nodded, wondering whether Sue was just being honest and a little tactless, or determined to muscle e in. She was certainly difficult to weigh up: smiley and friendly, but with a distinct edge of superiority? 'Well, we'll certainly have to be patient.' She stood. 'I've got to get on, sorry. Can I assume that we have no other possible leads from forensics?'

Sue yawned and stretched her arms straight above her head. 'Sorreeee! Had a late night.... So, yeah, nothing new at the moment, but Claire and I are going over everything again one more time.' She stood up and smoothed out her plain grey skirt.

Jane noticed enviously that her legs were nicely tanned. Holiday, or tanning salon? Jane decided the latter. She could imagine Sue going in for beauty treatments. Maybe it was time she started?

Sue smiled. 'I just thought... do you fancy meeting up for a drink sometime?'

Jane couldn't remember the last time she'd had an invitation. 'Erm... yes, I'd love to. Probably have to wait a few days, though, until... you know.'

'Oh yeah, of course. No rush. I know a lovely little wine bar, a bit off the beaten track. It's not far from here, actually. It's run by a woman and she calls it girl friendly. By which she means we can have a drink without being chatted up by a middle aged MD. We could walk there after work one day.'

Jane nodded and smiled as the phone rang. Sue mouthed 'see you later' and closed the door gently.

'DCI Birchfield. How can I help?'

'It's Mauren Collings. I wonder if you could pop round to the hospital? Bob's started remembering things.'

*****

It felt strange locking up the workshop for the last time.

Building up the business had kept Armitage sane since he left the army, though he doubted anyone would call him sane if they knew what he'd done.

He patted Bess's head as she trotted up to him, then yanked on the padlock to make sure it was secure.

'You don't think I'm mad, do you girl?' The attention got her excited, and she was panting as he opened the Capri door and settled her on the back seat. He turned once he was in the front. 'Now, no back seat driving, alright?'

She barked and licked his nose. He laughed. He couldn't recall the last time he'd laughed out loud.

'Right Bess, let's go and tidy up at the house.'

Traffic was light, so he was confident of spotting any car that was tailing him. He cracked open the window to give Bess some air, and decided to go back the long way round. He headed east on the dual carriageway, past the area where Jack Cooper lived.

He could remember every detail. Jack's walking route from the pub, the chip shop, the bench where he sat to eat his fish and chips; the look of terror as he saw what must have looked to him like a Foxhound about to smash into him; the dead weight of his mangled body as he nudged him with his foot to make sure the job was done.

Armitage frowned as he turned off to loop round to the north, heading towards Bolton. It was a stupid thing to do, getting out of the car. Easy to leave a trace. But he had to do it, had to be sure Jack was gone.

He had to be the first because he was the leader; the one who killed that kid.

Armitage didn't care if the other two had survived. They'd have suffered with their injuries for the rest of their lives, and he thought that would have been better.

He just hoped he hadn't left anything around Jack's body. He breathed deeply. Nah, couldn't have done or the police would never have let me go.

*****

Jane stopped to read Jag's email on her phone as she walked from her car to the hospital entrance.

She stepped aside to make room for a frail looking old man who was pushing a rosy-cheeked plump woman in a wheelchair. He looked like he was going to strain himself. 'Do you want a hand?'

'No, love, ta very much. I'll have to get used to it. She's my daughter. Just come out after an operation on her heart.' He laughed. 'I'll need one before long, looking after her.'

'Well, take care.'

'You too love. God bless.'

His cheery self sacrifice touched a nerve and Jane felt teary all of a sudden. She told herself not to be a fool, and read the email quickly.

'I have gone through notes (thank you!) and think it would be worth following up on something Phil wrote about some photographs taken at the scene of the first incident. A fragment of a feather was found. Phil seems to have put it to one side, but wondered if it might be from the insulation of a jacket. I haven't seen any other reference to it, or any follow up. I could be wrong, but I couldn't find anything. Just thought it would be worth another look, just in case? Will bother you again if anything else occurs to me!'

So everyone had missed this, including the super-efficient Sue. Jane held back her indignation when she realised she'd missed it too. She called Alex Gledhill.

'Alex. Where is Armitage now?'

'He's in his car, last seen heading north. We think he's going home, ma'am.'

'Who's on watch at his place?'

'Eric Sykes, ma'am.'

'Good. Our search warrant is still in force. Tell him to get in there now and look for a padded jacket, like a puffa jacket. If he finds it, check whether it's torn then photograph it and bag a sample of the lining. We're looking for feathers. Got that?'

Alex's voice was deadpan. 'Feathers. Yes ma'am.'

'Make sure Eric does it right now, and tell him to be quick. Armitage could be back at any time. This could be one of our missing pieces, alright?'

'Will do, ma'am.'

'Keep me posted. And monitor Armitage. Tip Eric off when he's about five minutes away.'

'Sorry, ma'am. The cameras won't cover us that far out in the sticks. We've got a car on the main road near the residential park. I'll ask them to radio Eric as soon as they see him.'

Jane pushed her phone into her jacket pocket as she walked quickly along the corridor. She tried to ignore the pressure building up in her head, as she remembered her temporary blackout before the team brief. 'Think of something else, Jane,' she told herself, repeating it every few steps until she reached the ward.

Her phone beeped again. A text this time. Allan. *'Sorry for everything. I want you to have my share of the house. Hope you're ok x'*

She stared at the screen, and didn't look up when the ward sister called out to her. 'Nice to see you again...' She touched Jane's arm and stepped back as Jane flinched as if she'd been wounded. 'Are you alright?'

Jane put a hand up to her eyes and shook her head. 'Sorry, yes. Just had a message from my ex -' She stopped, and her eyes widened slightly. She'd said it, out loud. Allan was now her ex. 'I'm really glad I'm out of it now.'

The nurse patted her arm. 'You're sure? You look a bit shaken up to me.'

Jane smiled. She felt her steel armour plating sliding into place. She'd survived far worse than this. His message would have been laughable if it wasn't so pathetic. 'Let's go and see what Bob's got to say, shall we?'

The nurse briefed her as they walked through. Bob was sitting up in the end bed, nearest the window. 'Come to give me a grilling?'

Jane grinned. 'You look better, Bob. I know you must be because you're already giving me cheek. I'm really sorry; I can't stay long. Maureen said you'd started remembering. Can you tell me anything?'

'It's funny; I can't remember the night he's supposed to have hit me.' Jane's disappointment must have showed. 'Oh, but I have remembered something else. About the vehicle.'

Jane sat down and opened her notebook. Another missing piece of the jigsaw? 'The vehicle? Which vehicle, Bob?'

Bob scratched his head elaborately. 'I'd never seen anything like it. That must be why I remember, don't you think?'

Jane controlled her impatience. 'What do you remember?'

'I can see it now, in my head... painted black. I thought that was odd for an Army vehicle. It was seeing the lights on at night in here that did it. I remembered buying a new torch. Then it came back. My old torch started playing up when I was out that night. That's why I wanted a new one, see?'

Jane nodded, her pen poised, as Bob shuffled to get more comfortable. 'I'd seen that man going round the back, putting a cover on something under the tree. I went to look, and I saw it.'

'Can you describe it, Bob?'

Bob's eyes were bright as if he was reliving the moment. 'Oh yes, it's clear as day. Funny that. I'd forgotten all about it.... I only saw the front end, it was wide, but narrowed down to a point – like a stubby pencil, I thought. It didn't have a bumper, either. Just looked like a block of metal covering the front. It looked solid as a tank.'

He rested his head back on the pillow and looked up at the ceiling. 'Have I been any help?'

Jane took his hand in hers and squeezed it gently. 'You've been more than a help, Bob. Just one more thing... You saw the man who assaulted you putting the covers on the vehicle, did you? It was definitely him?'

He smiled slowly, his eyes closing. His voice was faint as he drifted off to sleep. 'It was him, alright. I remember it clearly now.'

He turned his head to look at Jane. 'Can you tell my wife I remember her name, too?'

32.

Allan sat back in his leather swivel chair reading the front page of the Ashbridge Free Press: *Police roadkill suspect named.*

It was the first edition since the buyout, and he was proud of it. All in all, he reckoned it was proving to be a very good deal. He was feeling very pampered on his first day.

He had been allocated an eighth floor office, one floor below the chairman. It had sliding doors onto a balcony with spectacular views over the city. The new teak desk and conference table teamed up nicely with the brown leather chairs and a plush dark grey carpet. His new car – a Lexus Hybrid, black – was being delivered later today, and his gorgeous PA Ruby had just phoned to ask how he liked his coffee.

His luck was definitely in, though he'd still thought about Jane. He wasn't surprised she hadn't replied to his text, but at least he'd tried.

He could predict her reaction. The break up would all be his fault. But, given time, she might come to appreciate that he'd been the one to bring their relationship to an end. She was always telling him to be more assertive. Well, he had been, and now he was getting on with his new life, as no doubt she would be.

He put the newspaper down and lifted a couple of pages from his in tray. The first was an invite to join the company's health club, which would give him VIP membership of a gym just down the road. The brochure was full of muscle-bound blokes in tight t shirts, and page three models in skimpy tops. Allan shook his head, and decided he might as well join, if only to sit on a bike and admire the talent.

The second was a real eye opener: a letter inviting him to lead a new Society of Editors campaign to raise reporting standards and fight fake news. He was so shocked he had to read it again to make sure. It said he'd been recommended by the Society's board members. But, scanning their names, he'd never met any of them.

He stood up and paced the room, reading it again. This was unbelievable! A chance to make a name for himself nationally.

He had a big grin on his face, and it stayed there when Ruby walked in with a tray of coffee and biscuits.

He invited her to sit down at the coffee table, and blurted the words out before his brain was fully in gear. 'I've just had some very good news. How do you fancy helping me celebrate with a quick drink after work?'

To his relief, she didn't look at all put out. 'Well, yes. That would be great. I'm meeting a girlfriend at 7, but ok till then. What are we celebrating? As if I didn't know!'

He held up the letter. 'This!'

'Ah, of course. Well I knew you'd be pleased.' She swept her hair off her face. 'Roger told me this morning how delighted he is, too. Can I just say, though, I don't normally go out for drinks with my boss, but as this is a special case...'

He laughed. 'Yeah, thanks, I get it. I'm on my own in a hotel all week, so you've taken pity on me. It's ok. But, funny you should say that, I've never gone out for drinks with my PA – mainly because I've never had one. A PA, I mean...'

*****

Eric struggled with the lock on the caravan door.

The warden told him it was the right key, but it didn't seem to fit. He twisted and pulled, growing increasingly stressed. Then suddenly, it opened, and he was in.

The smell of dog and drains hit him first, but he put everything out of his mind apart from his mission: hunt the jacket. He looked round: shouldn't take long in a place this size. He'd wondered why all the secrecy. After all, they'd got a search warrant. Then Alex had reminded him they wanted Armitage to relax; to think he was in the clear. Fair enough.

The bed was unmade and there was nothing stored underneath, so he started on the cupboards. Nothing. Kitchen units? Nope. His options were thinning, but he saw a narrow door that looked like a broom cupboard so he tried in there. It was a cupboard. With a broom inside.

He'd spent ten minutes getting the key and getting inside, and he had no idea how far away Armitage was.

Eric tried to calm himself. He sat down on the bed. Think!

He glanced over to the kitchen, taking in the dark wood doors, the fridge, and oven, and the second door that led out to the back. Then he saw the only place he hadn't checked because it seemed pointless. The dog's bed. If his jacket was torn, he might have let his dog use it for a warm blanket or something. That was the sort of thing his dad would have done. He'd told Eric 'Never throw anything out. You might need it one day.'. Eric didn't dare point out that was why the house was a tip.

He walked over, anxiously checking his watch yet again. His phone beeped. A message. 'He's just passed us. You've got about five minutes max.'

His heart lurched as he knelt down. He lifted up a grubby grey woollen blanket by its corner, careful not to disturb anything. And there it was – a shiny black puffa jacket.

He pulled it out quickly, and turned it round in his hands, searching frantically for a tear, talking to himself out loud to try and stave off the panic.

Where is it? Maybe there isn't one? Anyway, it could be really tiny. Will I have time to get a picture of it and put it back without him knowing?

He found it, about three inches long, on the seam near a pocket. It looked like a jagged tear. He could see the white lining material inside. Eric took in a deep breath. Result!

Hereached for his phone to take a picture. He'd put it on the worktop next to the sink. Then he heard car tyres crunching on gravel.

There was no time to think. He had to get out. He crouched low so he could peer out of the window. The car was about 20 yards away. No choice. Have to go out by the other door.

He tried the key. It fitted! Eric grabbed the jacket off the floor and as gently as he dared, pushed the door open, and closed it with a sigh of relief.

He was about to run towards the trees when he remembered. He'd left his phone behind.

*****

'Give me the latest on Eric, then pass me on to George, Alex'

Jane talked loudly into her phone as she hurried down the main corridor that led to the car park, ignoring the judgemental frowns as she pushed through a line of people santising their hands as they waited to be seen at reception.

'He got in, ma'am, and he was messaged to say Armitage was five minutes away, but he hasn't responded.'

'Crap!' She nodded an apology to a man who held the door open with a disapproving shake of the head as she marched outside. 'Have you tried again?'

'Yes, ma'am. It's rung out, then got cut off. We can't get anything now. Like he's switched it off.'

'Or he's in trouble. Right. I'm on my way there now, send me directions will you? Mobilise anyone in the area to take up position at the caravan. No blue lights, no sirens. Out of sight, right? And get George to phone me on the mobile right now.'

She connected her phone to the car with Bluetooth and secured it in its holder.

George was onto her before she'd turned out of the car park.

'George. First, can you send Ross out to Broad Farm straight away. He can link up with me there. Armitage is back home, and he might be holding Eric... Yeah, I know. No, you stay there, set everything up for when we bring Armitage in – interview room, duty solicitor on hand, the works... And God help him if he's harmed Eric.'

She flicked on the blue lights and put her foot down.

According to Alex's directions, she'd be there in 20 minutes. After what happened to Jag, she knew it would feel like the longest 20 minutes of her life.

*****

Armitage put his key in the lock, then stopped. The door was already open.

Bess started growling, so he walked quietly back to the car and put her in the back. He pressed his ear against the door. No sound. He eased the handle down, bounced on the balls of his feet, then threw it open and jumped in, his head jerking round quickly to scan both ways.

All clear. But the other door had swung open. Whoever had got in, left that way in a hurry. He reached out to pull it shut, then, as he turned, he saw a mobile phone on the worktop.

'What have we here?'

He thought he heard movement outside, so he gently opened the window above the sink. Footsteps on the gravel. He took two steps to the other side of the caravan and peered cautiously out of the window on that side, just in time to see a man jogging into the trees.

His mind was fully engaged now. Who'd want to break in? The local lowlife? Not likely. He hadn't even got a colour telly. Seymour? Looking for evidence to get himself off the hook? No chance. He wouldn't have the guts.

There was one possibility: Ashbridge Police. But why? He knew they'd keep an eye on him. But what were they looking for?

He had a sudden moment of alarm. Had he forgotten something? He got down on his hands and knees and began searching, then stopped.

Whoever broke in must be relaxing now, thinking they'd got away with it. But he'd got the phone. Should be easy enough to find out who it belongs to. Maybe make a few calls...

But then, that would delay him, and what would it achieve? He was growing tired of the games. He'd a good chance of making a run for it, so why bother about some ham-fisted police search?

He moved quickly, but precisely – his mind made up. He shut down the phone, then threw a few clothes onto the bed; the ones he'd saved to help change his appearance – a button down shirt, clean pair of jeans, a branded sweatshirt he bought on ebay, a new pair of trainers, ditto, and a baseball cap.

He grabbed some old newspaper and matches from under the sink, and went out to gather wood from the pile he'd made behind the tree at the back.

He knelt down on the grass and built a pyramid of paper, sticks and scraps of wood left over from the building work at the workshop, and set it alight.

It took straight away. He jogged back into the caravan and started dragging out the contents: the little kitchen table where he'd sat alone night after night, making plans; the old rocking chair he'd had since he got married, and the only thing he'd kept after the break-up; the towels, the bedding.

The fire grew in intensity, and the heat kept him at a distance. Now he was having to throw stuff on from a distance. It felt great to be out in the open, watching the flames destroy everything so he could start his life over again.

It was like a ceremony, and he'd been waiting for this moment a long time.

He threw Bess's old blanket on last, then stopped. He'd put his jacket under it to give her some extra warmth. So where was it?

It didn't take him long to work it out.

*****

Maureen's first thought when she saw smoke rising to merge with the grey clouds was that one of the homes had caught fire.

She switched the kettle off and walked quickly down the path to take a look. Just a bonfire. It was coming from behind that man's caravan. His car was there, too. What was he up to now? Weren't the police supposed to be watching him?

She tried to think logically. There was no law against having a bonfire, was there? But she didn't trust him: not after what he did to Bob.

She stepped back out of sight as the man walked up to the car and opened the back door. His dog jumped out and started bouncing around. He grabbed its lead and walked her off towards the trees.

She turned to go back in and cried out when a man stepped out from the bushes.

He held a finger up to his lips. 'Shhhh. Best to keep quiet. It's OK, Mrs Collings. It's me, PC Sykes. Remember?'

Eric hid a smile as Maureen made him take his shoes off before she'd let him inside. But he could understand why. It was a little palace compared to Armitage's dump: covers over the seating, a fitted carpet, scatter cushions, and a proper kitchen. He put Armitage's jacket on the table.

Maureen took a closer look as the kettle came to the boil. 'What are you doing with his jacket?'

Eric was only a novice, but he knew this could count as a positive ID. 'How do you know it's his?'

'I see him most days, don't I? Horrible man. But he always wore that on his morning walk. Up to recently, anyway.'

Eric sat down, uninvited, then realised his mistake and stood up quickly. Maureen poured the tea and smiled to herself. A young man with manners, she thought: now that's a rarity. Bob had forgotten any manners he used to have.

She turned and pointed to the chair. 'Take a seat. Your tea's just coming.'

'Thanks. So when did he stop wearing it?'

'Oh I don't know, a couple of weeks ago, perhaps. Why are you so interested?'

'It could be important, Mrs Collings. Evidence.'

'Well, if you say so. But look at the state of it. Can you take that filthy garment off my table? Thank you...Now, chocolate biscuit?'

The adrenaline was beginning to fade now, and Eric concentrated on writing his notes in between eating biscuits and answering questions from Mrs Collings, who now insisted on being called Maureen.

Then he cursed under his breath. 'Can I use your phone, please? I've lost mine.'

Maureen rolled her eyes good naturedly, and held out the handset.

He froze, embarrassed. He'd be lucky to stay in CID after this. 'Erm... have you got the number for Ashbridge Police station, please?'

Maureen gave him a look, then opened a drawer and handed him the phone book. 'It's in there. Under police, I expect.'

Her sarcasm was the least of his worries. He was going to get such a bollocking for this. He turned to flick through the directory, then spun round as the door banged open.

Armitage was smiling, but there was nothing pleasant about it.

'I might have known you'd be here, you little runt. Breaking and entering. Stealing property. You should know better, sonny.

Tell you what. You just give me that jacket, and we'll say no more about it.'

33.

Maureen tried to sidle out behind him, but he swung round and caught her arm. 'And you can stay here, alright? You've caused me enough trouble.' He pushed her into a chair. 'Now sit down!'

Maureen stood, outraged. 'How dare you barge into my house and push me around!'

It was enough to distract Armitage temporarily. Eric grabbed the jacket, and held it behind his back as he weighed up his options.

Armitage was built like a tank, and he wouldn't stand a chance against him. There was no way past, even if he tried to run for it. He wasn't even wearing shoes. But even if he could escape, he wouldn't abandon Mrs Collings, who was now breathing hard and looking very scared as Armitage forced her down into the chair again.

He breathed in, thinking through what Ross would do. He tried to channel Ross's self condience, and looked Armitage in the eye. 'Thomas Armitage, I am arresting you for the murders of John Cooper, Colin Flynn and Andy Fry. You do not have to say anything -'

Armitage moved in close and laughed in his face. 'You're off your nut, mate. I'll give you ten out of ten for guts, though. Now give me that jacket.'

'If you want it, you'll have to take it off me by force, and that would amount to assaulting a police officer. Are you sure you want to add that to the list of offences?'

They heard the crunch of gravel at the same time. It sounded like several cars braking to a halt nearby. Armitage barged into Eric, knocking him down with a punch to the side of his head, then grabbed the jacket. Eric held on and it ripped again in the struggle. Maureen screamed. Armitage got the jacket with one final pull, and yelled in rage as he ran outside.

****

Jane got out of the car, and pointed in the direction of the scream. George nodded.

'Ross. Go!'

She watched as Ross ran towards the static caravan, with George walking behind.

To her left, she could hear a fire crackling behind another caravan, and she saw what looked like Armitage's dog looking out from the driver's seat of a Ford Capri.

On another day, it might have looked comical, but she had no time to appreciate it.

Ross reappeared hanging on to Armitage's waist as he attempted to run towards the car; his strength carrying them both along.

George took a few paces and stuck his hand into Armitage's chest. It must have felt like running into a brick wall. Armitage stopped and bent double, fighting for breath.

Ross straightened his tie and brushed his hair out of his eyes. He winked at George; 'The long arm of the law, eh George?'

George smiled and turned to Jane. 'Do you want to do the honours, ma'am?'

'Hold him for a minute. We need to find Eric.' She moved towards Armitage's caravan, then stopped as Eric called out: 'Ma'am? George? I'm sorry about my phone. I couldn't phone in...'

Jane strode up to him as though she was going to thump him, and Ross winced as he saw Eric's swollen and bruised face.

Instead, she smiled. 'I'm just glad you're in one piece, Eric. Did Armitage do that to you?'

Eric nodded. Maureen came out and stood next to him. 'This boy is a credit to you. He stood up to that evil little man. He was going to arrest him, then you turned up.' She held up the jacket and gave it to Eric. 'Here.You forgot this.'

Armitage spat on the ground and struggled against George's grip on his arm. 'He broke in and stole it! You should be arresting him. Let me go!'

Jane shook her head.

'Arrest him George – three counts of murder; assaulting a police officer; and attempting to pervert the course of justice. Oh, and we can now place you with the vehicle that was used to kill three men. Take him in. I'll join you there.'

Armitage yelled. 'What about my dog?'

Jane walked up close and stared him out. 'You'll never see that dog again, I guarantee it. But don't worry. Like the rest of us, she'll be a lot better off without you. I'll see you later.'

She nodded to George and Ross as they pushed Armitage over to their car.

Jane watched the dog as her owner was driven away; her eyes widening, her ears flat against her head. The Capri's windows were slightly open, and as George's car disappeared from view, she could hear Bess whining.

She sighed and turned to Eric. 'Come on, let's get you seen to.'

'I'm fine, ma'am.'

'I know you are. You just have to accept that you bring out the mother in us. Doesn't he, Maureen?'

*****

Jane made calls while Eric was being checked at the Urgent Treatment Centre.

The dog handling unit was happy to pick Bess up and keep her at the station kennels. 'We'll make sure she finds a good home, ma'am.'

Roy Cooke sounded like he'd won the lottery when she told him about the arrest, but went very quiet when Jane said they should challenge the Army about the cover-up that had hampered the investigation, or wilfully obstructed it, more likely.

'Now we need to think this through, Jane. Very carefully. We've got our man. What good will it serve stirring things up with the Army? How's it going to look? All the victims were ex-Army. Haven't they suffered enough?'

'They could have given us all the info on Armitage early in the investigation. They didn't. That decision may have cost lives.'

'Well, I hear what you're saying, but... Let's talk tomorrow. You've got enough to do tonight, interviewing Armitage. And well done, Jane! A quick result, too.'

Jane sighed deliberately loudly. 'OK, sir, thanks. I'll see you tomorrow. This is down to the whole team, not me. They did all the work.'

He laughed. 'You're too modest, Jane. Anyway, thanks muchly. Ciao.'

Jane felt like spitting. *Ciao?* Who the hell says ciao? Especially in Manchester?

She drove back with Eric, who sat with the jacket on his lap, now in a clear evidence bag.

She smiled at him as she pulled up at the traffic lights. 'Well, we needed a missing piece, Eric.'

He blushed. 'Is this it?'

'Nah. Sorry.' She laughed as she saw his disappointment. 'Sorry Eric, that was cruel.'

Eric was all ears, his embarrassment forgotten, loving the privilege of having DCI Jane Birchfield to himself. She told him what Bob Collings had given them the vital missing piece, and he told her how Maureen had identified Armitage as the owner of the jacket.

He wrote her response down when he got back to CID. He wanted to remember it forever. 'Brilliant, Eric, well done. We've got another detective on the team!'

*****

Armitage accepted the offer of a duty solicitor, but made a full confession.

George just switched the tape on, and Armitage seemed to relax. He spoke quite calmly. By the end, he looked relieved.

Jane thanked him for his co-operation, and he laughed: 'Does that mean I don't get done for perverting the course of justice?'

'Well, for what good it'll do you, we might go easy with you on that one.'

His smile faded as the reality began to sink in, but he showed no sign of weakness. 'I don't expect you to understand, but I did what I had to do. I made them pay.'

George shook his head. 'And now you're going to pay. Big time.'

When he'd been taken down to the cells, Jane sipped water and looked at George.

'What he did was brutal, shocking. But so was what happened in Kabul.'

'If he's right. He could be making it up, or exaggerating.'

'To justify killing three ex-soldiers? Nah. You can see how much he still feels it. At one stage, I started to wonder. What would I have done?'

'An eye for an eye...'

'Yeah. Sometimes you wonder. Is that the way it should be?'

'Must be something in the Bible about it.'

'An eye for an eye, a tooth for a tooth... '

George shuffled in his seat. 'That just means the punishment should fit the crime. There's a phrase to make everyone think they're right, ma'am. The fact is, you can't go round like a vigilante every time something happens you think is wrong.'

Jane winked at him. 'I didn't know you were a Bible scholar, George. But you're right. I always try to understand why people do stuff like this. You can see the headlines about Armitage when it gets to court. He'll be a monster. But his life was changed by being in one place at one moment in time. It turned him from a regular guy into a killer. I find that scary.'

'The main thing, is we got the bastard.'

Jane laughed and stood up. 'Thanks George.'

'What for?'

'Reminding me what my job is. Now get yourself home. And thank you.'

George paused at the door, pulling at his shirt collar. 'Are you ok, ma'am?'

'I'm fine, George, yeah. You?'

'Only I've been thinking... well, maybe I'm not in such a hurry to retire.'

'Really? That's great news. What's brought that on?'

He looked awkward and Jane couldn't work out why. Eventually, he looked up and smiled. 'I suppose I like working here. With you, ma'am.'

Jane kept her voice light and the smile bright, until the door had shut behind him.

George had never come closer to expressing his feelings. She felt herself gulping for air and trying desperately not to cry.

*****

They leaned back on the indulgently comfortable white sofa, and clinked glasses together.

'Well, congratulations... boss.'

Allan watched as she tilted her head to drink her Kir Royale. 'Cheers, Ruby. To us.' She gave him a look and he grinned. 'We'll be a good team, I think, don't you?'

She crossed her legs and took another sip. Hers was half gone and he'd hardly touched his. 'Yes, I think so, too. I like people who have a sense of humour. Don't take themselves too seriously.'

He nodded and decided to catch up by downing his martini cocktail in one. 'I'll drink to that.'

They laughed and he ordered the same again from their obsequious waiter. She leaned in to whisper. 'He's a real piece of work, that one.'

Allan found himself drawn in to gossip mode. 'What do you mean?'

'Last time I was in here, he tried to pick me up. I was with a group – men and women – and he got really upset when I turned him down.'

'Well I can understand that.' He stopped. 'I meant, you are attractive, so ...'

'Really? You think so? That's nice. You know what? You're alright, too. We really will make a good team.'

Allan covered his awkwardness by going to the bar to order a platter of snacks.

He walked out onto the street with her just before 7, struggling over the most appropriate way to say goodnight. Then she turned at the bottom of the steps and stood on tiptoe to kiss his cheek. 'Goodnight Allan.'

He went up to his room, boiled a kettle, put a sachet of breakfast tea in the plain white mug, and wondered why he hadn't kissed her too.

He checked his watch. 7.15pm. He yawned. It was probably just as well she had to go and meet her friend. One more drink and it could have got interesting. He snorted at himself. He knew he'd never have the courage to try it on.

The night stretched ahead, and he could still smell her perfume.

And all he had to look forward to was going through the manual for his new car, and ordering room service.

*****

Jane lay back on the sofa in her bathrobe, her head wrapped in a towel, her face shiny with moisturiser.

She didn't want to think about anything tonight, so she decided to binge watch Dr Foster on catch up, eat crisps and drink Malbec.

But the distractions weren't working. If she wasn't plotting how to get Roy Cooke to commit to prosecuting the regiment, she was wondering what Allan was doing, and whether she should reply to his text.

The wine wasn't slowing her brain, it was making her more reckless.

She paused the tv, and started thumbing her reply...

*****

Allan's nap was interrupted by the trill of his new Galaxy Note.

His first thought was that Sue had come back and wanted to meet up. He bounced off the bed and grabbed the gadget.

A message from Jane, and all hope of a restful night was gone. *'Thank you for giving me your share of the house. I gladly accept. Jane.'*

Was that it? Was that all she had to say? How much more reasonable could he have been? The more he went over it, the more angry he felt. He knew he should just delete it, send it to trash where it belonged. But something stopped him and he couldn't understand what it was.

He suddenly felt the need to get out of the room. He pulled on a pair of jeans and a jacket, slammed the door behind him and went down to the bar.

34.

Jane drove slowly, enjoying feeling coccooned in the car, as the houses thinned out on the road towards the Peak District.

She put the sun visor down as she crested the brow of the hill, and followed the sat nav instructions. *'In a quarter of a mile, bear right.'*

She'd had time to think, and a bit too much to drink, last night. As she sliced a banana into her muesli this morning, she'd decided to do it more often. It had helped her make her mind up how the next phase of her life was going to go. She realised she was in sole charge of her destiny, starting from now.

Roy Cooke had been as spineless as she expected. He'd fiddled with his cufflinks and blurted out a refusal to authorise any action against the Royal Lancashires, even when she'd told him about Brigadier Watts' intimidation of Seymour.

She'd told him she was determined to see it through. And she was on her way to see the Brigadier now. Roy had no idea, and George, loyal as ever, had promised to cover for her.

She just wanted to look the brigadier in the eye, confront him. It was the only way to know if he was lying. She smiled to herself as she imagined what her mum would say if she knew she was about to take on a brigadier.

She indicated right, and turned onto a quiet country lane studded with impressive houses bordered by high fencing and solid gates that looked as if they could withstand a bulldozer.

His place was called 'Royal Court'. It was approached along a hundred yard gravel drive bordered by perfect lawns and shrubs. Jane pulled up just out of sight and looked through the trees.

It was built of light coloured stone, with a wide curved bay window and a large conservatory. There was a white Range Rover parked outside a garage the size of a stable block. It shouted money and influence, and it made Jane even more determined to rattle his cage.

She got back in the car and drove up to the entrance, slamming the car door loudly and holding the door bell down. She could hear it ringing some naff tune repeatedly and grinned as she heard a woman's irritable voice 'Alright, alright. I'm coming!'

The door was opened by a picture perfect woman; the image spoiled somewhat by an angry expression.

'Yes. What do you want?'

Jane held up her ID card. 'Tell the Brigadier that Detective Chief Inspector Birchfield would like to speak to him. Thank you.'

She recognised his voice straight away, calling from somewhere inside. 'Who is it Mel?'

'The police. To see you.' She opened the door grudgingly and Jane stepped into a parquet floor hall with military portraits on each wall, and a flag suspended from the banisters at the top of the oak staircase.

The brigadier came in through a side door, wearing new looking jogging trousers and white trainers, and a Royal Lancs sweatshirt. He was smiling, and put his arm round Mel, who Jane thought looked young enough to be his daughter.

'Hi. You wanted to see me... erm?'

'Jane Birchfield. We spoke on the phone recently.'

'Ah yes, of course.' He squeezed Mel's waist and kissed her cheek. 'Darling, could you rustle us up a coffee, please?'

Jane turned to look at a portrait to hide her surprise. Not his daughter then...

Mel walked down the hall, and the brigadier smiled at Jane. 'Shall we go into the conservatory and enjoy the sunshine while we can?'

Jane followed him into a sunlit space that wouldn't have been out of place at a top hotel. He pointed to an L-shaped sofa with a cane base and deep purple seat cushions.

Jane was annoyed for feeling envious. Then Mel walked in and she pulled herself together. 'I'm here on official business. You may prefer to do this privately.'

The brigadier just smiled and stretched an arm across the top of the seatback, and stroked Mel's hair. Affection, or ownership? Jane wasn't sure. 'Oh, Mel and I don't have any secrets from each other. Fire away.'

Mel nodded her agreement. Jane had to admit, she was a stunner. Dark glossy hair, perfect complexion and no evidence of make up. The perfect couple.

She cleared her throat. 'Well. You'll be glad to know, brigadier, that we have arrested a man in connection with the hit and run murders.'

'Call me Ronnie, please. That's marvellous news. Congratulations. All done and dusted then.'

'Not quite.' Jane stopped as a young girl in tight black jeans and white t shirt walked in carrying a large tray. She bent down next to the brigadier and put the tray on the coffee table. He winked at her: 'Thanks Sal.'

Jane registered Mel's disdain, as Sal smiled and walked away like she was on a catwalk. Mel poured the coffee, the sunlight catching a collection of gold bangles on her tanned wrist.. It was obvious that Sal didn't qualify for an introduction, so Jane just noted the name for future reference and wrote *servant girl!?* next to it.

She decided to go for it. 'So, as I was saying. We've got our man. But I'm here to advise you that we are considering pressing charges against the Army – your regiment – for obstructing our enquiries, and you personally for intimidation of a key witness.'

He was good. He didn't blink; he didn't even change his expression. 'Really? Well, I'm surprised, to be honest. It's rubbish, of course. Do you want to elaborate: it's Jane, isn't it?'

'It's DCI Jane Birchfield, sir. I'm afraid you need to take this seriously. Just to be clear, I am not charging you at this moment. You are helping us with our enquiries. But as you know, your regiment has consistently claimed to have lost all record of a soldier called Thomas Armitage. We also have written testimony from a key witness in the investigation that you warned him off revealing Armitage's identity. Or should I say, threatened him?'

Jane paused to sip her coffee, playing it as cool as she could, even though the adrenaline was racing. 'I'm sure you'll understand when I say that looks very much like an attempt to obstruct a murder investigation. As I say, I'm not arresting you right now. But I would like your reaction, and I will of course be taking notes.'

He looked at Mel, who was taking an unnatural interest in the seam of a scatter cushion, then stared at Jane. She could almost see the calculation going on behind his eyes.

'I could say a lot of things, Detective Chief Inspector. First of all, I admire your courage. I only wish it was backed up by sound judgement; which is something I instil in people under my command.'

He leaned forward, elbows on his knees. 'But you want my reaction for the record, so here it is. Get your pen ready... It's total bollocks. I don't know how you formed that impression, and I certainly don't know what Seymour is talking about.'

'You deny threatening him in any way when he came to your house?'

'I -'

'He did come to your house, didn't he? We can agree on that?'

'Of course. He's a nice enough chap; just a little obsessed with details, army history. He wanted my input to a little pamphlet he was putting together. I helped him.'

He reached out a hand towards Mel, and she held onto it with both hers.

Jane flicked open her notebook, and read it slowly. 'This is what Mr Seymour told us about what happened. He told you about the allegations Armitage made against Cooper; concerning the incident that led to him being awarded a medal. Specifically, that Cooper murdered a child, and possibly other members of a civilian family. Mr Seymour told us: *'He said Armitage was a troublemaker who was set on destroying the regiment's good name, and anyone who repeated his allegations would face consequences. Let's just say the gesture he made left no doubt in my mind.'* Do you recall making that throat slitting gesture, brigadier?'

His face appeared to be set in stone. 'I really don't know what you're talking about.' He stood up, roughly pulling his hand away from Mel. 'I think we're finished here.'

Jane didn't move. 'I don't. We've only just scratched the surface,sir. Can I just be clear? And remember, this is on the record. You maintain that none of this actually happened? That you and the regiment did not mislead a murder investigation by conveniently losing Armitage's record, and you did not threaten a key witness? I should warn you, sir, that these are very serious offences, and that our investigation is continuing. Now would be a good time to tell us the truth.'

He sighed and put his hands in his pockets, apparently back in control. 'Are you actually calling me a liar? Let me, in turn, warn you that these are very serious allegations to make when you have not a scrap of evidence. All you have is your own theory, and the word of one ex-soldier with an axe to grind, against mine.'

He turned to Mel and smiled, raising his eyebrows, then looked at Jane. 'If you really want to destroy your career and make a fool of yourself in one hit, then be my guest. I can't stop you.' He stopped, and walked quickly over to a sideboard, where he picked up a black diary.

He walked back to Mel, flicking pages. 'Mel? Which night are we having Simon Hopkirk round for dinner?' She took the diary and started looking through it. Jane just smiled and made a point of writing in her notebook. 'Well, thanks for your time, Brigadier. And you, Mel. We will need to talk again, I'm sure. So please don't go anywhere.'

Mel threw the diary onto the sofa and looked at her husband apologetically. 'I couldn't find it.'

He walked towards the door. 'Lovely to meet you. Let me show you out.'

Jane drove back onto the lane and parked up in a lay by a hundred yards away. She could see the hazy outline of the Manchester skyline in the distance.

She'd thought her future was there. She'd pinned her hopes on getting the promotion Hopkirk had promised. She knew she'd probably blown it, but for the first time in her career, she wondered how much she cared.

She got out of the car and leaned back against the bonnet, feeling the gentle warmth of the sun on her face. A thrush hopped onto a fence post, singing its heart out.

Jane smiled and whistled back. She laughed as the thrush cocked its head to one side then flew away. She never could whistle in tune.

She watched it dwindle to a tiny speck before it disappeared into the haze.

35.

There were two memos on her desk when she got back.

The first was from Lorry: *I told Seymour it was up in the air whether he'd face charges. He decided he would testify. He gave me names of soldiers who would have been close to Armitage in Afghanistan. I'll follow them up.'* She'd handwritten a sentence at the end... *Mark sends his best wishes, ma'am.. We hope you'll come to our wedding next year!*

The second was in Doreen's over-excited writing: *The chief Constable phoned! He wants you to call him back, straight away! Doreen x*

She'd written it 20 minutes ago. She called Alex Gledhill. 'Can you get Armitage up to interview room 1 please? Cheers.'

*****

Armitage looked different. He'd had a haircut and a shave, but there was more to it than that. Jane thought he seemed at peace with himself. She could identify with that.

He drank his coffee slowly, but attacked the custard creams eagerly. Jane reminded him of his rights and switched the tape on.

'Tell me about Brigadier Watts, Thomas.'

'I should have killed him as well.'

'Okay, fair enough. Why?'

'He wouldn't listen. He knew what they did, but he did nothing. I told him. The full story. Said I'd swear to it on the Bible.'

'What did he say?'

'He told me I was a liar and if I repeated the allegations, he'd shift me out of the Army in a flash.'

'Will you swear to that in court?'

'Bloody right I will.'

Armitage gave enough corroborating evidence to justify bringing the brigadier in for formal questioning.

She rewarded him by allowing him to see Bess for a few minutes. She watched as he sat on the cage floor; stroking the dog's head in his lap.

She turned to Alex. 'How does a man who can be as gentle as that become a triple murderer?'

Alex shook his head. 'I wish I knew, ma'am. Makes you wonder if someone else drove him to it.'

'Funny you should say that, Alex.'

*****

The PA asked if she could be in Simon Hopkirk's office at 1615.

Jane said she'd be there, then walked to CID, sat on George's desk and asked for a wine gum.

'How is everyone?'

George grumbled. 'Lorry can't shut up about getting those names from Seymour.'

Ross called out: 'Not true. She can't shut up about getting married.'

Jane laughed. 'It'll be your turn one day, Ross.'

'It's not going to happen, boss.'

Eric chipped in, much to everyone's surprise. 'What about Amy at the Feathers?'

Ross threw a ball of paper at him. 'Nah. She's all yours, mate. Anyway, who said you could take part in the office banter?'

Eric flushed briefly, but summoned up the courage to throw the paper back.

Jane called them to order. ''Where is Lorry, anyway?'

Ross sighed. 'She's gone shopping with Mark. Wedding outfits, ma'am.'

'That's ok. It's allowed. But remember, it's not quite over yet. We've still got a few statements to compile, before we can hand it over to CPS. But they don't foresee any problems. I've filed a report on Brigadier Watts, requesting the go ahead to bring him in for questioning, and a warrant for Armitage's records. That won't be so straightforward, but we'll see.

'Whatever happens, you're an amazing team, and I don't tell you often enough. I appreciate each one of you. It's been an absolute privilege to work with you. Tell Lorry I said so, and I'll call her. OK... that's all.'

Ross broke the silence after Jane had left. 'Is it just me, or did that sound like a farewell speech?'

*****

Jane cleared her desk and waited till the corridor was clear before walking as quietly as she could down the stairs, carrying a cardboard box under one arm, a handbag over her shoulder, and her briefcase in her other hand.

Phil was propped up against a stack of pillows, looking washed out.

Jane put a bag of jelly babies on his table. 'Your medicine. Take three, three times a day.'

Phil smiled. 'Yes, nurse.' He patted the bed. 'Thanks for coming to see me. Take the weight off your feet.'

'What's the verdict, Phil?'

'Heart artery knackered. They're going to put a balloon in to open it up so the blood can get through. They reckon that'll sort it. Should be on my feet again soon. Back at work in a month or two.'

Jane snorted. 'You wish.'

'With all due respect, ma'am. Nothing will stop me.'

He looked so tired, it was hard to believe. But Jane knew work was his life. She'd always felt the same. But as she pulled out of the car park for the six mile journey to Greater Manchester HQ, she wondered if that was true any more.

*****

She got there early, and parked up in a corner of the car park that was catching the last of the sunshine.

She looked at herself in the mirror on the sun visor and wondered why it had taken her 20 years to realise there was more to life than the relentless search for promotion.

She'd felt driven from the minute she'd joined the force, but looking back, perhaps that was more about feeling the need to prove herself as a woman in what was – and still is – very much a man's world.

But her standards had slipped in the early stages of this investigation, she knew that. It was almost laughable. Her head had been turned by Allan's offer of marriage.

The dashboard clock flicked to 1610. Five minutes to go.

She glanced at the imposing square block of glass and steel that was regional HQ, the windows reflecting the late afternoon sun.

She flicked through her messages to find a series from Allan going back three months. She pressed delete.... *Delete the entire conversation?* She hesitated for a second, then pressed delete again.

Jane locked the car, lifted her face to the sun, and closed her eyes as she listened to the birdsong struggling to be heard above the drone of traffic.

She straightened her shoulders.

She was ready.

Printed in Great Britain
by Amazon

21583486R00159